WHERE THE RIVER RUNS GOLD

Also by Sita Brahmachari

WHERE THE RIVER RUNS GOLD

SITA BRAHMACHARI

Orion

ORION CHILDREN'S BOOKS

First published in Great Britain in 2019 by Hodder and Stoughton

1 3 5 7 9 10 8 6 4 2

A CIP catalogue record for this book
is available from the British Library.

ISBN 978 1 51010 541 6

Typeset in 12/17.25 pt Adobe Garamond Pro by Jouve (UK), Milton Keynes
Printed and bound in Great Britain by Clays Ltd, Elcograf S.p.A.

The paper and board used in this book
are made from wood from responsible sources.

Orion Children's Books
An imprint of
Hachette Children's Group
Part of Hodder and Stoughton
Carmelite House
50 Victoria Embankment
London EC4Y 0DZ

An Hachette UK Company
www.hachette.co.uk

www.hachettechildrens.co.uk

For Ada

With love and hope seeds

Step over the threshold.
Be brave, hold true

'We have this option ahead of us – we have to take the
option to protect the natural world . . . that's where the future lies.'
David Attenborough (2019 World Economic Forum)

THE EYE
OF THE STORM

Ten Years Ago – The Night of Hurricane Chronos

Nabil had been out foraging on a piece of scrubland in the Western Quarter. The air was thick with heat and dust, but otherwise there had been no warning signs. From a gasp, the storm built quickly. *Probably another false alarm*, he thought, peering up at the glowering sky, but he couldn't risk leaving baby Themba all alone in the world. He shoved the herbs and mushrooms he'd collected into his backpack, abandoned his bike, set his face to the howling wind and struggled to make his way across Kairos City.

How Nabil survived that journey through the eye of the storm he would never know. A wall crumbled in front of him; he swerved, yelped in pain as his ankle twisted, but still failed to dodge a shard of glass that sliced into his cheek. The pavement lifted from below and opened up great craters which he had to leap across, stopping only momentarily to catch his breath and wipe the cloying blood now trickling into his mouth. He stood transfixed as the face of the ancient clock on Kairos Central Station was snatched clean away and the orb of time spun through the sky before dropping with a deafening thud in front of him.

Is this the end of time? He struggled for breath as panic and exhaustion took hold. But still he dug deep and did what he had come to do in every waking and sleeping moment in the month since Tia had died . . . so soon after the joyful birth of their baby Themba. He let the memory of the warm glow he had felt that first time he'd held Themba in his arms flood through him. Ever since, lost in space and time, he had searched and searched for signs of Tia's presence to guide him out of the darkness. Nabil fell to his knees, his hair smeared across his face, cheeks indented from the force of the gale. He tugged with a strength he didn't know he had and finally pulled the long golden hand of the clock free.

He felt as if the giant hand was anchoring him, lending him a steadying weapon in his struggle to push on through the storm. As he stared at his clasped fist, a shower of powdered masonry crumbled over his skin. Above, a loud crack shattered the air and a gargoyle fell from the old museum, splitting its head open. Its long, grey tongue shot out, mocking him. Vicious omens whispered in his ear. He pushed on, desperate to keep the darkness from his heart, but the uprooting of the great trees of Kairos City, the brutal bowing and breaking of his beloved oaks filled him with the deepest sense of foreboding he had ever felt in his life.

Nabil shunned the desperate cries, the raw stink of fear in the air, as he rose to his feet and forced himself on. His blood pulsed with one aim only: to see his baby son again, to keep the last being in the world he truly loved, safe. *Themba, Themba, Themba*, he called, begging the wind to carry his voice to his child.

With every step the wind blew stronger and yet Nabil's mind grew steadily quieter, set as it was on one single course. Time's hand, clasped in his, had grown unbearably heavy, but still he clung to it until finally, from out of the dust and debris, emerged the outline of his warehouse home.

With the windows blown out, the wind howled through the wide empty frames. Beds were upturned, abandoned blankets lay on the floor. He called out to Tia's sister, Lottie. Breathless, he paused to listen but not a soul stirred. Nabil ran to the storeroom and collapsed against the heavy metal door, screaming Themba's name.

Swiftly unbolting the door, Lottie stared in horror at Nabil's bruised and bloodied face. Afterwards she spoke of how he resembled an ancient warrior, dug up from a battlefield clasping a golden arrow in his hand. Gently she coaxed the clock hand from him and placed his son in his arms. As Themba gurgled and grinned, Nabil raised his head and listened to the piercing cries of another soul.

He kissed Themba's mop of soft curls, reluctantly handed him back to Lottie and limped on through the debris of the warehouse, following the insistent cries. Pieces of tarpaulin and odd fragments of lives flew past the windows – a red shoe, a bright-green headscarf, a piece of sheet music. Nabil braced himself, clinging to the banister as he climbed up the rusty spiral staircase.

In front of him a ginger kitten mewled loudly, its fur blasted flat against its ribs, spine arched, clawing at a pillow. Had he struggled all the way up here for this? As he bent down and reached out towards the kitten it grew silent, but now a newly energetic cry rose from a red blanket behind the animal. Nabil moved cautiously towards the bundle and the kitten swiped and hissed. Whatever it stood guardian over felt Nabil's presence because it opened its lungs and the bleating cry grew into a full-throated scream.

Nabil's hands trembled as he carefully unwrapped a coarse grey blanket to discover a baby girl with jet-black hair, naked except for a daisy chain strung around her body. As she peered at him with her tear-washed eyes, her expression seemed to question him: *what will you do with me?* Nabil quickly covered her soft skin, noticing that his skin and hers were exactly the same hue. Now only her face was visible staring into his. By her side was a basket containing a nest of edible leaves streaked with berry stains, with a golden locket at its centre.

'Shh, shh. Did your mama go out foraging and get caught in the storm? Shh,' Nabil repeated over and over as the kitten wrapped itself around his ankles and began to purr. Nabil cradled the baby closer. He studied her expression, so unlike

Themba's. Questions sparked from her like shooting embers from a fire. Her eyes shone sharp and bright and seemed to ask *Can I trust you? Will you keep me safe?*

Tia appeared in his mind's eye, standing behind him and smiling. He could almost feel her breath on his cheek as the darkness in his heart lightened. *Was I supposed to find you here, baby?* he whispered, cradling her in his arms. A voice floated to him through the specks of ash and dust.

We'll call her Shifa – the one who heals.

PART ONE
OVER THE THRESHOLD

Chapter One

Shifa sat on her bed brushing her hair over and over, sweeping through the length from the crown over her shoulders, splaying it out across the tiny gap between her bed and Themba's. One side of her parting was now the tangle-free silken 'raven river' as Nabil had named it, and that her twin Themba loved to twist around his fingers to get to sleep. Sometimes she thought her hair belonged more to them than her. Her papa, Nabil, who was always saying 'never cut your crowning glory', would not be happy, but she was doing this for him as well as for Themba. In five years' time it would have grown again *if she wanted it to.*

Daisy came purring up the bed and claimed Shifa's smooth mane as her pillow. The old cat had grown so thin that she could feel each one of her ribs underneath the scraggy ginger coat that Shifa now stroked with the back of her hand. Daisy gazed at Shifa with her dull green eyes as if to say, *Don't leave me.* Shifa attempted to block the thought

11

that upset her the most about leaving home – unless Daisy was some kind of miracle cat and lived to a ridiculous age, Shifa knew that when she said goodbye to her tomorrow, it would be for ever.

'Should I cut a strand for you too?' Shifa sighed as she began smoothing through the other side of her parting.

'Five years away will feel like for ever for them,' Aunt Lottie had shouted at Nabil from the warehouse window as they left and Lottie's words had whirred around Shifa's mind all night. As usual at bedtime, Themba had reached across the narrow gap between their beds, taken hold of a strand of Shifa's hair and begun tangling it around his fingers. She'd lain on her side and watched her papa, wracked by tears, wrap himself in his own grandfather 'Baba Suli's' coat. *Strange how my great-grandfather can feel so real to me through Papa's stories,* Shifa mused. Nabil was clutching a tiny photomemory in his hands. What had disturbed him so much that he had felt the need to wrap himself in Baba Suli's coat, which belonged as their guardian and protector at the entrance to their story hive? At the sight of Nabil's distress Shifa had been about to climb out of bed to comfort him when Nabil, kneeling, had leaned forward, rested his forehead on the floor, rocking back and forth to do what he said he didn't believe in – pray. Shifa wondered then, *Is he praying for himself or us?* Shifa shivered and enveloped herself in her blanket. Watching Nabil she had the oddest feeling that it was not only her papa who was praying but

Baba Suli too had come to join him . . . kneeling inside his coat.

But this morning all had been restored to its rightful place and her papa had put on a brave face and set out early with Themba, giving her a longed-for birthday treat of a lie-in snuggled up beside Daisy.

'You're going to have to let me go, Daisy!' Shifa sighed when she'd finished brushing her hair. Gently she eased her hair from under her cat's tummy. Daisy miaowed a complaint and settled again in the indent that had been left by Themba's head. Shifa gave that side a final brush and smoothed over her daisy-patterned dress. It felt weird trading it for her usual shorts and T-shirt but it was her one dress and if she couldn't wear it on her birthday when could she? Despite her papa's odd reaction when Aunt Lottie had given it to her, it was comforting to know that it had once been worn by her mama, who according to Lottie, as a grown woman had been just about Shifa's size and height. In any case, she might not look too out of place in the palatial agora if what Lottie said was true and this vintage daisy pattern and material called cotton was gold dust to Paragons.

She stood up and stretched out her long, lean arms, climbing on her bed attempting to catch a glimpse of more than a fragment of herself at a time in the tiny misted mirror. She sighed, remembering how her papa's scowl had dampened her joy after unwrapping the dress. 'What's the point of that? Where's she going to wear it at Freedom Fields?' he said. Shifa didn't see the harm in pretending to be a Paragon for a day, especially on her birthday. At least Aunt Lottie understood how much she had longed to own something beautiful just for the sake of it.

But she had to grudgingly admit that her papa was right. She knew that even in the city they couldn't afford to eat out, or visit the galleries, cinemas and theatres, let alone shop in the grand agora marketplace. The thought always lit flames of outrage in her gut and she'd be flooded with all the clamouring 'how come' questions that she'd ever asked. She got that after Hurricane Chronos the ARK Government had set out a new way, but how could it be right to divide people into 'Paragons', 'Freedoms' and 'Outlanders'? To Shifa, even the names seemed like someone's cruel joke.

Maybe this is my protest dress, my 'cotton' armour that my mama Tia once wore, to make me my most wild and rebellious!

Shifa grabbed her ARK ID and a seed-packet envelope off her bedside table and shoved them into one of the deep pockets of her dress, loving that she could stick her hands down inside them and feel properly comfortable.

Fired up now, she bent down and tied the laces on her once-white canvas pumps – her best ever clothes-bank find, but now slightly greying and worn.

She twirled around. 'What do you think, Daisy? Will I pass for a Paragon?' Daisy opened a sleepy eye and closed it again. 'Don't you judge me now!' Shifa sighed. 'It's my birthday and I'll do what I want to!'

14

Shifa left Daisy sleeping, wandered into the communal room and knelt at the upturned crate that her papa had cobbled into a table. Her great-grandpapa Baba Suli's coat was back in its rightful place, guarding the secret doorway to their story hive, as if announcing that normality was restored. *As if* . . .

Shifa picked up the Freedom Fields brochure, its cover adorned with yellow sunflowers and smiling faces.

Freedom Fields Family
'Stronger Together'
Education, Healthcare, Work Experience, Training
Food, Fresh (air), Fair (treatment), Freedom and Fun
A Family for Life

Saliva filled Shifa's mouth and her stomach groaned as she turned to the well-thumbed 'Catering and Hospitality' page. The image showed bronzed, healthy young recruits sitting around a table laden with glistening strawberries, apples, eggs, cereals and bread. At least from tomorrow, they wouldn't have to wait in line for hours at the food bank each week only to receive the same bland goods: a scoop of vitamin powders, rice, pasta, corn, flour – and whatever Paragon surplus 'treats' past their sell-by date were on offer.

Shifa scanned the room, taking in the rickety furniture and the stacks of bike parts, wheels and other random finds waiting to be traded. The metal water buckets for washing, filled yesterday from the compound tap, were lined up on the cracked floor and already running low. Anyone walking in here would wonder what there was to miss in their cramped home. But then, 'just anyone' would not know about the story hive and the secret treasure that lay behind all their recycled finds.

Shifa's stomach rumbled again. She skirted around the buckets to the sink, held a cup under the tap and just about managed to quarter-fill it with a trickle of drinking water.

She reached into the back of the cupboard to find half a cob of stale bread and an unlabelled jar of something green and pickled. Shifa took a spoonful of dry vitamin powder and mixed it to a watery paste. It was supposed to dissolve but never did. As usual it coated her tongue and stuck to her back teeth. *Disgusting*. She chewed the dried-up bread and pickles as speedily as she could. *Better not to taste for too long, just get it down.* As she swallowed, she caught a flash of a blue-black uniform through the frosted glass of their window and instinctively crouched low following the silhouette of the pointy-capped beak of an ARK Enforcement officer, or 'Crow', as named by Lottie and Themba long ago. A small card dropped on to the mat, followed by a larger envelope. The shadowy figure moved on. The large envelope fell on its back with the Freedom Fields sunflower seal face upwards. Shifa turned it over.

She picked up the official-looking envelope addressed to Nabil and laid it against the bottle vase on the crate table, eyeing it suspiciously. She didn't see how it could be 'Private and Confidential' if it was about them going to Freedom Fields, but still . . .

The postcard was addressed to her and Themba.

Happy 11ᵗʰ birthday Themba and Shifa Aziz. Congratulations! You're trained and ready to become Freedom Fields Recruits. Take this to your food bank where you will receive your birthday celebration Paragon donation hamper.

The stirrings of excitement fluttered in her. This would mean extra food for their farewell party in the warehouse tonight! Maybe there would be enough to share with Lottie and her forager friends – in Shifa's dreams, a whole cake with icing.

Shifa shoved the birthday postcard in her pocket along with her ID and seed packet, unbolted the door and let herself out. *So annoying*, she thought, as her papa's rhymes, invented to keep Themba on track, sprang into her mind too, uninvited, whenever she went out.

Step over the threshold.
Be bold,
Be brave,
Hold true,
To all that I have taught you.

Daisy came padding through from the bedroom and curled herself around Shifa's ankles. 'How come you always know when I'm leaving? Sorry, Daisy. I have to go.' Shifa sighed, carrying Daisy to her frayed chair cushion, where she would sit and wait for her till she returned. It broke Shifa's heart to think of how long Daisy would wait here, crying for her after they had left for the farm. Daisy set up her usual high-pitched protest that tore into Shifa and finally brought tears to her eyes. She wiped them away with the hem of her dress and opened the door.

Behind her the enormous mismatching hands of the old station clock collided into twelve o'clock.

Chapter Two

Shifa clung to the grey-shadow walls of their block, moving swiftly towards the compound gates, past the park with the broken swings, but as she rounded the corner she stopped in her tracks. There, towering over her on the huge wall that surrounded the compound, was an enormous painting of a cherry tree exploding into pink blossom, with the word 'Graffitree' emblazoned along the length of its trunk.

Shifa had heard about an underground movement of artists breaking ARK law by painting trees, flowers, plants and bees on walls all over the city, but she'd yet to see them for herself. She gasped at the beauty of the giant painting. If she closed her eyes and opened them just a little she could imagine that she was standing in front of a real tree. What would it smell like? Sweet? Aunt Lottie thought the Graffitree artists were likely to be 'Outlanders', or 'Foragers' as she preferred to call herself and her ever-growing band of friends. Lottie said only people with free thought could think up such a beautiful protest against the Freedom Fields Family. *If I was a Forager and could paint like my brother, I would fill this city with Graffitrees*, Shifa thought.

There had been an assembly at school when they had been warned that painting on property without permission was not art but an act of vandalism, a scourge on the city. The Parliament had made a new ARK 'Crimes Against Buildings' law that they were all warned would be severely enforced. *But how can painting a beautiful blossom tree in a city that's lost its trees be a crime?* Shifa's musing was answered by the familiar buzz of a drone creeping up on her, forcing her to move on.

She thought she understood why the artists took the risk of breaking ARK law. These trees took up space and could be enjoyed by everyone. Except for the private parks and gardens of the Paragons where her papa worked, it was ARK policy that all other land in Kairos City be turned into housing compounds or Freedom Fields allotments to grow food. The message was clear – land was too precious to waste on anything that could not be eaten and food production was firmly under the control of Freedom Fields. But Shifa longed to see the great trees of Kairos-City past that Nabil told stories about – the oaks, chestnuts and weeping willows. The blossom tree was a reminder of how beautiful the city must once have been. *How could a reminder of nature's beauty be seen as dangerous?*

A sharp-jawed Crow, face hidden under the brim of her black cap, stun gun in holster, leaned against the security gates. Shifa felt in her pocket for her ARK ID, ready for the questions that her dress would prompt, but as she drew parallel, the Crow glanced at her and away as she began talking into an earpiece about 'departures' and 'extra guards'. The Crow shot Shifa's ID a cursory glance and ushered her past.

Making her way along the cracked pavement, Shifa kept her head bowed to avoid being scanned by a new opticare surveillance port positioned on the opposite side of the street. She preferred them to the bulging eyes of drones – at least opticares were stationary so that she could memorise the location of new installations. A rat scuttled across her path and froze, and Shifa froze with it. For a second, she saw her own reflection in its eye. To think that people were so desperate that they were hunting rats for meat, pigeons, beetles and cockroaches too.

She had not believed it the first time her papa had returned home to tell them that Daisy must either stay at home or travel with them. The idea that people were hungry enough to eat cats and stray dogs was too gross. Papa had told them that even before Hurricane Chronos, he had never eaten meat, having come from generations of vegetarians getting their protein from nuts when there had still been enough in the time of the bees. The thought of eating something that had once been a living, breathing animal or insect, made Shifa want to heave.

She was almost at a run now as she set out towards the Warehouse District. Shifa slowed her pace and scanned the familiar building. Lottie had hung up the brightly coloured bunting she and Themba had made last night inside one window, and in another a rainbow-painted sheet screened the inside from the out. Flute trills floated out.

'Aunt Lottie!' Shifa called up.

She had been amazed to hear from her papa after their 'heated discussion' last night that the invitation was still on for their warehouse party this evening. At the sound of Lottie's music, an idea floated through Shifa's mind. *What if Lottie's words struck home and Papa was praying for an answer. What if he's changed his mind about sending us into service after all?* Maybe after the party they could run away together and find a new kind of life somewhere outside Kairos City?

The playing stopped and Lottie's beaming face appeared at the window. Her bright ribbons were plaited messily through her straggly hair as usual.

'Thought I heard you, Shifa Aziz! Look at that dress on you! Beau-ti-ful! Want to come up now and I'll braid your hair for the party?' asked Lottie. 'Sorry for the duff atmosphere last night . . . How's Nabil today?'

'OK! He's taken Themba on an outing. Can't come up, sorry! Won't be allowed braids for graduation tomorrow,' said Shifa, swallowing. 'I'll see you later, though!'

'Don't be late! I want to savour every minute with you and Themba tonight,' said Lottie, blowing her a kiss. 'Where are you off to, anyway?'

22

Shifa cupped her hands against her chest into the shape of a skep-heart, their secret hive code for the Flower Tracks.

Lottie smiled and blew Shifa a kiss. 'Enjoy! But be careful! Security's tightening up.'

Shifa raised her eyes to the sky. As if she, who had discovered the Flower Tracks – *well technically Daisy had* – needed reminding that their garden had to stay secret.

'Your hair looks so beautiful today! Happy birthday, Queen of Shifa!' Lottie called after her.

What Shifa loved most about the path between the warehouse and the Orbital Bridge was that the street clearers could never keep pace with the speed at which the weeds and wild flowers grew here between the cracks. There were always traces of green shoots growing in amongst the crumbling buildings. Shifa picked the heads of a small purple lilac flower, placing them carefully in her seed-packet envelope. *I'll give these to Papa*, she thought, *to plant after we've gone to the farm. Maybe by the time we return it will have grown into a small tree!*

Shifa's mind wandered to the day she'd found her first wild flower and begun her seed collection. She still felt the excitement rise in her when she remembered discovering her first poppy in Kairos City, how she'd felt the velvet skin softness of its leaves and been amazed that nature could make something so delicate and beautiful. One of the things that filled her with excitement about being sent off to the farm was the idea of discovering new flowers, collecting seeds and bringing them back for all to enjoy on their Flower Tracks. *I don't care if it's against the rules, I'm taking my seed packet with me.* An ant crawled across her palm and Shifa couldn't help thinking that if wild flowers were allowed to grow then more insects and birds might return to the city. She longed to hear the hubbub of nature that Nabil had spoken of in the city when he was her age, the trill of bright birdsong instead of the eerily quiet streets that hummed with drones, electric cars and the low buzz of generators.

Shifa stood on the bridge and peered down at the queue already snaking out of the door of the food-bank container. She descended the filthy steps, treading carefully and avoiding the walls that stank of pee, and joined the back of the line.

After a long wait, she finally reached the front and handed in their birthday postcard. Sweat coated her forehead as a Crow held up his wrist screen and scanned her ARK ID. As he did, Shifa recognised his face. It wasn't only their green overalls that marked ARK Protection out as different from Crows. The simple sign was written on their faces. To Shifa everyone who had ever given her food from the bank had also offered a smile, as if they really cared. But the smile was now gone and . . . Shifa glanced down at his overall pocket. *Since when have ARK Protection started wearing stun guns?* 'Stephan' according to his name tag called to a worker at the back of the container and a pair of hands appeared holding a small box with Shifa and Themba's names written on the front. He handed it to her and she flicked open the lid to find a bread roll and one small sponge cake, no bigger than Shifa's fist. *Not even any icing or the faintest flicker of a smile.*

'*Thank you*, I think are the words you are looking for. Well? What are you waiting for?' Stephan asked.

Shifa mustered all her courage. 'Thank you but please can I take something else . . . for my family and . . . it's for my brother and me . . . we're twins? Maybe we should have two?'

'Stephan' seemed almost at the point of wavering but before he could respond someone grabbed hold of Shifa's arm, yanking her backwards and pushing ahead of her in the queue.

Why had she even bothered? Was she supposed to feel grateful for this? *This is why I shouldn't get my hopes up, ever!* she told herself, feeling a sudden urge to get away. She sprinted back up the steps and over the bridge, not stopping until she reached the underpass. Sweat trickled down her back. She doubled over as she reached the top, clutching the box in her hands.

Just inside the entrance to the underpass a teenage girl clung on to a squealing, open-mouthed baby, skinny as a chick.

Shifa thought of what Principal Daviala had warned about giving to people in need. 'No one has ever been forced to join our Freedom Fields Family but I'm afraid those who don't aren't thinking of the greater good, and brutal though it may sometimes seem, Outlanders must face the consequences of their decision to opt out.'

At least there would be no more school and no more lectures from Principal Daviala when they left Kairos City tomorrow. Shifa placed her birthday box on the ground next to the girl and opened the lid. 'Would you like this?' she offered.

The girl's eyes widened at the sight of the cake. She shifted, eyeing Shifa warily. 'It's OK . . . I just want you to have it.' Still the girl seemed unsure. 'I'm Shifa, what's your name?' she ventured. The girl shook her head, not willing to trust her. Shifa had heard that Foragers were being tricked and bribed into joining the Family.

'Thank you,' she whispered before taking a huge bite of the cake, eating at a speed that showed she was afraid someone would swoop in and take it from her. Shifa winced when she noticed the girl's gums bleeding as she ate. She scanned left and right to check for opticares, then leant in close. 'If you go to Number One in the Warehouse District, there's a woman called Lottie – my aunt – she helps people . . . Look for the one with the rainbow sheet and bunting in the window.'

The girl flinched as she snuggled her baby closer in the crook of her arm. Her baby began to cry, a hollow hungry cry, and the girl peered up at Shifa. 'My name's Halonah, and this is my Honey,' she said with a shy smile.

*

Emerging through the underpass, Shifa skirted the high walls of Paragon Park where her papa worked in the stately gardens – *not free for Freedoms* unless they were workers. Shifa laid her head against the wall and listened to the mechanical hum of beedrones, but also here and there a little sweet birdsong – she sniffed the air at the scent of lilies like the ones she had managed to grow on the Flower Tracks. *How come Paragons are allowed to enjoy beautiful flowers and we're not?* The familiar twist of anger reared up in her as she passed the imposing entrance gates and peered through the bars at the mass of colour, and felt a deep ache of injustice at being shut out.

Chapter Three

Shifa headed across the well-tended Kairos Piazza with its gigantic tree sculpture. When she was younger, she had been impressed by it, but once Papa had shown her photographs of real ancient trees, the sculpture had started to look dead and lifeless. Its Solarmirror leaves reflected the sky and absorbed the sun but never turned golden or floated to the ground.

She leant against one of the trunks to tie her loosening lace. *The Graffitree blossom has a thousand times more life in it than this*, she thought. In her mind a flurry of pink blossom floated over the agora, settling as a carpet of sweetly scented flowers. A drone buzzed behind her head. She attempted to ignore it as she strode on, Nabil's rhymes scrolling through her mind: *'No time for dreaming, unless you want screening. Don't go into the agora marketplace unless you want a bitter face!'* Honestly! How old did he think she was!

Shifa hurried across the commercial quarter to the agora marketplace where an army of brown-overalled sanitation workers were sweeping the streets; others worked in metal crates, suspended at dizzying heights, cleaning the windows of luxury flats above the agora. *What must it be like for them*, Shifa wondered, *to peer into the lives of Paragons? I wouldn't mind seeing it for myself!*

Shifa strained her neck to survey the crystal dome with its circular roof garden, the Solarmirror in the centre so clean and clear it looked like sky. Nabil always hurried them past the agora, telling them it was full of useless expensive things for Paragons that would only make them *want, want, want*. But now for the first time Shifa really took in the wealth that oozed from every shining facet, and she understood why Papa always marched them on to avoid Shifa's *inquisition,* as he called her questioning.

She stopped in front of a Crow and felt for her ARK ID.

'Shifa Aziz. What's your business here?' the Crow barked.

'Hairtakers.' Shifa attempted to make her voice matter of fact.

The shorn-haired Crow admired Shifa's hair, as people often did, following its lush length down her back to her calves; she stood aside to let Shifa pass. 'You'll get top price for that in there.'

Inside, the air was perfumed. A screen announced the sickly scent to be 'Essence of Forest Glade' and flashed an advert of where to buy it in the agora perfumerie. Bland, calming music streamed waves of electronic boredom. *It doesn't make you feel anything*, Shifa thought. *Not like Lottie's music.*

The inside of the agora was all lit up: the sun ricocheted off the roof from one gleaming window to the next. The first 'street' took Shifa through Orchard Stores, where the shops sold Freedom Fields produce – oranges and grapes. The sight of their plump, dark purple skins made her mouth water. She scanned the display for a glimpse of strawberries as shown in the Freedom Fields brochure, but there were none.

A window screen played an advert: 'Landowners! Want to grow your own designer fruit? Buy a miracle – Beedrone – 50,000 groits (enquire within for credit options).'

Shifa gasped. *Fifty thousand groits*. Who would ever be able to afford that? Shifa stared at the screen as the strange mechanical yellow-and-black orbed creature with splaying tentacles flew through a grand garden, collecting nectar and flying on to the next flower. *Spooky*, Shifa thought, and nothing like the beautiful tiny delicate winged bees that Nabil had described Baba Suli and their ancestors keeping.

'Why can't everyone have beedrones then?' Her own childish voice when the beedrones had first been sold returned to her – and her papa's reply. 'Too expensive for everyone to own . . . but maybe one day.' Her little-girl's voice rang in her ears so clearly now, always questioning.

'But Papa, are they more expensive than *us* pollinating?' she'd asked.

Shifa winced as she remembered the argument afterwards between Papa and Lottie about Paragons being rich enough to spread their wealth instead of putting children to work so that they could hang on to all their old luxuries now that the bees were gone.

Nothing as beautiful as the skeps we make, Shifa thought as she watched the film of the beedrone returning to its container hive, and she wondered how it was possible that the latest version of the miracle beedrone was still so far out of the reach of everyone but Paragons.

Shifa smiled as she remembered Themba's little-boy voice when Nabil had first taught them to make a skep hive on the Flower Tracks.

'What's the point of making skep hives when there aren't any bees left?' Themba asked, as he cut his fingers on the sticks he was attempting to bend into shape.

'We have to keep the family tradition going, or it'll die out, won't it?' Papa replied.

'Like the bees died out,' said Shifa.

'Yes, but look!' Papa had peered inside one of their skeps on the Flower Tracks and found a nest with two tiny blue eggs in it, and an urgently singing mother bird. He told them she was called a thrush, and that they should step back so as not to frighten her. 'Don't worry, your eggs are safe here. Seems like we've attracted another little family to our garden. You see how nature can regenerate? We've got to keep our family skep-heart beating.'

A small child grabbed the ends of Shifa's hair. Shifa moved aside.

'Sorry about that!' His mother laughed, unclasping her child's podgy hands and pointing at the screen. 'He's obsessed with flowers and bees,' she explained. 'He'd much rather be in our garden than here!'

'Me too!' Shifa said, walking on.

Shifa read off a giant scrolling screen and found what she had come for: the Hairtaker, number eleven, Beauty Emporium. Suddenly she felt sick with nerves, her legs shaking. She shivered, unused to the air cooling, and wrapped her hair around her like a shawl to cover her goosebumpy arms. She sniffed the air and inhaled a strange smell wafting from a cafe with a sign boasting 'Freeze-Dried Rare Coffee'.

She peered inside the cafe at a small group of teenagers sprawled on comfy sofas. They were wearing the latest SmartTek jackets, network devices in every pocket, drinking coffee and chatting, flicking their hair in drama-sweeps and admiring their shiny new Feetskins with personalised patterns. The fit-like-a-glove Feetskins were one thing she was excited about owning but she had a hunch that Freedom Fields issue would be bland and practical. She looked down at her own greying pumps and in a flash it struck her that the Paragons would take one glance at her feet and know she was a Freedom. As one girl patted her plait, her long nails shimmered. There was no way you could garden or do pollinating work with nails as long as theirs.

Shifa smoothed over her dress. Maybe Lottie was right about the cotton vintage flower pattern being sought after, but for going out at night maybe, not for a day of shopping or hanging out in the agora. *I feel more out of place here than anywhere I've ever been. What makes fashion?* Shifa wondered. *Who starts the idea?* Despite the trend to design your own Feetskins, all the girls' clothes, hair and teeth were more or less a uniform. But now she inspected closer there was a difference – as one girl lifted her cup Shifa could clearly see her sunflower tattoo. She must be one of the chosen few scholarship girls that Principal Daviala kept telling Shifa she could aspire to be one day.

Turning right, she walked past the shops, reading the signs on one side of Pamper Street. Shifa paused for a moment to peer through the Nail Palace window, riveted by the flying-saucer-like domes where Paragons chatted as their nails dried. *It's like I've landed on another planet.* The next shop was Massage Junction, then Aroma Healing, Hairs and Graces, Extensions and finally . . . she checked her reflection in the Hairtaker's window. A security drone swooped out of nowhere, she turned and it clicked in her face, sending her tumbling backwards into the shop.

Chapter Four

'Steady!' Shifa was caught by a woman wearing a sunflower-emblazoned, crisp white coat, titanium blue lipstick and a cone of plaited hair. She had fake-straight sparkly teeth and her blue eyes were so bright she must have been wearing lenses. She smelt of rose perfume. Shifa became painfully aware of the sweat patches under her own arms.

As she propped Shifa back to standing, the woman's manicured hands were already reaching under Shifa's head, weighing her hair, feeling its thickness with a tentative touch, as if she coveted it but was also afraid that she would catch something unsavoury from its strands. *Who was I kidding thinking I could pass for a Paragon? I might as well be wearing a 'Freedom' stamp across my forehead!* It hadn't even occurred to the Hairtaker that she might be coming to *buy* a length of hair.

'My name's Nita,' she said, in a bored, matter-of-fact tone. 'I'll be your hairtaker today. You'll find instructions and everything you need for your prep through there.' She pointed to a cubicle door.

A lock clicked behind Shifa. The floor and ceiling of the changing room gleamed white and stank of Chemisan. Shifa scanned around for an opticare but found none.

An automated voice clicked on. 'Welcome to the Agora Hairtakers. Rest assured this facility is protected by the ARK privacy law, denying access to drones and opticares. Remove all clothing and jewellery. Place your belongings in the laundry hatch provided where they will be steam cleaned and returned to you. Please proceed to the shower area indicated by illuminated arrows.'

Shifa placed her daisy dress in the hatch as instructed. Wrapping her arms and hair protectively around her torso she felt painfully aware of her protruding ribs and hips. She followed an arrow that led to a footbath of purple Chemisan that she had no choice but to walk through.

All this for a haircut? It was humiliating. *Does she think she's going to catch something off me?* Shifa's chest swelled with anger and suddenly she wished she was back at the warehouse sitting at Lottie's feet as she braided her hair, but there was no going back now.

Shifa stepped into a large shower room. Steam began to pour through holes in the walls. She picked up the bottle of odourless 'Hair and BodySan,' coated her skin with it and waited for the water. The shower head began to spurt a constant, powerful hot jet of water as she lathered the liquid into her hair and steam enveloped her. Shifa closed her eyes and felt the muscles in her neck and shoulders relax as the unfamiliar hot water ran over her skin. *What would it feel like to shower in this luxury every day?* She arched her back and felt the silken sheet smoothness of her wet hair for the last time.

An amber light flashed on the wall beside the shower and after a couple of minutes it turned red. The flow of water halted abruptly and a warm jet of air blasted her so hard that she had to cling to the wallrail. As instructed from above, she now walked back through to the changing room. She smiled for the first time at the sight of her freshly laundered daisy dress that had dropped into a tray under the hatch. As she put it on she realised that it had turned from cream to white and the yellow flower centres now glowed bright.

Nita directed her to a seat and Shifa stared at her reflection in the large wall mirror, attempting to detach herself by imagining she was watching someone else as Nita began combing through her hair.

'Good, good, no dead crawlers . . . And the length is impressive . . . Unusually healthy and glossy too.' Nita spoke to the back of her head as she opened her sharp metal shears. Shifa held her breath and was unable to stop the flow of tears as Nita made a clean sheer cut at the nape of her neck. She caught the length of hair in a pouch-like contraption attached to the chair. Smiling to herself and stroking it like a long tail, Nita picked it up and placed it on a sheet of satin cloth on a counter behind her.

'Can I keep a tiny strand of it? For my brother, when we're in separate dorms. He twists it around his fingers to get to sleep . . . he can't sleep without . . .' Shifa's explanation faded as Nita pointed curtly at the price list on the wall.

Full Length Hair 500 groits
Mid Length Hair 250 groits
Keepsake strands will be deducted by ring thickness:
Large (100 groits) Medium (60 groits) Small (40 groits)

Nita unclasped a necklace containing three golden-coloured rings and held them up for Shifa to choose the size.

'Well? What's it to be?' Nita prompted her.

'It's my birthday today, and my brother's.' Shifa spoke the words at Nita's reflection.

'Nice try! But we don't barter in the agora.' Her smile appeared and disappeared in the glint of an eye.

'Small,' Shifa whispered, feeling the jagged ends of her hair where it now ended just below her ears.

Nita took the small golden ring and a length of Shifa's hair and passed it through. She stapled it at one end. It wasn't much but it would be enough for Themba's night-time entangling.

'Plaited or unplaited?' Nita asked.

'I'll sort it,' Shifa muttered, desperately trying to stem her tears.

'Raise your head now, look straight ahead. I need to log your change of appearance,' Nita ordered, and swivelled Shifa around in her chair. She seemed for a moment taken aback by Shifa's tear-stained face as she handed over her ARK ID. Nita pressed the card against her handheld screen and waited.

'Oh! It *is* your birthday!' Nita pointed to the screen where Shifa's date of birth was recorded. *As if I need proof of it!*

Nita raised the screen to take a new ARK ID photorecord, then seemed to change her mind.

'I'll tell you what – I don't usually do this but as you've brought me such lush hair, I'll neaten it up a bit for you while you dry your tears.' Nita swivelled her around and began snipping away, cutting it slightly shorter at the nape, evening out the jagged edges. She watched Nita's jaw soften as she worked, her sunflower tattoo grow and shrink as she opened and closed her scissors. Here was her chance . . .

'What's it like on the farms?' Shifa whispered.

Nita leaned in close to Shifa. 'We can't discuss that. Not that there's anything to hide.' She nodded reassuringly. 'Follow instructions, take everything in your stride and you'll be fine. There! That's better! Suits you actually! And much more practical in the heat of the polytunnels. In a few days' time you'll thank me for this! Happy Birthday!'

Shifa stared at herself in the mirror and tried to muster a

smile. If anything, the short hair made her dark eyes take up even more of her face. She definitely looked older and maybe that wasn't such a bad thing . . . but it felt so strange, like losing a part of herself.

'So that's four hundred and sixty groits altogether. How do you want to be paid?

'Three hundred and sixty on credit and the rest in groits?' Shifa said, handing Nita the Food Bank card.

'You've got it all worked out, haven't you!' Nita whispered. 'Just don't be too smart at Freedom Fields – they don't like that!'

Shifa's fingers smoothed the shiny surface of the golden groit notes. She'd never seen any this new before.

In the hair extensions shop next door, a price list was displayed in the window: '1 whole head of hair extensions = 1,000 groits'.

How can they make so much profit? Why wasn't I paid more? For a moment she'd been proud of the price she'd managed to get along with the tiny box containing Themba's strand. Now she felt sickened and deflated and, staring in the window, she caught herself wearing the 'bitter face' of Nabil's cautionary rhyme. With the groits she had in her pocket she wouldn't even be able to afford to buy a quarter of her own hair. How long would it be, she wondered, before a Paragon was swishing her head around, glorying in her new hair?

I've seen enough, Shifa thought as she strode to the nearest exit, down through Fashion Street and the Feetskin Emporium. On a stand outside was a Feetskin display, and despite her resolve to get out of the agora as fast as she could, she found herself pausing and picking up a pair in her favourite mossy-green colour. They were so soft and smooth, with grips on the undersides too – no wonder Paragons loved them so much.

A shop assistant hovered near the display eyeing her suspiciously. 'They're a hundred groits,' she said, checking out Shifa's cropped hair and greying pumps, and signalling for her to put the Feetskins back.

Instead Shifa reached into her pocket and took out her groit notes. She paused to enjoy the look of surprise on the assistant's face, then handed the shoe back.

'Actually, I've changed my mind. Not my colour!'

On her way out of the agora, a man in white overalls emerged from a service entrance. She hung back for a moment and watched him dump a small box into a yellow Paragon Giving Container. She waited for the worker to return inside and scanned around for opticares – it was worth a look. She climbed the metal ladder and peered inside. The box had 'Cakes and Confectionery' printed on the lid, stamped with a sell-by date of yesterday. Shifa glanced around again and then opened the lid to find ten fairy cakes, all iced in pastel colours. Her stomach gurgled. Enough cakes to share at the warehouse party. She plucked one from the tray and took a small bite. The sponge was soft and only slightly drying, but the icing was deliciously sweet. She placed it back in the box – she would finish it later. Was this stealing? Would her papa lecture her for taking them? She thought of the pathetic cake the Paragons had 'gifted' her and Themba for their birthday, and wondered if the Crows scavenged in the boxes first and took some of the best gifts for themselves. Surely just this once it could not do any harm to take what had already been rejected by the Paragons.

Chapter Five

One of these cakes is for Halonah, Shifa decided as she approached the underpass. But as she entered, a pungent reek of Chemisan filled her nose. The walls and floor had been power-hosed clean, new opticares blinked at her and a notice had been placed on the wall.

Outlanders relocation programme in action by order of Ark Law.

Shifa shuddered. Apparently more Foragers had been 'relocated' over the last weeks than ever before. If only she'd offered to take Halonah and Honey to Lottie this morning instead of heading straight to the agora – she could have gone to any old hairtakers. *I could have done something to help*, she berated herself, the sound of Honey's hungry cries haunting her every step.

She walked quickly now, desperate to get home before Papa and Themba so that she could hide the Food Bank card and groits. Nabil was a proud man and it would be easier for him to find the groits and Food Bank card after they'd left than accept them from his daughter's hand.

All the way home she had willed for the cherry blossom Graffitree to have survived the day, but it came as no surprise to smell paint well before she reached the compound. The delicate floating petals that had trailed across the wall, wafting on the breeze of the artist's imagination and catching hers, had already been painted over, pitch-black. She felt for the few seeds she'd collected in her seed packet today that she would give to Papa. If tended with care and planted on the Flower Tracks they might grow . . . A rhyme of Themba's came to her and was some comfort – *Shifa, I think you'll find that no one can take away the blossom that's floating through your mind.*

Daisy's sharp miaow punctured the air as Shifa unlocked the door. She checked the time – only four o'clock. Nabil had said he and Themba would be back just after five. At least she still had plenty of time before they returned. She placed the cakes on the crate table, picked Daisy up and cradled her in her arms. The old cat reached a paw up to Shifa's hair and miaowed sharply as if scolding her for her missing mane. 'I know it feels weird but I had to do it, Daisy! For Themba . . . and Nabil.' Shifa sighed and set her down.

Shifa took her strand of hair out of the box and laid it beside the cakes and the official envelope addressed to Nabil. 'Isn't that the strangest birthday collection you've ever seen?' Daisy sniffed at the hairtaker's box.

Shifa picked up the 'Private and Confidential, URGENT' letter. *What harm could it do to peek inside?* Nabil always said that as far as Freedom Fields was concerned they should not keep any secrets. Shifa eased open the envelope, managing to break the seal cleanly. She sat down at the crate table and read . . .

For the sole attention of Nabil Aziz, hereby
known as 'The Carer' of Shifa and Themba Aziz.

On behalf of the ARK Emergency Government

In partnership with The Freedom Fields Family
of the Kairos Lands.

Following approval of your recent request to
include a legally binding amendment seeking
assurance that siblings Shifa and Themba Aziz
will be placed together on Freedom Fields Farms,
please find enclosed your final pledge.

Failure to present this document at your
wards' Graduation Ceremony will result in
yourself and your wards being removed from the
Freedom Fields Family and all the benefits it has
afforded you to date.

(Refer to your ARK contract for the
consequences of severance and debt repayment
clauses.)

Concerning the many questions you have
addressed to us, we would like to assure you once
again that your wards will be safe in our hands.
Please find attached a response form to frequently
asked questions.

We wish to remind you that the Freedom Fields
Family is the trusted partner of the ARK
Government. While we have been fully functioning
as a nationwide enterprise for the last decade as

an 'emergency' response to the devastation that
Climate Chaos has wrought throughout the world
and on our land's natural resources and economy,
we have a longstanding record of building our
portfolio of schools, healthcare, welfare and
food production for well over half a century. Our
Youth Recruit-led Food Production and Pollination
Service is proving an invaluable pillar in our
portfolio to rebuild our great Kairos Lands.

We of Freedom Fields hope that this letter
serves to reassure you that our Family offers the
very best future for your wards.

Signed

On behalf of Freedom Fields

Freedom Fields Family is a subsidiary of PoV Bank
and Technological Services

In Loco Parentis Pledge

I .... hereby
freely and in full knowledge of the rules,
freedoms and obligations of The Freedom Fields
Family by appointment of the ARK Government,
do hereby place Freedom Fields in loco parentis
.... and ....
for the period of five years (or until termination
of the Ark Government Partnership) for the
purpose of essential Food Research, Production
and Pollination Services.
Exceptional circumstance guarantee for sibling
same-farm placement. Amendment Approved.

Signature: ....
Printed Name and Status: ....
....

Freedom Fields Family is a subsidiary of PoV Bank
and Technical Services

Shifa's hands trembled as she held the contract. To see their futures in black and white like this made leaving home feel all too real. *In loco parentis* . . . She had never heard those words before but she was in no doubt about what they meant. This was the legal proof that they were being handed over – *if Papa signs it.* Did his request for the amendment at the last minute show he still wasn't sure? That he didn't trust them? She swayed and steadied herself on the crate table.

Daisy padded to her side and was now circling Shifa's ankles. 'It's OK, Daisy. It's going to be OK! Maybe we don't have to go away . . .' The contract had filled her with foreboding, but perhaps the answers to these questions would still her nerves? Shifa crawled after Daisy and nestled in the comfortable folds of Baba Suli's coat to read the answers.

Strictly for Carers

Please refer to the brochure to refresh your knowledge of all aspects of your wards' Freedom Fields Service Adventure. It is there to answer any questions you may have related to their needs including:

Nutrition
Education
Health and safety workplace training
Healthcare
General wellbeing and recreation
Work/life balance
Life after service

In addition you will have received comprehensive briefings from your Freedom Fields school. Please be aware that although it is a proud and exciting moment of independence to graduate into Freedom Fields Service, a minority of students may become emotional at the point of parting and it is useful for all concerned if you, 'The Carer' remain calm and convey a positive and confident attitude demonstrating your total trust in us as being one Freedom Fields Family.

Update: What is the current state of Food Production?
While there has been some limited improvement in our ability to feed all our citizens, we are still some way

Freedom Fields Family is a subsidiary of PoV Bank and Technological Services

Food, Fresh (Air), Fair (Treatment), Freedom and Fun

off fulfilling our quotas. As you are aware, this is due to threats to, or extinction of, natural insect and bird pollinators, trees and plant life, combined with population shortages following Hurricane Chronos. The destruction of our ARK Species Lab containing the diversity of all our plant and tree life has been an incalculable blow to our world. Despite taking drastic steps to change farming methods, scientists believe that the regeneration of our Kairos Lands may take many decades.

Whether your ward has been selected to work on a pollination farm or research facility, they will be making a vital contribution to helping boost quotas of food production in the Kairos Lands. Plant pollination by the delicate fingers of children is an effective method of ensuring the production and variety of food that will eventually be available to all ARK citizens. As we rebuild our Lands, we are proud to have been able to fulfil our pledge to supply basic nutrition through food banks to all Freedoms.

Why isn't the Farm address given to Carers in advance? Please understand that it is a mammoth task to coordinate the graduation and distribution of thousands of young recruits to new farms around our vast lands. Our experience shows us that location information is most effectively recorded following the settling-in process when recruits are fully registered.

Will I get regular reports from the Farm?
Of course! Carers will be sent a quarterly update on recruits' progress. Recruits are not encouraged to write letters home as this hampers settling and can cause homesickness.

When are Visiting Rights and/or Carer Communication granted?
Each farm operates a fair and rigorously monitored system of credits and debits. We are sure that your wards will soon receive the number of credits required to trigger visiting rights. Recruits do not return home under any circumstance throughout their five years of service.

N.B. Carers should be sensitive to the fact that the majority of Freedoms were made orphans at the time of Hurricane Chronos and therefore do not have visitors.

What happens if recruits become ill?
In the event of illness, Freedom Fields will ensure that all healthcare is provided free of charge to recruits.

NB: A Housecarer is employed on each farm to assist in the settling and welfare of all recruits.

Carer communication can be arranged in truly exceptional circumstances, and at the discretion of Freedom Care professionals.

What happens if recruits do not abide by ARK law while on the farm?

For the safety of everyone, recruits will be monitored through opticare surveillance. Each farm has full security and boundary controls. In addition, storm barns installed on every farm ensure your ward's personal safety. ARK law is known to all our recruits but the individual rules of each farm must also be adhered to.

In the unlikely event that you 'The Carer' should be taken ill or found guilty of a serious crime under ARK law and placed in an ARK Correction Facility, rest assured that your wards will be fully catered for by the Freedom Fields Family.

*Reminder:

In accordance with your longstanding ARK Contract, at the point of your wards' Graduation your personal Freedom Care and Work Insurance Guarantee will be terminated.

Shifa stroked Daisy's back over and over but the ash cloud that settled in her heart refused to shift as she placed the letter back in the envelope, pressed the sunflower seal and sent it flying towards the door.

Chapter Six

Desperately needing to hide away from too much reality Shifa crawled through the coat tails of Baba Suli's frayed old coat that guarded the entrance to their story hive. She bent down, carefully pulling apart the frayed wine-red lining of the side vents. Every time she passed through the coat flaps she thought of her papa as a baby wrapped snug inside when, at the end of his long journey across mountains, deserts and sea, Baba Suli had finally made it to the Kairos Lands. An old man and a tiny baby with all the rest of the family devastated by war. Mother, brothers, sisters, aunties, uncles all died except ... not lost, not extinguished, her papa insisted, because he refused to let their stories die with them. Shifa loved it most when Nabil spoke in Baba Suli's voice as if he was summoning him into the room.

'Once there was a golden city, in a golden time, where the trees stood tall, and the wild-flower fields bloomed, where the honey was aplenty, a time of sweetness and simple kindnesses, where skeps were given as wedding presents for newly-weds to start new lives together. One such skep was gifted to me and my wife Shifa long ago in our beloved kingdoms of Skyranum. It probably feels like a fairytale to you but it was a long and arduous journey I made with my grandson Nabil over deserts and oceans . . .'

Shifa gently opened the coat flaps and eased away the towers of empty crates stacked behind. The ones above her head were immovable and formed a heavy rooftop of recycled finds – random pieces of wood, string, old glass bottles waiting for Nabil to make into one of his garden sculptures, now collectors' items among the Paragons. Hard to believe that once upon a time there had been enough room for all of them to crawl inside this tiny hexagonal cocoon that Themba had named their 'story hive'.

Shifa thought of this as the Flower Tracks of the compound, because Nabil had been inspired to build it soon after he'd rediscovered his storytelling voice on the Flower Tracks. Daisy laid a paw on her arm and Shifa stroked her head and wondered how their family would have survived these last few years if she had not disobeyed her papa and ventured out on one last hunt for Daisy that day three whole years ago. She would never forget crawling underneath the giant Freedom Fields billboard, following a trail of weak cries, and discovering Daisy stranded on a ledge, winded, bruised and half starved to death. Shifa had held her close, then lifted her head to discover the piece of rough scrubland that had become their saviour.

'It's your garden, Shifa – you found it!' Nabil had declared when she'd taken him and Themba to see it. Growing flowers and plants there just for the sake of it, not even for food, had been Shifa's idea. It had done them all good. Disobeying the ARK law had seemed to make Nabil grow stronger and his shadow times had become rarer. Sometimes Shifa thought that as they tended their secret garden it tended them back.

She snuggled close to Daisy and whispered in her ear, *It's all our garden, Daisy. I saved you and you saved us, isn't that true?* Shifa's silent thought somehow conveyed to Daisy as she stroked her tummy and the cat purred in answer. *When I'm away I'll talk to you every day – listen out for me.*

Before yesterday, the last time that she remembered her papa crying was when the Crows had come to claim his books. He had sat Shifa and Themba down and prepared them for the visit in a calm, logical way, seeming to back the new ARK law as tough but necessary. The arguments made sense: the destruction of the forests meant urgent recycling was needed. Paragon Digital Libraries would retain all the important books and with patience, in time, these libraries would be opened to Freedoms too. But after they had taken his books he'd sobbed all night anyway. It was Baba Suli's collection on trees, wild flowers, birds and beekeeping that he missed the most. Shifa smiled as she remembered Themba's rhyming note that had brought Nabil out of the darkness that time.

'Dear Papa, I think you'll find
That no one can take away the trees that grow in
  your mind.'

Their story hive had been born when their papa had revealed to
them the secret they must never tell – that he had not, after all,
allowed the Crows to take away all of his books. Here, their
minds and hearts had travelled far across Kairos City to the
times before the devastation of Hurricane Chronos. Here they
had read contraband pages that they had discovered in
unlikely places around the city, and with these finds their
story hive had expanded into wild deserts, alien planets, raging
rivers, bird and butterfly aviaries, the tallest snow-capped
mountain ranges and the sweetest flowering meadows – a
world away from the rules and regulations of Freedom Fields.

For a while now Shifa and Themba had grown too big to
share the space, so they ventured in and out by themselves,
placing new treasure finds in their book boxes. Shifa's
was full of ripped-out pages of reference books about wild
flowers and birds, and story fragments she'd found tucked in
crevices around Kairos City, all containing folds of knowledge
that she read and memorised. From one random page she'd
learned how to make a flower-shaped origami envelope out
of scraps of paper. When she squeezed the top, the flower
head opened like a mouth allowing her to place her precious
seed finds inside. This was the seed packet she would take
with her to Freedom Fields.

Hidden behind a brick in the old Kairos Library walls, she had even found a giant reference-book page about river life, with glinting waters and illustrations of fish called rainbow trout. Ever vigilant for opticare and drone swoops or a patrolling Crow, she would normally read the pages quickly before walking on by, desperately holding on to the words, names, images and snippets of stories, and hoping that new hands would discover them after her. That, Lottie had told her, was Forager lore – 'passing on knowledge and power in secret'. But the river reference page had Themba's birthday written all over it. Only when she found pages about plants and wildlife would she keep anything for herself and fold them into tiny squares to make into seed envelopes, destined for her treasure box.

Shifa carefully placed Themba's box on the floor beside her own. His had grown surprisingly heavy with his sketchbooks, scraps of maps, paints and collage art. She turned her box towards her and ran her fingers over the title on the cover, *Encyclopedia of Wilderness Flora and Fauna*. The golden writing had somehow survived but the rest of the cover was so worn and torn that only one patch gave clues to its former glory – a picture of a small yellow buttercup. Nabil had told them a story that if you place this flower under your chin and the skin turns golden, it means you like butter. 'What's butter?' Shifa had asked.

Taking out the river page for Themba, she unfolded it to its full size. She dusted off her dress, took her flower-head seed packet out of her treasure box and allowed a thought to sprout in her that one day she might be free to write her own story in a real book, with her own name on it, and maybe Themba could illustrate it. If they could find a good place to hide it till a future time when books were free for everyone again . . . She closed her eyes and smiled to herself as she pictured a stranger from the future opening the cover of their book and reading. She tried to imagine a title but nothing came. But then how could she know where her story would take her until she and Themba had travelled beyond the crouched confines of their hive? Nabil was right. It was not that their hive had shrunk but that they had grown and needed to fly free. Despite her fears Shifa did feel the buzz of anticipation to see the Kairos Lands for the first time in her life.

A scuttling behind her brought her back to herself, and she recoiled from a shiny brown cockroach. As Shifa shuffled back, Nabil's box fell off the crate shelf and the contents, wrapped in a coarse grey blanket, spilled out over the floor. They had each sworn on Story-Hive Law – Themba's idea! – to respect the privacy of each other's treasure boxes, unless invited to share in finds. Shifa gasped as she picked up a golden locket on a chain. She had not intended to pry, only to place the groits and Food Bank card on top of her papa's book box so that Nabil would find them later.

Daisy padded over and began to tug and tease at the blanket so insistently that Shifa had to firmly move her aside. 'Let me get a look-in, Daisy!' Nabil had never spoken of this necklace before. Then it dawned on Shifa. *It must be my birthday present!* She found herself grinning. She had always longed for a piece of jewellery of her own and had hinted as much. Her heart raced as she carefully inspected the delicate, dented locket and unhinged the clasp, to find . . . four tiny wilted daisies inside. Daisy prowled around restlessly, her engine-purring like a lion's.

Shifa closed the locket and placed it back in the box, quickly gathering Nabil's torn-out pages and placing them on top, pausing again as she spotted the first origami seed packet she'd ever made for her papa. The paper was worn and thin but it held something firm inside. She could not help herself. Shifa teased apart the edges and glimpsed a tiny photomemory inside. She had never actually held one in her hands before. *This is what Papa was crying and praying over?* Shifa's temples pulsed as she raised her head and listened for Nabil and Themba coming home. She knew she shouldn't snoop but she couldn't help herself. Shifa opened the seed envelope and slid out the photo with trembling fingers.

It showed a woman with shoulder-length, curly auburn hair, just like Themba's. As Shifa drew the photomemory closer it took her a moment to realise that her mama Tia held only one baby in her arms, its head half covered by a bright red blanket. She held her breath. *Let it be me she's holding.* The idea of seeing herself as a baby, held in her mama's arms, made her heart swell and her chest convulsed with a rushing tide of emotion that had been surging in wild waves all day.

Why would Papa lie? He had told them many times that he had no surviving photomemories of their mama. That everything had been lost in the mayhem of Hurricane Chronos. Shifa turned it over to find Nabil's distinctive calligraphy handwriting. On the bottom right-hand corner was written:

Themba Aziz
Firstborn son of Tia and Nabil Aziz

Shifa frantically searched in the seed packet and book box for a photomemory of herself and her mama but found nothing. Maybe it was simply that they had been photographed separately and somewhere floating around Kairos City there was a photomemory of her inscribed on the back with her name. That would be it – Nabil would have wanted to be fair. In any case, she reasoned, what would Themba make of seeing such a photomemory?

Daisy set up a noisy miaowing. Shifa quickly rearranged everything and crawled out, closing the story hive in behind her. 'I think I'm going to get a locket for my birthday, Daisy!' She curled up inside Baba Suli's coat and waited for her brother and Papa to come home.

Chapter Seven

Nabil wheeled his bike in and propped it against the wall. The wooden seat he'd adapted for Themba to perch on when he'd been younger now contained a sack of foraged items with wilted leaves protruding from the top.

'Hi Papa!' Shifa called, and his mouth fell open at the sight of her peering out of Baba Suli's coat. He stared, as if trying to take in the girl before him. He nodded solemnly and walked over to the table and picked up her strand of hair. 'For Themba?' he asked.

Shifa nodded. Her papa reached out and hugged her close. She heard the emotion swell in his chest as it had in hers at the hairtakers. *Why did it feel like she had cut so much more than her hair?*

'I see you're wearing your birthday dress!'

Shifa nodded and pulled away from him, suddenly understanding that seeing her in it might be painful to him. Nabil was standing on the Freedom Fields envelope. He bent down and picked it up.

'A letter came for you. From Freedom Fields. It says it's urgent.'

'Ah! Yes!' He picked it up. 'I'll deal with that later,' he said, dropping it on to the table. He took a mushroom from his pocket and crumbled it in Daisy's saucer. 'Not much, but all I could find!' The cat sniffed at it, sat down and began eating.

'Themba's waiting for us at Lottie's. He's pretty hyped up, so we'd better get going. I've just got something I need to do first!' Nabil pointed in the direction of Baba Suli's coat.

'Me too!' Shifa smiled to herself as she walked through to the bedroom.

Shifa placed her hair strand on top of the river page and began folding it gently – Themba would not be happy if it was too creased to read. He'd want to memorise every word. As she folded, shiny turquoise, silver and golden lights from the fish scales and tails brightened her mood and lit her mind with new possibilities for where the locket had come from . . .

What if it had belonged to Mama Tia and Nabil had been waiting for today to give it to her? What if Tia had made the daisy chain with her own hands? Then it would be the most precious thing in all the world. *My mama was a Forager and loved flowers too!* Shifa felt breathless with anticipation and a new connection forming to a mama she and Themba had no memories of. A sudden sadness enveloped her to think that her Mama Tia would have been

63

alive today if the infection hadn't taken her. Despite what Lottie said, she understood why Nabil had needed them to have the protection of Freedom Care.

When she returned to the table she found the living room empty but the tails of Baba Suli's coat still swinging back and forth.

Nabil returned on his hands and knees holding the groits and Food Bank card, his brow furrowed with a deep scowl.

'What's this?'

Shifa shrugged. 'From my hair. We'll have loads to eat and you'll need groits to visit us.'

Shifa understood his look of wounded pride, but she had not expected his anger.

'You had no right to do that for me! Did you go through my belongings?'

'I didn't . . .' Shifa turned away so he would not see the crimson flush of her lie snaking up her neck. 'I just slipped them in the side. I didn't want you to find them till . . . later.'

'Filthy groits for your beautiful raven river, Shifa.' Nabil groaned and slumped on to Daisy's chair, thudding his elbows heavily on the crate table. Shifa watched the lower planks of wood bend and snap and the envelope fall between the cracks. The chair rocked back and Nabil fell on to the floor, his arms stretched above his head. He seemed transfixed for a moment as he stared up at the giant clock.

Daisy pawed at Nabil's chest.

Shifa knelt down beside him. 'Are you all right, Papa?'

As he sat up, he kept one hand firmly clasped around something that glinted gold. He shifted it over to the other hand and placed it in his pocket, staring at the letter on the floor.

'Our table's broken,' he muttered.

Shifa nodded.' You can fix it, Papa!'

He smiled sadly and squeezed his daughter's hand. 'My Shifa, always believing we can fix everything.' As he looked into her eyes Shifa thought, *Poor Papa looks more broken than the table.*

Themba leaned out of the warehouse window, grinning and waving, his mass of auburn curls dancing along with the hand-dyed bunting. Shifa was so taken with the sight of his hair's golden glow in the dying sun that she almost forgot what she had done to her own hair. The expression on Themba's face turned from joy to shock as she drew closer.

'Come on up!' Lottie called as they climbed the spiral staircase. Nearing the top, Daisy wriggled from Nabil's arms so he set her down. The old cat padded straight for the window, to her usual spot of sunshine on her nest of coloured cushions. At least Daisy was safe at the warehouse – these days, accompanying them here and to the Flower Tracks was her only bit of freedom.

Lottie walked over, held Shifa's face in her hands and kissed her on the forehead.

'You didn't get that haircut at the Flower Tracks! A haircut can be liberating! Happy birthday, beautiful! What do you think?' Lottie opened her arms and twirled around to have her decorating efforts admired.

The place was strewn with Lottie's brightly coloured blankets and festooned with bunting. In the centre of the room was an uneven row of crates covered by a cloth that Lottie called her 'banquet table', with bottle vases of herbs dotted at intervals along it.

'Thank you. It's lovely – smells good too!' Shifa inhaled deeply . . . rosemary and thyme. For a moment Shifa closed her eyes and imagined herself in one of the open meadows she'd seen in the Freedom Fields brochure. If only they could all go there together, or Papa and Lottie could come and live nearby . . . Shifa set her box of iced cakes in the middle of the table and opened the lid.

'Come and see what I found, Themb!'

He was staring at her and clutching an enormous parcel on his lap but he remained on the cushions with Daisy and refused to come to the table.

'What did you do with *my* hair, Shifa?'

'I think you'll find it's mine!' Shifa laughed and stepped towards him with her parcel. 'Happy birthday, Themb! Here!'

'Here, too!' Themba thrust his package towards Shifa but he was already immersed in reading the text and pictures on the wrapping of his own.

'It's all about fishing . . . How to cast a line out . . .' Themba was reading sideways now and, as she'd predicted, seemed more interested in the wrapping than what was inside. She hoped it would make up for the thinness of her hair strand. Themba unravelled the page as if it was as precious as gold.

Daisy craned her neck and stared at Shifa accusingly as her hair strand tumbled to the floor.

'What's up, Daisy?' Shifa laughed as her cat sniffed at it.

'Eugh! Daisy doesn't like it either!' She began to paw at it, suspiciously. 'It's weird – not attached to your head, like a dead thing.'

'Technically, I suppose it is dead now! It's to help you sleep when we go to the farm! Glad you like it!'

'I liked it better on your head.' Themba bit the inside of his lip, closed his eyes and twiddled the ends around his fingers. 'It *could* work.'

Shifa nodded, glancing over at Lottie who was already welling up with tears. Her papa shook his head as if to say, *Hold back, keep it calm*, as they always tried to for Themba's sake. *Change the subject. Change the subject.*

'I saw a blossom tree painted inside the compound today, until they blacked it out,' Shifa said breezily. 'I wish you could have seen it, Lottie. What did you think of it, Themb?'

He shrugged. 'I didn't see it.'

'Papa?'

Nabil shook his head.

'But it was enormous!'

'Sure it wasn't one of Shifa's dreams?' Nabil winked at her.

'Shifa the dreamer, Shifa the dreamer,' Themba teased. 'Open *my* present then!'

'You've got to see this to believe it!' Papa ushered Lottie over.

Themba had been making something for ages, tiresomely banning her from their bedroom while he worked on it in secret, but what she unwrapped was beyond anything she'd imagined; a multicoloured collage of Kairos City and all the paths of their lives in it.

'Me and Papa found a few bits of the old city where a map shop used to be . . .' Themba pointed to a tiny section of sepia-and-faded-green map pages. 'Papa remembered some places, how Kairos City used to be. They call this bit an Ordinary Survey map,' Themba announced, relishing this specialist piece of knowledge over Shifa.

'Ordnance Survey,' Papa corrected, laughing.

Lottie was pointing excitedly. 'There's the old Hippodrome where me and Tia went to see our first film!' She traced her hands over to the great dinosaur spine of something labelled the 'Darwin statue'. 'I forgot about that!'

'Thank you, Themb. All I know is it's definitely not ordinary.' Shifa grinned, attempting to take in all the detail.

The strangest thing was that Kairos City looked more like countryside, it was so covered in green spaces, parks and woodlands. Even the Kairos River snaked a different course. Shifa supposed the wider flood plains had forced the city to shrink away from its tidal banks. She trailed her hand around a spot where she thought she might have walked once with her papa.

Shifa laughed. At the top of the map, contained in its own shiny separate world, was the Paragons' Quarter: the agora, the ARK Government Globe, Paragon Park where Papa worked, the Garden Belt and villages, Consular Homesteads, and the glittering new 'state of the ARK' Kairos Central Station, where they would set off from tomorrow.

Shifa laid her precious collage on the floor and got Themba to sign and date it in the bottom corner. He laughed as he did. 'Like I'm a professional artist!' If only they cared about art at Freedom Fields schools. If Themba were a Paragon he would probably be hailed as a genius. He might not always be able to follow the rules or filter whatever he was feeling from his words, but he could make whole worlds come alive in paint and pencil. Themba had added light everywhere, making the stubborn murky grey of the Kairos River glisten and shine silver here and golden there.

Shifa attempted to hug him, but he squirmed out of her grasp. You could never give Themba a hug unless *he* needed one. Shifa nodded towards her strand of hair as he wound it around his fingers.

'My present doesn't look much compared to yours.'

Themba reached up to Shifa's short hair and his eyes shone. 'But it is much! I know it's much. You cut off your river of hair because you care . . .' Shifa turned away to hide her emotion.

Nabil patted Themba's shoulder and handed him a package. 'This one's from me.'

Themba unwrapped the cloth to find an artist's notebook and a small box. The paper of the art book was marbled – Shifa had seen her papa making it with nettle juice, oil and water, and she'd been mesmerised by the pale cell-like swirls into which he'd dipped the paper.

Themba picked up the box, on which Nabil had written in calligraphy, slid it open and gasped as he discovered a rusty, gold-tipped pen and four small vials of ink: one gold, one silver, one copper and one black. Some of these she was sure had been used on her collage. Themba rushed at Nabil and hugged him. 'You said I couldn't have them!'

'Changed my mind!' Nabil laughed.

Themba held the pen, pressed the soft vial and filled it with copper ink. 'Should have signed Shifa's map with this,' he said as he swirled his name in copper on the page.

Nabil nodded. 'But remember, Themba, Shifa's collage has to stay with me.'

Themba puckered his lips. As always with Themba, the argument went around and around. He tried everything, even arguing on Shifa's behalf that if he could take his present . . . why couldn't . . . ?

'That's enough, Themba! We agreed, remember? You're not taking the map and that's that. It'll get confiscated and you'll be in trouble before you start!' Nabil finally snapped, holding out his hand for Shifa to pass it to him.

70

'I'll take it with me in here!' she told Themba, tapping her head. 'Like you said to Papa about the trees . . . and that blossom I saw today. I'll carry it in my mind.'

Themba shrugged. 'Like I'll have to imagine your hair's attached to your head?'

Themba's perfect logic always made Shifa smile.

Lottie laughed too and raised her head at approaching footsteps, waiting to see who appeared. Shifa felt pure joy as she sprang up and greeted Halonah holding baby Honey in her arms. She nodded shyly at Shifa.

'You found us! This is Halonah. I told her to come and find you,' Shifa gabbled in excitement.

Lottie took Halonah gently by the hand and led her into the warehouse.

'I thought they'd taken you away,' Shifa said.

'They tried but we hid.' Halonah kissed her baby's forehead. 'As quiet as quiet my Honey was, as if she knew she had to be to survive.'

A drift of pink blossom floated through Shifa's mind all through the eating of cakes, Lottie's flute playing and their birthday celebrations. Nabil didn't even spoil it by questioning her about where the cakes came from. As they laughed and sang and Halonah handed baby Honey to Shifa, she thought her heart would explode with conflicting emotions and unanswered questions. She was sure now that Nabil was waiting for special time with her to give her the locket. As she closed her eyes to make a wish she struggled to still her mind, each wish stampeding into the next, clamouring for attention. In the end Shifa settled on twin wishes. The first she knew could never be, but wishes were all a leap of faith so if she made a truly wild one first, a wish to halt time in a moment of happiness, maybe there was an outside chance that the second wish could come true.

Let this moment last for ever.

Let Papa and Lottie have found a way for us all to stay together.

The party was nearing an end. Lottie found a mattress for mother and baby to sleep on. Halonah was so exhausted that she slept through her baby's cries. Shifa watched as Nabil picked her up and rocked her in his arms so tenderly that she soon calmed.

'You're good at that, Papa!' Shifa whispered.

'I've had enough practice!' Nabil whispered back.

When he had finally settled Honey, Shifa took a deep breath and plucked up the courage to ask. 'Papa, please can we go to the Flower Tracks one last time?' She peered over at Themba who was deep in concentration practising his calligraphy as Lottie held a torch above his head. 'Just the two of us?'

'It's risky.'

'Please, Papa.'

Lottie looked up. 'You should go and talk, tonight of all nights, just the two of you!'

Nabil re-examined his daughter's newly cropped hair and nodded, his knotted brow declaring that there were things he needed to speak of too.

Shifa took a deep breath as they stepped into the night.

Chapter Eight

Nabil paused on the Orbital Bridge to admire an unusually bright starlit night for Kairos City.

'To think that when I was your age we had to wear pollution masks because of all the carbon fumes and now the Kairos air is cleaner but the great trees are gone. And this constant heat . . .' Nabil wiped the sweat off his forehead. Shifa could never understand how humans could have not worked together to prevent Hurricane Chronos and its worldwide wrecking wave. Whatever the differences between humans in different lands, why couldn't they put them aside to see that they were all born from the same earth? The way Shifa saw it, humans were the family and the earth, sky, sea, planets and universe were the humans' guardians. Not taking care of the planet felt like destroying the thing that most cared for you. When Nabil had tried to explain that in the build up to Hurricane Chronos some countries had struggled to make deals, and there were leaders who had even refused to believe the science of Climate Chaos, she had hardly been able to believe her ears. But tonight there was no sign of weather turbulence. The air was still and the clear moonlit sky glowed a deep sapphire colour.

They continued to walk in silence until they reached the familiar sunflower-festooned Freedom Fields billboard. Nabil stood watch as Shifa scrabbled underneath it, knowing just where the dip in the ground was to slip under, then Nabil quickly followed. They sidestepped down the steep bank together before taking up their usual places on the low benches by the shed where they kept their skep collection.

Shifa leaned forward and pulled off a lavender head and rubbed it under her nose, breathing in the potent scent. The Flower Tracks smelt even more magical at night. She had always thought that if anything would give them away here it was not their whispered voices or the sound of their trowels tilling the earth, but the rare delicious scent of their wild garden and the insect and bird life that had begun to seek it out. In the day time she would watch, mesmerised, as the tiny white butterflies danced on the white and purple flower heads she had named her butterfly bush. Now she was amazed to find that delicate green moths with pink winged borders crowded around their heads.

Shifa picked up a dandelion head and blew the wispy seeds up towards the sky.

'They say if you pluck one of those feathery heads and want to send a wish, turn in the direction of where your loved one lives, then blow and the seed ball will convey your message faithfully,' Nabil said, picking another head and and blowing the seeds towards her. 'And if you want to know if your loved one is thinking of you, blow again – if a single aigrette is left you know that you're not forgotten.'

'What's an aigrette?' Shifa asked

Nabil pointed to the wispy seed head that remained on the stem.

Shifa waited patiently. These stories were always a precursor to what he really had to say. She lay on the warm ground and surveyed the sky. The evening air was fresher than the day but still far from cool.

'I think it's a hare in the moon!' Nabil whispered.

Shifa followed Nabil's gaze skyward.

'Papa, can we talk about real things tonight? You know I don't believe in omens, good or bad. We haven't got much time.'

'Stories *are* real!' Nabil insisted.

Shifa nodded. Themba and Nabil were so alike in that way. Themba through his art, Nabil through his stories.

'This is one of Baba Suli's I want you to take with you . . . OK?'

'OK!'

'Long, long ago there was a hare, a fox and a monkey that decided to live together. So in the spirit of community they made an agreement to care for each other and any stranger who came their way. Together they made a pact never to harm another creature. So, the Manito—'

'What's that?' Shifa sighed deeply. *No point fighting it!* she told herself.

'A spirit of nature, a supernatural force.'

'OK,' said Shifa. 'And . . .'

'The Manito appeared to them in the form of a woman and decided to put them to the test.' Shifa turned towards Nabil now. Maybe this was about her mama after all. 'Off she went to the forest and the hare, fox and monkey all welcomed her. She was hungry and they had no food, so one by one she set them the task of going out foraging for her. The fox went first, the monkey second. Even though food was scarce they collected fruit and vegetables and gave them to the Manito to eat.

'Finally, it was the hare's turn but it found nothing at all to bring back to the Manito. Not a single scrap. So the hare instructed the Manito to build a fire. "I have heard men eat flesh . . . so I will give you mine!" the hare said, and braced itself to leap on to the fire, but the Manito caught the hare just in time and said,

'"You have been so unselfish, little hare. You have given me yourself and so, in return, I offer you a gift too."' Shifa sat up, smiling . . . waiting for the locket. '"A gift to carry you up to the moon in my arms, so that everyone on earth, when they look up, will see that the hare is in the moon and be inspired by your kindness. See it now?"'

Shifa smiled because, now she looked, she could just about trace the shape of the hare in the moon!

'I really don't want to go tomorrow, Papa.' Shifa's voice wobbled. 'I read that contract on the table . . . And I know you haven't signed it yet . . .'

Nabil sat up and held both of her hands. 'I thought you understood, Shifa. If I knew another way that was safe for you both . . . I couldn't risk what happened to Tia happening to you.' Shifa held her breath. Nabil's shoulders stooped. 'When I opted in I never imagined that farm recruits would be needed for this long. I assumed it would only be for a few years and you'd get to go to school, be looked after if you were ill . . . and after that things might readjust. I never thought I'd actually have to send you into service.'

Shifa nodded, her eyes glistening. She felt foolish now to have allowed herself even the tiniest glimmer of hope.

'But here! This is for you to take with you . . .' Nabil whispered, reaching in his pocket and handing Shifa a small velvet purse. Her heart leapt. So it was for her after all. She loosened the drawstring and took out the dented golden locket.

'It belonged to your mama. I've been saving it for you,' Nabil whispered.

Shifa's heart swelled as she sprang a tight hug on Nabil. 'Thank you, Papa. Don't be angry with me but I knocked over your treasure box today and saw a photomemory of Mama with Themba. I thought you said nothing survived.' She turned to Nabil and he stared back in wide-eyed horror.

'Why weren't we both in the photo?' she asked.

Nabil rubbed his palms hard over his face and picked away at a sprig of thyme. He seemed frozen, unable or unwilling to respond.

'Papa! What's the matter?'

'I've been trying to find a way to tell you this since you could speak,' he said eventually, his voice emerging more like a painful wail. 'Lottie said I should have told you the truth years ago, but there never was a right time and I never found the right words. I have not been honest with you . . .'

Shifa clasped her mama's locket and Nabil's words, stumbling and hesitant at first, melted into her. She was inside her papa's story, breathing every step of his journey as the hurricane hit Kairos City, and the closer he came to home and the landmarks she knew, the greater the pull in her was to stand up and run away from whatever he was about to tell her. Because in the growing wildness of his telling, the gravel soarness of his voice, the wind's roar, time's mismatched hands, Daisy's miaow – she could feel a new truth straining at the leash to be spoken.

'Shifa. I'm not your birth papa. This is your mama's locket but Tia, Themba's mama, died a month before I found you on the night of the hurricane. I brought you up as if you were twins.'

Trust and truth and love . . . Those were the important things, and here Nabil was telling her that her whole life had been a lie. There was no photomemory of her with her mama because there were no memories of her mama. Not even

Nabil held the key to those.

Her papa held his head in his hands. They were both sobbing now, and great wrenching painful tears fell to the earth and watered the ground of the Flower Tracks they had planted together. For the first time ever this place offered no comfort.

Shifa stared at the wilted daisy chain in her hands. This was all that was left of the mama she would never be able to picture. She would never even know her name.

Nabil placed his hands over his heart. 'Shifa, I named you after my grandmother.'

'All those family stories you've told me . . .' Shifa gulped back the tears, hot with betrayal and anger.

'Some families are made, not born.' Nabil reached into the shed and took out two half-finished skeps, handing one to Shifa and holding one himself.

Her hands worked automatically, weaving softened sticks and grasses in and out to make a tiny hive. *Papa is not my papa, Themba's not my brother, Lottie isn't my aunt . . . and my mama left me all alone with nothing but a kitten to mind me. Daisy's the only being in the whole world that has a memory of my true mama.* Shifa gasped as she failed to bend a brittle stick into a soft curve, flinching as the sharp edge splintered and drew a thick tear of ruby blood from her skin. Nabil reached over to help her but she snatched her hand away.

'No more stories, Nabil,' she warned, sucking the soft pad of her finger so hard that it began to throb. 'Am I supposed to thank you now for all your kindness? Are you the brave, kind hare in the moon? If you were, you would have told me the truth years ago. You're a coward, Nabil. My name isn't even my own!' Nabil kept his head lowered as her words lashed him. 'Why do you think you have the right to decide anything for me? If my mama was a Forager, then I could choose to be one too. I'm not going away tomorrow. How can you sign me over when you're not even my papa?' Shifa climbed on her hands and knees up the steep slope. She stood at the top of the slope looking down on the Flower Tracks and hurled the skep with all her force against the brick wall. Its hollow heart shattered in an explosion of twigs, seeds and dust.

Nabil and Shifa walked towards the warehouse in silence, but the hurt between them drummed louder with every step they took. Despite her threats, Shifa would leave tomorrow – Nabil knew as well as she that her love for her brother meant that she could not allow Themba to go into service on his own. The journey between the Flower Tracks and the warehouse had never felt so long.

Lottie stood at the entrance, waiting for them, holding out her arms in relief to see them back safe. Shifa brushed straight past her and walked up the staircase to find Themba curled up with Daisy on the cushions, both asleep, Shifa's hair strand intertwined between Themba's fingers.

She lay next to them and whispered into Daisy's ear, 'I didn't know you saved my life before I saved yours!' Daisy purred in reply as Shifa held her close, the soft pads of her paws reaching up to her face. 'Please be here when we get back,' Shifa pleaded.

'What's wrong with your eyes?' Themba asked as he stirred.

Shifa shrugged. 'An allergy to something on the Flower Tracks.'

Themba reached sleepily for her locket. 'Is this your birthday present?'

'Careful, Themba!' She tugged it away from him.

'I was only looking. What's the matter with you?'

'Sorry. It's . . . delicate, that's all.'

Themba examined her face. 'Did the locket make you change? Has it got powers?' Themba laid his head on Shifa's lap. 'Don't be sad, Shifa, you're my best sister. I'll look after you.'

Lottie stayed inside attempting to contain a screaming, scratching, clawing, wailing Daisy, and as they walked away from the warehouse for the last time, baby Honey started howling too. At the sound of their cries Nabil's back stiffened and the tears Shifa had attempted to hold inside her broke. She didn't know what or who exactly she was crying for – Honey or the motherless baby she had been, her loyal Daisy who she might never see again, or maybe it was more than any of these.

Perhaps she was grieving for a time, only hours ago, when she had believed she knew where she belonged. Nabil reached for Shifa's hand, but she snatched hers away even though her eyes were so awash with tears she was hardly able to see where she was going. She stumbled but refused once more to take his hand. Nothing could ever be the same between them again.

As they approached the newly painted black wall of the compound Shifa peered down at her dress, now covered in grime, and her true mama's dented locket. The Shifa who had set out to the agora that morning drifting on a breeze of pink blossom was unrecognisable inside and out to the Shifa she was now.

Once home, Shifa took herself straight to bed, refusing to play along with Nabil's pretence at normality. As Nabil wished her goodnight, he whispered, 'There are people we know on the farms – housecarers who'll look out for you.' Shifa shrugged and turned away, wondering for the first time how she would sleep without Daisy snuggled by her side.

She imagined stroking Daisy over and over and fell into a troubled sleep.

Chapter Nine

The ceremonial doors opened to the orchestra playing a rousing version of the Freedom Fields anthem.

Teachers stood in the aisles, ushering students to the front seats. The bright yellow seats that surrounded the stage in semicircles were reserved for new graduates. The red velvet benches behind them were for Freedom Fields VIPs and carers were to sit in a roped-off area at the back.

Shifa turned as Nabil took his seat. Strange how she had always struggled to think of him, as Freedom Fields preferred them to call their carers, by his first name because up until yesterday he had never felt like 'Nabil' her 'carer'. He was always 'Papa', but not any more.

Once everyone was seated and the anthem's last note had stopped reverberating around the hall, the general murmur of voices gradually stilled making the unexpected blast of noise from above all the more of a shock. Themba placed his hands over his ears at the drill-like judder of ARK AIR taking off above them. All eyes rose and fixed on the roof as if by some miracle they could bore through it and catch a rare sighting of one of the only remaining fleet of aircraft in the land. So strange to think that in Baba Suli's time the skies had been full of great winged aeroplanes taking off and landing in Kairos City every few minutes.

What if Ark ministers had brought news that everything was to change and they were no longer needed to go into service? Shifa allowed herself a second to dream of that scenario as the orchestra prepared itself, instruments raised, bows and breath at the ready. A single trumpet pumped out a flat note setting a ripple of giggles off around the hall that was instantly silenced when Principal Daviala hurried in flanked by Freedom Fields VIPs. They seated themselves while their principal paused in an aisle close to Shifa and rearranged her shiny yellow cape hood with petal edges. It looked home-made and over-theatrical. *Was it supposed to be a sunflower?* Whatever it was, it made her look even more in a flap than normal as she fluttered her way on to the circular stage.

Behind her the familiar advert for golden sunflower-drenched fields was projected from the enormous screen.

'Good morning, soon-to-be graduates!' Principal Daviala's shrill, over enthusiastic voice sounded through the hall.

'Good morning, Principal Da-vi-ala,' they echoed back.

'And don't you look a picture!' She grinned, her arms swooping across the rows of yellow uniforms. 'My golden graduates!'

She looked at the roof above and over to the Freedom Fields VIPs. 'And what a privilege to have a surprise visit from our venerable ARK Parliament Education Minister. Such a shame she couldn't stay. But she wishes me to extend her congratulations to you all. This is indeed a proud moment for our school community.'

Principal Daviala's voice wobbled slightly as she read from a script. 'We at Freedom Fields Conservatoires pride ourselves on being open-access educational establishments. Our school of course is particularly proud to be one of the first specialist pollinating schools, attracting worldwide attention for our advanced scientific methods and state of the Ark pollinating training tunnels and techniques. Of course we have an excellent staff team of eminent scientists to thank for that. Suffice to say that what our children don't know about hand pollinating crops isn't worth knowing!' Principal Daviala laughed and a few of the Freedom Fields VIPs and teachers applauded.

'Today we celebrate our Freedom Fields Family's achievements and we welcome carers too as members of our family. Our vision is that one day we'll be equipped to provide for *all* our citizens, from cradle to grave.' She smiled as she pointed up to the fields of happy children on the screen behind her.

She took a moment to compose herself. 'Forgive me. Always an emotional day as we celebrate fulfilling our contract of care and bringing our students up as' – she opened her hands in anticipation of the call and response – 'one . . .'

'Family,' the hall rumbled back, on cue. Shifa felt numb and by the time she opened her mouth to echo the words the moment had passed.

Shifa's attention was caught by the Freedom Fields VIPs beaming with pride. Looking over to the rows of ARK Freedoms taken in by the Family after Hurricane Chronos, Shifa wondered why it was that they never looked truly happy.

'Now it's time to look forward into your bright futures,' Principal Daviala was saying. 'Precisely at this moment, across Kairos City and up and down our great Kairos Lands, a small army of Freedom Fields students are graduating. And by tomorrow some of those graduates will become your new best FFFs – Freedom Fields Friends. But now without further ado it is time for the swearing in. Could graduates please be upstanding to speak their pledge.'

Shifa nudged Themba to standing.

'Repeat after me: we, of Freedom Fields Family, Kairos City, swear that we will do our duty to serve our lands . . .'

Shifa mumbled the words that they'd been learning off by heart for months now, but they blurred into a dull indecipherable chant and she found she couldn't continue.

'That from this day forward we will do our best to serve the family, to pollinate crops and provide food for the greater good of our lands,' the other students chorused as one.

'In excellent voice!' Principal Daviala praised. 'Now it's time to invite each row forward to receive your coveted sunflower tattoo, signifying your lifelong badge of honour, to wear with pride alongside your friends and family at Freedom Fields.'

Principal Daviala glanced to the back of the hall. 'Carers, please be upstanding when your ward's name is called. May I make a polite request, to save time, that you refrain from applauding until the end of every row. An official photomemory will be sent to you shortly.'

'Shifa Aziz.'

Shifa skimmed the audience and saw Nabil stand and form a skep-heart towards her. Automatically her fingers cupped together, but she could not bring herself to raise them to her heart. All through the ceremony she had felt hollow, like something inside her had shattered along with the skep she'd dashed against the Flower Tracks wall. Her dream of last night returned to her and she felt nothing more substantial than a dandelion aigrette as she floated on to the stage and Principal Daviala took her hand. 'Congratulations, Shifa! Keep up the good work!' Up close she realised that the tattoo stamper worked like a fat staple gun. A line of cartridges were arranged on a small table in alphabetical order, ready to load.

Professor Autumn stood by Principal Daviala's side to confirm the name and number of each cartridge. Shifa braced herself for pain as her principal positioned the stamper in the tender skin wing between the thumb and finger of Shifa's right hand and pressed down. It pinched slightly but didn't hurt. Shifa splayed her fingers and inspected the bright yellow sunflower now embedded for ever on her hand. The seeds in the middle had been scattered in a strange configuration of seed code.

Now Principal Daviala called for Themba. Shifa still wasn't sure if having a surname that begins with an 'A' was a curse or a blessing. *As it's not even my surname, what does it matter?* she thought as she prepared herself to assist with Themba if needed, but he offered the principal his hand without fuss.

'Hari Basrat.'

'Lily Erith.'

'Yusuf Falola.'

'Anton Gebhard.'

Themba cheered as his friend Anton took his place on stage. He was still so tiny. It seemed ridiculous that someone as small as Anton would be working soon.

'Violet Halloway.'

'Poppy Irskine.'

The names scrolled on and on, then Principal Daviala welcomed the first of the ARK Freedoms to the stage and the whole staff team stood up, as was the tradition for children adopted by the Family. As 'Freedom' was the surname given to all of them, after a while the first names too fused in Shifa's mind.

'Luca Freedom,' Professor Autumn called out. *Who would I have been if I was adopted as an ARK Freedom?* Shifa wondered as she attempted to read Luca's expression. How did he manage to make his face into a blank page? He was one of the tallest boys in the school and when he shook hands with the teachers he towered over most of them, too. In his uniform he could easily have passed for a cadet on the screen behind him. He glowed with health, as all ARK Freedoms did. Shifa guessed it was the constant supply of food, never having to go hungry at weekends or holidays. That, and the daily swimming lessons. It seemed so unfair. Why shouldn't all Freedoms learn to swim in the school pool? She had often asked but never been given an answer. Shifa wondered if it was because ARK Freedoms were already being trained up to work as security forces.

The endless rows of ARK Freedoms queued up and Shifa forced herself to pay attention. She wondered how it had been possible to be in school all this time and never really find a true friend. She had asked once if Chiara could come home but Nabil had not been keen. She supposed it was because their lives contained too many secret places. More secrets, as it turned out, than even she had known about.

Finally, the last of the ARK Freedoms received their tattoo and returned to their seats. After a few more of Principal Daviala's flourishes, the orchestra struck up the anthem again and the students and carers filed out into the food hall, where tables were laden with bread, cereals, pastries and apples for their traditional send-off banquet.

Themba tucked in straight away, stuffing his mouth full and clowning around shoving a whole apple into his cheek pouches!

'*You* should try to eat more.' Nabil smiled at Shifa as he sipped at the treacly coffee that had been poured into tiny cups.

'I can't. I feel sick with nerves,' Shifa whispered.

Nabil frowned, 'Shifa, I—'

'The shuttle is now ready to escort you to Kairos Capital Station,' boomed Principal Daviala over the intercom system. 'Carers are asked to say their goodbyes. Thank you once again for your warm send-off. Please be ready to leave from the main hall in five minutes.'

Principal Daviala approached Nabil, smiling and offering Nabil her hand.

'You must be very proud today, Mr Aziz!' Shifa had heard her use the same stock line with other carers.

'I'm their father. I've always been proud of my *children*.' Principal Daviala frowned at Nabil's deliberate use of the discouraged attachment word – 'Papa' as well as 'Mama', 'daughter', 'son', 'my children', were not welcomed. The phasing out of them, Freedom Fields argued, was an act of kindness intended to make all Freedoms feel like equal family members.

A sudden anticipatory hush fell on the hall.

'Was there a particular reason for the official ARK visit earlier?' Nabil asked.

'A regular inspection! They do like to keep us on our toes! But Mr Aziz, talking of official business, I believe you have some belated documentation for me,' Principal Daviala said curtly. Nabil handed over the envelope. Shifa flushed crimson with rage as Principal Daviala pulled out a page to check for Nabil's signature. 'Everything in order. Very good.' Immediately she had it in her hands the principal turned to Themba, who was now clinging to Nabil's arm.

'Come along now, Themba, let's not make a fuss! What do we say? We're all in the same ARK together!' Nabil's frown grew into a scowl. *Light and positive*: the words from the contract scrolled through Shifa's mind.

'Now! I expect, Mr Aziz, that you'll need to get off to work now.' *How patronising!* Shifa thought. *Dismissing him as if he's one of her students.*

Nabil planted a last kiss on Themba's forehead and whispered something in his ear that made Themba grin and Principal Daviala tut as she guided him away. Nabil took a tentative step towards Shifa and held out his arms to hug her but she could neither be comforted or comfort him.

Nabil bit his lip and let his arms fall by his sides, then enunciated loud and clear, without a care who heard. 'I love you to the ends of the earth, Shifa. Be bold, be brave, hold true.'

She answered him with silence, not even offering him their sign of a skep-heart to show that despite his lies, she loved him too.

Chapter Ten

The Sky Shuttle navigated the roundabout and joined the slipstream of traffic on to the Orbital. In this small distance, Themba had already picked at the seat covering enough to wear away the material. Shifa pulled his hand away. He seemed shocked, as if he'd been unaware of the damage he'd done. She bit her lip as she watched him transfer his fingers from the material to the dry patch of skin on his neck and resume itching. Once again she gently pulled his hand away. *Please let this not be the start of his tense Themba ways.*

'Papa! There's Papa, like he promised me!' Themba shouted as he jumped out of his seat and pointed towards the bridge as they sped towards it.

Nabil's tall, gaunt figure was unmistakeable amongst a small gathering of carers and Foragers. Was that Halonah holding baby Honey – waving to them? There was Lottie, standing next to Nabil, her bright hair ribbons floating. As the shuttle approached, Nabil and Lottie dropped a rainbow-coloured sheet over the ledge; on it, in deep blue paint, were written four enormous words.

DARE
DREAM
BELIEVE
IMAGINE

Whilst the shuttle was passing under the bridge Lottie and Nabil must have hauled the sheet up, run over and lowered it again so that they could keep sight of them and their message for the longest time. Shifa and Themba strained to follow events as a Crow patrol descended and attempted to grab the banner from Lottie's hands, but she fought back and released the sheet on to the Orbital, raising her arms in triumph. It got caught on the underside of the bridge where it hung for a moment before ballooning with air and blustering free, caught on a slipstream it sailed towards them. Everyone in the Sky Shuttle was on their feet now, roaring, waving and pointing as the four words spread – *like hope blossom*, Shifa thought – among them.

The navigator's voice barked angrily through the intercom. 'Return to your seats immediately. Irresponsible stunts like that are the cause of accidents on the Orbital.'

Shifa kept sight of the bridge until Nabil, Lottie and the others became silhouettes, then stick shapes, then dots on the horizon, before finally melting away.

'Goodbye, Nabil,' she whispered, and as she spoke his name she wondered how much she really did know the man she had for so long believed to be her papa. The words on the rainbow banner scrolled around and around her mind – *dare, dream, believe, imagine.* Maybe those words were true for Lottie but it felt to Shifa that Nabil had lost his hold on them and given up.

She would just have to get on with it now and take care of Themba as best she could. Shifa cast a look at Themba's sunflower tattoo. The seeds at the centre were arranged differently to hers.

A Freedom Fields cadet was making his way up the coach ordering them to settle down. As he touched the headrest opposite her, Shifa inspected his tattoo, its central scattering of seeds different again. She rubbed her thumb over her own. *We're all branded and coded now,* she thought.

'Back to your seat,' the cadet ordered Anton, who had come to sit with Themba.

'Please can he sit with me?' Themba asked.

The cadet shook his head. 'You'll sit where you're told. This isn't a summer camp.'

Themba's hands trembled as he took his sketchpad from his chest pocket and began sketching what he saw through the window. 'It's not fair! Why can't Anton sit next to us?' he complained without attempting to lower his voice.

'Shut up, Themba.' Luca, who was sitting nearby, spat the words between clenched teeth.

'Don't tell him to shut up!' Shifa snapped back.

Luca shrugged. 'Sort him out then or he'll get us all into trouble before we even get to the station,' he mumbled.

Themba was shading in the huge wings he had attached to the Skylight train of his imagination. Shifa guessed that Freedom Fields had refused to allow the graduates to see images of it to keep it a surprise, but no one could have dreamed up anything like Themba's mythological sky train! Shifa hoped he wouldn't be too disappointed with the real thing.

She and Nabil had worked so hard to prepare Themba for this day, but Shifa had not expected to feel so adrift herself. She felt for the locket around her neck and wondered how it had got dented. Try as she might to block them out, she could not still the questions. Where had her mama gone on the night of the storm? Had she meant to come back to her? Shifa's insides churned and, for a moment, she thought she would be sick. *I wish I had never found out.* She envied Themba, meandering somewhere deep in his retreat into art. At least he'd found a way to carry his secret story hive with him – flying in and out of reality as and when he chose.

Out of nowhere a strong gust buffeted the shuttle sideways. Panic and fear rippled through the passengers as the front of the shuttle veered dangerously, before the driver managed to pull it back on track.

'Silence!' the driver's voice boomed over the intercom.

A cadet patrolled up and down the coach again, eyeballing everyone as he went. Themba carried on sketching as the cadet drew parallel. Being ignored seemed to annoy him.

He snatched Themba's book off him and began flicking through the pages. Themba sprang out of his seat in outrage but Shifa took hold of his arm. 'Let me get it back, Themb. Leave it to me,' Shifa reasoned.

'The Skylight with wings! In your dreams!' the cadet sneered and tossed the book back into Themba's lap.

A recorded, softly reassuring voice sounded over the intercom. 'To begin this new phase of your lives, Freedom Fields proudly offers you a guide to the landmarks of our beautiful Kairos City.' Themba clung tight to his artbook and squished his nose against the window. 'Our great capital is still in the process of reconstruction and replanting. For those who have not had the opportunity to travel far beyond your compounds, this journey is an opportunity to witness some of the latest developments you'll be contributing to through your pollinating service. The great Kairos Central Station is situated, as its name suggests, in the old centre of Kairos . . .'

Shifa leaned forward for a better view around Themba. She spotted a small orchard of sapling trees, bending and arching in the wind. The new attempts at tree planting never seemed to get very far before a new gale hit.

'And on your left,' the voice continued, 'is the Solar Globe – proud home to our Kairos ARK Government. The largest building in Kairos City and the first powered entirely by revolutionary Solarmirror suntraps.' The sun's glow settled on the Globe and glinted sharply at them.

'Hurts my eyes,' Themba complained, squinting. Shifa raised her arm to screen him from the worst of the glare. His head knocked against her shoulder and he let it rest there.

Themba reached up and attempted to twist a short strand of Shifa's hair before he remembered that her long mane had gone. He sighed deeply and reached into his pocket, took out Shifa's strand of hair and began twisting it around his fingers. Luca raised his eyes to the sky and frowned.

'Why don't you try to get some sleep, Themba?' Shifa whispered, glowering at Luca, who turned away. Shifa felt Themba's head grow heavy and his breath thicken into his familiar sleep snuffle. With Themba snuggled close, Shifa's own eyes grew heavy but she forced herself to stay awake, not wanting to miss seeing with her own eyes how Kairos City was being rebuilt.

The coach slowed to a stop at a junction where people appeared from tents on the edge of the road.

'Foragers,' Shifa whispered. Two boys and a girl of about her age climbed on to rickety bikes and trailed the shuttle. Shifa flinched as one of them banged on the side, like he wanted to make sure they'd seen him before he was left behind. Themba stirred and Shifa stroked his head to settle him back into sleep.

'Scum!' spat Luca, glaring at the boy. 'Serve them right if they get knocked down.'

Who are you, Luca Freedom? Shifa wondered. Sitting this close to him, she realised that his face wasn't blank at all. His grey eyes were hard as stone. Shifa turned her back on him.

They had passed through the Eastern Quarter and were entering the Garden Belt, where Nabil sometimes sought out extra work. Shifa had been here a few times before. These wide, clean streets must have once been beautiful boulevards lined with trees instead of giant stumps. But the gardens were vast. If only she could open the shuttle windows to hear the birdsong from the flock of . . . were those sparrows she saw darting around the garden? There were the white butterflies of her Flower Tracks too and something hovering larger, its yellow stripes glowing unnaturally bright – a precious beedrone in action, hovering, collecting nectar and pollen and moving on. Shifa could never see these gardens without feeling how wrong it was that she and other Freedoms were not officially allowed to cultivate even the smallest piece of ground.

They passed street after street of gardens and Solarmirror bungalows until the shuttle turned on to a larger road. She had never seen the communal cemetery before, where the unclaimed bodies of the victims of Hurricane Chronos were buried. Shifa wrapped her arm closer around Themba's shoulder.

An advertising billboard hung at the stone entrance.

PRIME DEVELOPMENT LAND FOR
FREEDOM FIELDS FAMILIES . . .
COMING SOON!

How could they build homes on a graveyard? Themba's head lolled against Shifa's shoulder as he slept. She closed her eyes too, taking comfort in his closeness. She drifted to her Flower Tracks dream, picking and weaving lavender strands, leaving only enough space for Daisy and Themba to crawl inside the safe hollow of her skep-heart.

Chapter Eleven

'Welcome to Kairos Central Station,' announced the automated voice.

It was 'all that glitters', just as Nabil had described it. Every surface dazzled. The centre of the building was a giant sparkling dome of diamond-cut Solarmirrors. To its left and right were two oblong structures covered in sleek mirror sheets. The central station resembled a giant jewel sandwiched between silver slices.

'Hurry up!' The cadet chivvied them off the shuttle into a communal holding pen.

'A hexagon,' Themba said as he surveyed the station angled on six sides too, like honeycombs. Nabil had once said that bees had been natural architects. *Well, the worker bees have arrived*, Shifa thought.

A siren sounded, Themba covered his ears and a hush fell over them all. On a screen above, a countdown began. Ten, nine, eight, seven, six . . . on the final count of one, gates to their pen opened leaving everyone on their shuttle no choice but to funnel along the fenced paths in front of them. They shuffled forward until they were gathered in the central diamond dome of the station where, for the first time, Shifa got a sense of the numbers of graduates. She estimated there were five hundred or so of them. She craned her neck and imagined herself to be a swallow soaring high and higher up to the balconies above. But as she looked up her gaze was met by an audience of Paragons peering down on the procession, as though they were the entertainment. If only she and Themba could grow wings, fly out of the domed roof and be free.

Once they were assembled in the middle of the dome, a transparent tubular wall rose from the floor, forcing them to huddle closer. Familiar music began to be piped out of surround-sound speakers. The viewers on the balconies joined in with the anthem. Voices rose up and swelled through the cavernous acoustic dome of the station. Once again Shifa only mouthed the words. It felt so fake for Paragons and Freedoms to be singing together, but if you didn't listen to the words it might have been almost beautiful. *How dare they, who'll never have to go into service, sing too?*

Welcome to our family
Where we look after you.
Welcome to our family
Where every day is new.

Welcome to our family
Where there's food and health and learning too.
Welcome to our family.
We'll take you in our hands
Till comes the day of harvest
When you help us feed these lands.

As the last note reverberated through the dome the balcony audience applauded, the floor juddered and the disc they stood on began to slowly descend. Themba clasped Shifa's hand. Through the gloom Shifa registered Themba's wide-eyed panic as the light-filled dome began to recede.

'It's just a lift,' she whispered, 'like the one at school.'

'Nothing like,' Themba gasped, trembling with fear.

A huge roof slid closed above them, the shiny glass gave way to brick walls; it was as though they were descending through an enormous chimney. Finally, the lift shunted to a stop. Shifa blinked as her eyes adjusted to the gloom. They were in an underground vault, supported by huge metal arches and spines that resembled the Darwin dinosaur skeleton of Themba's painting – this one had blood-rusted ribs.

What would Nabil think if he could see them in this dungeon? The sunlit fields of the brochure already seemed a long way away. Crows swooped everywhere and, in this half-light, cast giant shadow wings in every direction.

'Where's the sky? Where's the Skylight train?' Themba stuttered as he peered into the dark.

'This is just the way to it!' Shifa consoled him but her heart raced and her own voice wavered. Her whole body was already coated in a sweat that reeked of fear.

One side of the tubular glass wall retracted and they were shunted on to a conveyor belt that propelled them along at speed towards an assembly of Crows who stood at even intervals in front of a scanner, behind which were huge metal double doors.

A communal gasp of relief escaped as the doors swung open and sunshine brightness filled the platform on which the silver bullet of the Skylight train awaited them, its doors open and ready for boarding. Crows parted like a swish black curtain. Overhead electronic signals flashed – 'Destination: Freedom Fields Farms'.

Instructions played on a loop from hidden speakers as they waited their turn to pass through security.

'Hold your tattoo ID to the scanner. You will be allocated a ticket and a carriage. Proceed directly along the platform and board the Skylight. We thank you for your co-operation.'

They shuffled forward gradually and when it finally came to their turn, Shifa let Themba go ahead of her, nodding her encouragement as he tentatively placed his tattoo on the scanner. When they were both through the barriers the electronic voice ordered them to proceed to carriage twelve.

On their way Themba caught sight of Anton boarding a carriage and before Shifa could grab hold of him Themba veered off towards his friend.

'Oi! Where do you think you're going?' a Crow shouted.

'I asked to be with my friend, Anton,' Themba shouted back.

'And who might you be?' The Crow drew close, took hold of Themba's wrist and scanned his sunflower. 'Themba Aziz,' the Crow said, pronouncing Themba's name wrongly. Shifa willed Themba not to challenge her . . .

'Not "th" like "thumb" but "t" for "train",' Themba informed the Crow, whose eyes turned icy as her hand reached for her belt. Shifa gasped and glanced along the line. Why hadn't she noticed it before? All the Crows had weapons attached to their belts now.

'Continue to carriage twelve and board immediately,' said the Crow in a threatening tone.

'Please, Themba,' Shifa pleaded, tugging him away, but as she did Themba's face grew beetroot red and his breath came in short, sharp gasps.

'Remember – breathe, breathe, breathe and everything will come with ease,' Shifa whispered, almost running out of breath herself at the sight of Luca approaching.

'Listen to that engine purring,' Shifa coaxed, hearing the desperation in her own voice. 'Sounds a bit like Daisy.' But as the image of Daisy lying on her frayed cushion floated into her mind her own voice faltered. Her hand rose to where her locket lay against her skin and she formed her hands into a skep-heart. *Help me, Daisy. Stay with me.* The memory of Daisy crawling over Themba's map flashed through Shifa's mind.

'Soon we'll be on our way and you can get your artbook out.' As the words floated out of her mouth they felt like a gift from Daisy.

Themba unclenched his fists, his breathing grew calmer and he began to move forward again. Shifa watched in dismay as Luca passed them and continued to progress up the station until he finally boarded in carriage twelve. *Why him?* Shifa's heart sank.

Once they were all on board, a Crow appeared and began a headcount. Twenty graduates, ten boys, ten girls.

'Sit!' ordered the Crow as if speaking to patrol dogs, but there was nowhere to sit except for a communal mattress on the floor. Where were the seats? The passengers shared a look of bewilderment, except for Luca whose face was expressionless as he kneeled on the mattress. The others followed.

Themba clamped his ears as an emergency siren began to wail. Suddenly, the metal-booted feet of Crows pounded the platform, and someone sprinted past the open door but was hauled back. Shifa watched, hands clasped over her mouth, as a Crow raised her gun, finger on the trigger and fired at point-blank range. There was a gasp of horror from the carriage as the recruit slumped backwards and the Crow carried a limp body back along the station, head lolling over her arm.

Themba's mouth hung open and his nails clawed into Shifa's hand.

'Don't worry. They'll be awake in a few minutes,' said the Crow supervising their carriage. 'It's dangerous to run along a platform and it's our job to protect you. We can't have anyone going missing.'

'Stunned, not killed?' Themba whispered.

'Stunned, just stunned,' Shifa whispered back as she attempted to still the mounting panic that was growing in her.

The carriage door slid shut with a hiss, thrusting them into semi-darkness.

Themba howled. His wild lament echoed through the minds of every silent one of them.

'Where's the sky, Shifa? Where's the light?'

Chapter Twelve

There were no windows on either side of the carriage. A horrified silence crept over them, pierced only by Themba's heartbroken sob.

Shifa cast around to find one narrow strip of glass in the train's roof, filtering in just enough light to see the others' stunned faces.

As far as she could see, Luca was the only other student from their school. A low siren sounded again and built gradually from a drone to a roar as the carriage shunted slowly forward. Shifa had never felt claustrophobic crouched in their story hive, but now she struggled to control her breathing. Shifa closed her eyes and imagined she was stroking Daisy's back and gradually her breathing calmed. *Slow and even, slow and even*, she told herself, for Themba's sake. She opened her eyes again and found that she had been patting Themba's back over and over. The unspoken question spread like fire around the carriage, written in every fearful eye. *Why won't they let us see where we're going?*

Themba broke the silence. 'How am I going to draw the Kairos Lands if I can't see out of the window?'

'Up there, Themba!' Shifa pointed to the sliver of light. Above them the rusty ribs of the station had brightened a little into a pale grey sky.

A screen embedded in the carriage door lit up. Its raw strip light cast a clinical glow over the carriage, tingeing all their faces a sickly green. The monotonous drone of electronic SoundTeK music Shifa had last heard at the agora was streamed into the carriage. Themba clasped his hands over his ears.

'Make it stop!' he shouted.

Ignoring Themba and glancing nervously towards the opticares, the other passengers took off their backpacks and spread out, staking out their territory on the mattress. It was covered in rough orange canvas and the painted outlines of body shapes indicated an allocated space for each person. At the end of the mattress was a narrow corridor leading to a toilet. The middle row gave the clearest view up to the skylight. A girl dropped her bag next to Themba's and knelt down. Her tears flowed in a steady river down her cheeks. Shifa read her name tag – Yara. As she smiled at Yara, Luca reached over, picked up the girl's bag and dumped it in the body space in front.

'That's not fair. *She* was here first!' Themba complained.

'Tough!' Luca sneered. '*I* need to be in the middle to see what's going on.'

'Why should you?' Shifa snapped.

Luca raised his eyebrows and pointed to a wrist strap that read 'Supervisor'.

At the far end of the carriage two boys were squabbling over who would be nearest to the fridge and who would end up next to the toilet.

Luca strode over and pushed both of them on to the mattress.

'You'll sleep where you've landed. Any arguments?'

The boys shook their heads.

Of course he's in charge, thought Shifa. All ARK Freedoms would know how to impress the Crows. In a flash Shifa saw, as if from above, how the whole system was supposed to work – Freedom Fields were bringing up an army to serve them and ARK Freedoms were their role models.

A boy behind Shifa surreptitiously slid a toy bear out of his bag and hid it under his legs. Shifa reached for her locket and felt her heart calm as she rubbed her fingers over its dented surface. She imagined herself stroking Daisy. The picture she now held in her mind of Daisy protecting her baby self with a daisy chain around her bare body made Shifa's heart swell with love for the old cat. No wonder Lottie and her papa had always had a thing for daisies. But neither the locket nor her gratitude to Daisy could rid her of the ache of sadness at her parting memory of Nabil, arms outstretched, yearning for her to hug him, to make a sign, if only a skep-heart to show that she cared. But she had been

110

too caught in a vortex of confusion and rage to show him. *Look after him, Daisy.* In her mind's eye Shifa followed her cat down on to the Flower Tracks and placed her on Nabil's lap to comfort him. *Try not to think, try not think, try not to think.* Her words followed the rhythm of the train as she attempted to block out the dismal scene before her.

Themba held his book on his lap, writing.

Dare to dream.

Dare to believe.

Dare to imagine.

'That's right, Themba,' she whispered, signing a skep-heart.

The screen brightened and images began to appear showing the front of the Skylight heading out of Kairos City, as though they were once again passing the stately houses and gardens. On one plot, chickens roamed freely. Standing in the middle of a garden a woman holding an enormous handful of white roses lifted her head and held the bunch towards them like an offering.

'How can she see us?' Themba asked.

Luca smirked. 'How gullible can you be?'

Shifa clenched her teeth and attempted to dull the fire of anger sparking in her belly. She turned her back on Luca. This wasn't the place to get into a fight. All that mattered was for her to stay calm and to keep Themba calm too.

'The woman on the screen can't see us, Themba,' Shifa explained. 'This is just a film.'

111

'But I-I-I need to see where we're going,' Themba complained.

An echo of agreement spread around the carriage.

Shifa watched the next images pass – a field of horses galloping alongside the train. Luca was right, this was a fantasyland created for their entertainment. They could not have left Kairos City behind so fast.

Now a few golden-brown cows peered over a gate. The green of the fields was so lush it hurt Shifa's eyes. The dronecam swept over the countryside in one even curve, transporting them along a river that hummed with bird and insect life, its banks threaded with a delicate lacing of wild flowers.

Themba leaned close to Shifa and tapped his chest. 'River's in my pocket.'

Shifa sighed. 'Keep it hidden then.'

Shifa peered up to the sliver of glass above, through which the real sky remained stubbornly grey. The pink blossom Graffitree seemed more honest to her than any of these images. Onscreen, white blossom floated along a path where a woman held a lamb in a small enclosure of sheep. There was a general 'aww' at its sweet face, but Shifa noticed that its skinny legs were wriggling hard to be free.

Themba leaned forward and squinted into the screen. 'That's the same woman who waved at us before, with the roses!'

Sometimes Shifa was still taken aback by Themba's powers of observation. People got him wrong, thinking he

112

didn't see things in the 'normal' way – it was just that the world rushed at him with so much detail. He grabbed his art box and shoved it away in frustration. Pencils, brushes, inks, pens and paints spilled into Luca's space. Shifa quickly began to gather them up.

'Do that again and I'll take them off you!' Luca warned with gritted teeth.

The opticare in the corner tracked towards them.

'Why is the optispy staring at me?' Themba scowled into the lens.

Shifa placed a protective arm around him.

'Shh. Remember, Themba, call things by their proper names,' she reminded him.

Themba nodded as the opticare and he locked eyes and it eventually swivelled away. 'How can I draw the landmarks if everything's fake?' Themba whispered, tears threatening once again.

Shifa turned to the page in his artbook of his mythical flying Skylight.

'You know how! Leave the real world behind, spread your wings.' Themba's face softened as he studied the sky and picked up a grey pastel.

'Sky doesn't lie,' he mumbled and he began to smudge the floating clouds on to the page before stopping abruptly. 'Mmmm, moving too fast to catch now!' he complained.

'Or *we* are!' Luca was lying flat on his back with his arms behind his head, cloud chasing too.

The film cut out and was replaced by sunflower fields and a cherry-sweet voice that sounded uncannily like Principal Daviala's.

'Congratulations, Freedom Fields recruits, you have begun the greatest adventure of your lives. We are delighted to offer you the opportunity to travel on our triumph of ecologically sound, electrical engineering. This train has now left Kairos City. We hope you enjoyed the Kairos Lands screening, brought to you by some of our talented Freedom filmmakers. Following your meal we will be offering a chill-wave meditation.'

Shifa had no idea what a chill-wave meditation was and even Luca appeared sceptical.

'Please pay close attention to the following transit information. We trust you have now found a comfy place to relax. At this sound' – a soft-toned gong rang through the carriage – 'your fridge will unlock and the allocated carriage supervisor' – the voice cut out for a second and was replaced by an automated one – 'Luca Freedom' – the voice resumed – 'will be responsible for handing out your food supplies. Please ensure you place all rubbish in the recycle chute.'

An image of hands throwing rubbish in the chute appeared on the screen. *They must think we're stupid.*

'This journey is being recorded by opticare for your security and comfort. A report of your transit conduct will be live fed to your Freedom Fields Farm. Please respect your environment and leave your carriage in a clean and tidy state. Carriage twelve. You are the twelfth and final stop for the Skylight.'

A low groan echoed through the carriage. A gong sounded and the fridge light clicked on. Everyone sat up expectantly.

'Out of my way!' Luca demanded, clambering over hands and feet to the fridge. 'Sit down or you won't get anything.' He reached in and brought out a stack of small boxes and handed them out.

As Shifa opened the lid she read the words, 'This refreshment is to last you the whole of your journey. Please eat slowly to avoid carriage nausea.'

But Themba's mouth was already stuffed full. Shifa looked in her box, which contained slices of dried apple, a vitamin bar and bread.

Within minutes most of the boxes were empty.

'Slow down!' Luca ordered.

ARK Freedoms could never understand what it was like to be truly hungry.

'I feel sick!' Themba whined. Shifa checked through his empty lunch box and sighed. She handed him some rehydration juice too late as he gagged and started to retch.

'Get him up!' Luca shouted, lurching towards Themba.

'I'll deal with this!' Shifa guided Themba to the bathroom, holding back his curls as he vomited in the toilet basin.

'Make sure you clean up in there!' Luca ordered.

The clouds in the carriage began racing once again and the screen lit up. Tiny bubbles began to burst and flow into a silvery stream. Shifa yawned and lay down.

The relaxation waves were now replaced by a field of lavender. Shifa imagined herself picking bunches and weaving them into a skep, Nabil sharing what he'd learned from Baba Suli of how much bees had loved lavender. She breathed in the scent. Everyone in the carriage was suddenly sleepy as the Skylight pulled into the second station.

Shifa's head grew foggy, her thoughts drifting back to Daisy. Could a cat remember such a thing as protecting a baby? Shifa's fingers reached for her locket. Maybe Themba had been right and it did have a power in it – the power to summon Daisy whenever she needed her. *Do you think of me as your baby?*

Luca turned over in his sleep and as he did his arm knocked against hers. No tortured thoughts were keeping *him* awake. Shifa stared up at the endless grey sky above, and let the potent wave of lavender scent and Daisy's purring lull her into a deep and dreamless sleep.

PART TWO
POLLINATION FARM

Chapter Thirteen

'You have arrived at your destination. Welcome to Pollination Farm. Please make sure you have all your belongings with you.'

The automated voice was muffled, as if sounding through water. Shifa lifted her head to take in the bleary-eyed faces in her carriage. The grey rectangle of sky had been replaced by an inky black one peppered with bright stars.

Shifa's head was still floating when the carriage door slid open and light flooded in. She squinted at a woman with shaven hair, her lips drawn in a flat line of boredom.

'Get them unloaded, Jax,' a disgruntled voice ordered from further up the platform. 'I'm getting grief from HQ. As if it's *our* fault they're running late!' The gruff voice drew nearer.

'I'm Jax,' the woman said, placing a hand over her nose as the sickly smell of lavender essence mixed with vomit drifted out. 'And this,' she indicated the scowling man who now stood by her side, 'is Jermaine.'

'Eugh! This lot stinks!' Jermaine covered his mouth and nose.

'Get yourselves up and out into the fresh air as fast as you can,' Jax ordered.

Luca blinked at Shifa. Caught off guard in his between-asleep-and-awake state, he seemed as uncertain and confused as everyone else. But in a blink he remembered his supervisor status and the stony-eyed Luca returned.

'Hurry up!' he shouted as he stepped on to the platform. Jermaine offered him his hand. 'Good job, Luca! Your efforts won't go unrewarded. Now, help us rally the' – Jermaine cast a disparaging look in their direction and sighed – 'new recruits.'

Shifa took Themba by the arm. He attempted to push her away but she refused to let go. This was hardly a welcome committee.

The Skylight's engine revved and they stood for a moment in silence – watching its silver bulk pick up speed and roar away, it felt as if a cord connecting them to Nabil had been severed.

They seemed to walk for hours along a well-worn track, catching only vague grey outlines of the countryside distilled by torch and murky moonlight. Shifa made out a small rise in a hill, the solid shape of a machine etched in mist, the glinting white arms of wind turbines cartwheeling over and over, stumps of freshly harvested crops, of what she wasn't sure but she inhaled the unfamiliar wholesome scent. The air did smell fresher and she thought she heard water flowing in the distance.

For the first time since leaving Kairos City she began to feel a seed of excitement growing in her. There was a coolness to the night air that she had not felt for so long in the monotone heat of the city. A crescent moon shone brightly in the sky. *No hare in the moon, Nabil,* but perhaps there would be more freedom here than at home to explore nature? Her stomach gurgled – never to feel hungry for four whole years, that would be a start. Perhaps in the clear light of day her longed-for meadow fields blossoming with wild flowers would be waiting for them to run through. She heard Daisy's bird-warning bell chiming and imagined her prowling towards her through a meadow. *Think of all the flower seeds I can collect, Daisy!*

'How far now?' a boy behind her asked, but no one bothered to answer.

By her side, Themba was counting steps.

'One thousand three hundred and twenty-four, one thous—'

'Cut it out, will you?' Luca nudged Themba's shoulder. Shifa quietly seethed.

In the far distance a light illuminated a long path leading to a tall gate and the silhouette of buildings at the top of a gently sloping hill. To Shifa's tired legs, it seemed as far away as the moon.

Finally, feet dragging, the recruits reached the top.

121

'Welcome to Pollination Farm,' Jax announced as Shifa observed the Crows sitting at watch posts, scanning screens above the electric gates that now swung ceremonially slowly open.

They entered a large floodlit courtyard and Shifa squinted up to the windows of the old farmhouse. A cockerel weather vane spun on the chimney top. Below it the window frames wore white lintels, like eyebrows raised sceptically at approaching recruits. The front door was painted green and around it was a latticed frame – like the one Nabil had made for the Flower Tracks – through which a profusion of yellow roses climbed. Shifa longed to draw near enough to smell their fragrance.

The courtyard sloped down from the house towards two new barns, their red-painted roofs dotted with Solarmirrors. Here were the storm-proof barns she'd read about in the brochure, dug low to protect against the worst wind blasts. Behind the barns the flat fields were lit in eerie fingers of light that began narrow then spread wide in ghostly lengthening shadows.

Shifa glanced back at the house and caught sight of a silhouette – was that an animal or a small human that stalked across the window? *It's just your mind playing tricks on you*, she reassured herself.

Four cadets awaited them in the courtyard: two women and two men wearing the same grey-green uniform as cadets in Kairos City.

In the distance, from behind the barns, came a low

droning hum. Themba placed his hands over his ears and winced.

'Excuse me. What's that noise?' Shifa asked Jermaine, who was standing close by.

He stepped towards her, took her hand and scanned her sunflower tattoo over his wrist screen. She was desperate to pull away but held still. *How dare you take control of me like that?*

'So, *you're* Shifa.' He raised his arm and pointed down at her. 'Apparently she's the best you can hope for!' he called to Jax and then wandered off.

'Shifa! Come join us at the front,' Jax ordered. Themba reluctantly released hold of her.

'Don't look so worried! You've been singled out for your leadership qualities.' Jax nodded towards Luca. 'You have him to thank for nominating you.'

Shifa kept her eyes trained on the cobbled courtyard, but her mind raced. *What's Luca's game?*

'Girls! On the right, behind Shifa. Boys, to the left behind Luca!' Jermaine barked, raising his arm in the air. 'To the barns!'

When Themba attempted to sneak into the girls' queue a cadet strode over and plucked him away.

'I want my sister!' he yelled.

'He won't be too popular in there if he wakes the others,' Jax warned Shifa.

'Can I speak to him quickly?'

Jax shook her head. 'Not now, we need to get you all settled. The cadets know his . . . needs.'

'Please, we're twins. Can't I just say goodnight?'

'He'll be fine. The first night away from home's always the worst. Everyone's in the same boat!' Jax said dismissively, nudging Shifa on.

Shifa watched in horror as a cadet, with his hand clamped over Themba's mouth, dragged him along by his arms through the arched doors of the boys' barn.

To go against Jax's order now could mean trouble for both of them. Shifa swallowed hard and felt the spindly shoot of anticipation that had begun to grow in her as they walked across the fields, wither and die inside her.

Chapter Fourteen

Jax led the girls along a central corridor, lit by a strip of floor lights. The barn was divided into sections that held five beds in each area. Yara attached herself to Shifa and clung to her side, keeping pace.

Peering closer Shifa could just make out the shapes of sleeping bodies under the covers. Two feet appeared at one end of a bed. A blanket mound shifted and two other feet wriggled free from the covers at the far end. *So much for having more space than at home!*

Jax placed her hands to her lips to still the murmurings of disquiet, then showed the ten recruits to their spartan dormitory of five empty beds. Shifa quickly placed her bag on the end of one. Yara peered through her fringe and smiled shyly as if asking for permission. Shifa nodded and Yara laid her rucksack down beside Shifa's.

Jax issued instructions, recited so precisely that she must know them off by heart.

'There's a welcome pack at the end of your beds with toiletries and pyjamas, and you'll find a fresh uniform for tomorrow in your allocated storage cabinets.' She pointed to a row of cupboards, next to a door with an illuminated graphic of a shower on it. 'You can place the one you've been wearing in the laundry chute in the bathroom. Shower quickly now. There'll be time to unpack properly tomorrow. Lead the way, Shifa!' she ordered.

She headed to the bathroom, and was followed by the other girls into a long white-tiled room with communal showers, toilet cubicles, and floor-to-ceiling storage shelves with folded towels provided and pegs for hanging clothes. Shifa caught the self-conscious look on all their faces, the guarded body language as they began to undress. Still, it was a relief to climb out of her sweaty overalls. She wrapped the thin towel around herself before taking off her underwear. Why couldn't they have changing cubicles, or put curtains between the showers like they had at school?

The instructions on the wall read:

Step on to the shower plate.
Soap thoroughly.
Warning! No water wastage. Supply time limited.

Arms wrapped around herself, Shifa stood on the shower plate and gasped as a jet of ice-cold water rained down on her head. There were shrieks and complaints but Shifa braced herself – showering and strip washing in ice-cold water was nothing new to her. She quickly lathered her body and hair with the odourless soap. Despite the icy cold it felt good to wash away the sweat and fear of the day.

Once dry and wearing the simple pyjamas, Shifa opened the door of a toilet cubicle. She searched for a lock but found none. Light shone through a small, high window above her. She waited for the bathroom to empty then carefully climbed up on the toilet lid . . . and opened the latch.

The low drone she had heard on arrival growled louder. From here she could see that it emanated from inside a huge, illuminated pod like a giant grub. Between the bars of the window, dark shadows of small people moved slowly through dense vegetation. Shifa's hands trembled as she closed the window. It seemed there were shadow beings everywhere here.

She took a deep breath. *Be bold, be brave, be strong, hold true* . . . But even as she called on Nabil's words, they rang false in her ears. She reached for her locket – but now she could only hear Daisy's wildcat cries on the night of their separation. Sobs escaped from her as she covered her mouth with her hand.

There was a knock on the door and Shifa quickly wiped her face with her sleeve and stepped down, flushing the toilet behind her. She stepped out to find Jax waiting for her.

'Why are they working at night?' Shifa asked as she washed her hands.

'Your induction's tomorrow. Ask then. Get into bed now,' said Jax in a matter-of-fact tone. 'Your housecarer will be patrolling soon.'

Yara was already in bed when Shifa quietly tucked herself in. When she closed her eyes the memory of Themba's distressed wails haunted her. Her stomach cramped as she longed for Daisy to curl beside her.

The housecarer patrolled the barn. Shifa strained to catch sight of more than a skinny silhouette fleetingly illuminated when a torch was cast in their direction. Yara slept fitfully but suddenly bolted upright and swung her legs out of bed. By instinct Shifa shot out her arm and grabbed hold of Yara.

'Let me go! I want to go home!' Yara screamed. Shifa shook her head and placed her fingers over her lips.

'What's all the commotion about?' The housecarer's voice drew close. Shifa's attention was caught by the woman's feet, encased in fluffy backless slippers. Yara shrank back under the covers and held her breath as the torchlight rested on their bed.

'My friend,' Shifa whispered, pointing to the bottom of the bed, 'was having a nightmare, that's all.'

The housecarer sighed. 'Can't say I'm surprised – sleep balm can make you a little jittery. But Kairos City is no hop and a *skep* away, so perhaps it is the kindest way to get you to sleep through the journey.' Through the gloom Shifa could just make out the housecarer's long bony face and kindly eyes as she leant down to pick up a fallen blanket. Placing it on the bed she cupped her hands to her chest. Shifa leaned closer towards her. *Is she making a skep-heart?*

A hop and a skep? *Did I hear right?* Nabil said he and Lottie knew people on the farms who would keep watch over them. She could not be sure though. Perhaps she was imagining things she wanted to see. But if the housecarer *had* used their secret signal . . . Shifa placed her hands over her own heart and heard Daisy lightly purring . . . Who else but a friend of Nabil's or Lottie's would know what a skep was?

Chapter Fifteen

A cacophonous alarm shrieked into the sleep barn, like a million caged birds. Shifa sprang up breathless. Yara too sat bolt upright, her hair a bushy tangle and her huge hazel eyes darting around the dorm. Shifa couldn't help but smile at Yara's feet in her face as she moved them aside. Shifa wiggled her toes too. Yara pulled a face and, after a pause, they both began to giggle.

'First day hysteria!' A tall older girl emerged from the bathroom, her hair wrapped in a towel. 'Haven't you read the noise pollution rule?' She pointed to an enormous poster on the wall under the high window.

Pollination Farm Rules: Strictly Enforced

The girl stepped closer and tapped on the 'Orderly Conduct' rule. 'You'd better learn to keep calm, if you don't want a violation!'

'Give them a chance to settle in, Chirelle,' said the housecarer, coming up behind her. 'Woken up on the wrong side of the bed again?'

'Couldn't sleep with the racket this lot were making *and* Ailish was snoring all night,' said Chirelle, gesturing towards a dorm nearer the barn entrance.

'You'll be missing each other soon!' In the morning light Shifa saw that the housecarer's soft brown eyes matched her voice – firm but kind.

Chirelle rolled her eyes and sauntered away. Shifa read the poster. The rules were colour coded, with a key at the bottom:

Violation of green rules = debits

Violation of blue rules = recreation limitation

Violation of red rules = double shifts

Multiple violations = confinement

Now Shifa focused on the next column.

Green Violations:

Raised voices

Lateness

Low work rate

Failure to wear suitable uniform

Entering courtyard areas when vehicles are on site

Blue Violations:

Rudeness

Persistent low work rates

Failure to fulfil chores

Red Violations:

Straying outside designated areas

Fighting

Shift avoidance

Insubordination

Where were the credits? Shifa tried to still the worry that stirred in her, and calm herself with the hope that the housecarer might know Nabil and the thought that soon she'd see Themba and they'd explore the countryside in the daylight for the first time in their lives.

Once they were dressed in their fresh uniform, the housecarer gestured for them to gather around. 'Good morning! My name's Housecarer Hannah and, as my name suggests, I'm here to listen to any cares and worries you may have.' She smiled at her audience. 'This barn will be your relaxation zone for the next four years and the girls you see around you are your new family.'

'But we don't even know each other's names,' Yara blurted out.

'Well that's easily remedied.'

Hannah got each girl to introduce themselves. As they did Shifa tried to memorise the pairs in each bed.

Shifa–Yara.

Connie–Jacy.

Soraya–Caitlin.

Miri–Blessing.

Carla–Pooja.

'Any questions now?' asked Hannah.

Carla's hand shot up. 'Where are our weekend clothes?'

Hannah shook her head. 'I'm afraid you'll only have your uniforms, for now, to save on laundry.'

'But—' Carla was about to ask something else but reined herself in.

'Are you housecarer in the boys' barn too?' asked Shifa. 'Did you see my brother last night?'

'Themba, isn't it?'

Shifa nodded, noticing Hannah had pronounced his name correctly without sounding the 'h'. Hardly any stranger ever did that!

'Don't worry, Shifa. I stayed with him till he settled. He'll be fine once he's adjusted. I've known many boys like Themba – it just takes a little extra kindness and patience.' Hannah smiled reassuringly. 'Now, I just need to do a little check that you haven't brought any prohibited items with you and then we can go to breakfast.'

You could hardly call it an inspection as Hannah glanced over their beds.

'We all need a few home comforts!'

She reached Shifa and Yara's bed last. Shifa's seed packet was hidden in the deep pockets of her daisy dress. Her heart raced as she watched Hannah pick the dress up and let it unfold to its full length without inspecting the pockets, and lay it back down again.

'I do love a daisy,' said Hannah, as she stepped towards Shifa and tucked her locket inside her uniform. She leaned forward and whispered in her ear. 'I should keep that hidden if you want to hold on to it.'

As the girls lined up by the doors Shifa heard the unmistakable clank of heavy bolts being unlocked on the other side. The fear she kept dampening down rose in her again. Had they been locked in all night? And they were taking so long to open them. *How would you get in or out of here in a hurry?* Shifa felt breathless as she cast around for emergency exits and found none.

Shifa pushed the thought to the back of her mind as the girls climbed the steep ramp into the courtyard, where they passed by a small queue of ashen-faced recruits lining up and waiting to enter.

'Night workers to the right, day to the left,' a cadet shouted.

As the night shift recruits shuffled in, Shifa couldn't help but notice the sallow tinge of their skin. Nowhere had she ever read or heard anything about having to work through the night.

For a moment Shifa thought she must be mistaken as a girl brushed passed her, but no, it was . . .

'Kiki!' Shifa whispered.

She had deep-set orbs of darkness around her eyes that showed only the faintest glimmer of recognition. It seemed hardly possible that this was the same bright-eyed girl who had sometimes helped mind her and Themba on the compound when they were little, before her family had relocated.

The girl shook her head and Shifa caught sight of a purple birthmark on her neck. It was Kiki all right.

'Shifa!' yelled a familiar voice. She turned with relief to discover Themba tumbling out of the boys' barn, evading Luca's attempt to restrain him as he sprinted across the courtyard. He now clung to Shifa as if they had been separated for weeks instead of a single night.

Shifa held him tightly against her. He smelt fresh and clean at least but when she finally caught sight of his face she gasped to find that an angry purple bruise had appeared on his cheek.

'Where did you get that?' she asked, tilting his chin to inspect it closer.

'Luca. Kicked me in the night!' Themba flailed his legs and arms around to illustrate.

Anger flared in Shifa. For so long she had always thought that the deep connection she felt with Themba was because he was her twin, but seeing his bruised face made her fierce protective instinct rear up stronger than ever.

'Luca gets a bed of his own tonight,' Themba explained.

'Good!' Shifa sighed, stroking his face.

'It doesn't hurt bad.' He shrugged, reading Shifa's concerned expression. 'Housecarer Hannah put kindness cream on.'

Shifa scanned over to where Luca stood in a huddle talking to Jermaine and some cadets.

'Luca's got a blanky, like Anton's, you know!' continued Themba. 'I've got your hair, he's got his baby blanky!' Themba leant close to Shifa. 'I'm not supposed to say I saw it though or . . .'

'Or what?'

'Don't know.' Themba winced and shoved his fist in his mouth.

'Don't *do* that to yourself!' Shifa pulled it free.

'Be good! Stay quiet. Shut up or else!'

'Or else what?' Shifa asked, but Themba's attention drifted.

'There goes Jermaine the pain!' he sang as Jermaine strode across the courtyard.

Ailish tapped Shifa on the arm. 'Is that your brother?' Shifa nodded. 'Then tell him to keep it down.' She gestured towards Jermaine. 'He's only known as "the pain" behind his back! Watch out! He's got a vile temper! If he hears that kind of talk he'll put your brother straight on double shifts or worse.'

'Thanks for the heads-up,' said Shifa, shooting the older girl a grateful smile.

The recruits fell into formation again and walked along a gravel path that led around the boys' barn to the back of the old farmhouse.

Shifa gazed at the open countryside in awe. The land beyond the house sloped gently away then flattened out to reveal what had not been visible last night. Right in the middle of a wide path stood a giant tree, its trunk so dark it resembled gnarled rock. The great arching branches and gold-and-mustard leaf canopy spread out far and wide, casting dappled shadows over the fields. Their procession slowed and came to a standstill as the recruits admired this rare view of open farmland.

'Is that real?' Shifa asked Ailish.

She nodded. 'Best thing about this place.'

Shifa gasped. 'I think . . . it's called a cathedral oak.'

Ailish shrugged. 'We call it our survivor tree. They say it's a thousand years old. How do you know what kind of tree it is anyway?'

'My papa – carer – taught us about them.'

'I need to draw that for Papa!' Themba announced and refused to walk on.

Ailish glanced from Shifa to Themba as if trying to work out how brother and sister had turned out so different.

'Don't say I didn't warn you!' She shrugged and overtook them, heading towards a Solarmirror-panelled building running the length of the back of the farmhouse. Themba balanced his book on his knee as he transported the survivor tree to his page with broad pencil-sweeps.

'What's the hold-up about?' Jermaine appeared by Themba's side, his jaw clenched in annoyance. 'I might have known *you* would have something to do with it!' Shifa anticipated the scene that was about to unfold, whisked Themba's artbook from his hand and placed it in her own pocket.

'Shifa! Give it back!' Themba tantrummed, leaping up at her.

Jermaine placed a firm hand on Themba's shoulder. 'Now, calm yourself, Themba. You've seen your sister so you can return to your group now.' When Themba carried on protesting, Jermaine grabbed his arm and led him to Luca.

'I need to draw now! Tell my sister. Shiiiiiiifa!' Themba yelled.

She placed her fingers to her lips, willing him to be quiet as they walked on. Then suddenly he was. She turned to see him stuffing his fist back into his own mouth. *Did Luca make him do that?* Tears stung Shifa's eyes. She had never felt so helpless in all her life. She held her hand over her overall where her locket lay against her skin and her chest began to burn and heave, her breath catching in panic. She unzipped the overall and reached inside for her locket, rubbing the dented surface over and over to calm her and as she did she was transported . . . crawling on her hands and knees through the folds of Baba Suli's coat where she found Daisy prowling around a grey blanket, sniffing at the locket. *What are you trying to tell me, Daisy?* The old cat dragged the blanket closer to Shifa . . . *That you protected me like a lion and you were only a kitten—* Daisy miaowed sharply and pawed at Shifa. *I know . . . I know I have to be Themba's lion.*

Chapter Sixteen

The food hall contained two long tables stacked with steaming bowls of porridge, jugs of oat milk, rice, pastries, bread rolls and . . . were those strawberries? Shifa's stomach groaned as the smell of plenty filled the air.

She poured warm oat milk on to her rice. On tasting it her stomach began to relax. Here at least everything looked just as it had in the glossy Freedom Fields brochure.

'Why can't we all sit together?' Shifa asked Ailish, who followed her gaze towards the other long table where the boys sat.

'They don't welcome "mixing",' Ailish said, raising her eyebrows suggestively. 'Not that they have anything to worry about with us!' Shifa glanced under the table to see Chirelle and Ailish holding hands.

With her free hand Ailish waved to an older boy with a shaven head who sat next to Luca. 'That's our friend, Zeb,' she explained.

'Who's he, sitting between Zeb and your brother?' Chirelle asked Shifa.

'Luca! An ARK Freedom.' The words slipped from Shifa's mouth and immediately she regretted them.

'What's that got to do with anything? You think you're better than us?' Chirelle narrowed her eyes at Shifa and her face twisted into a scowl.

'I didn't mean anything by . . .' Shifa felt herself flush. *I should be more careful. I don't understand anything about this place or these people*, she warned herself.

'Don't go separating us out, then. We're all in this together.'

'Sorry!' Shifa mumbled.

Ailish waved her hand as if to say 'no worries'. 'You want me to ask Zeb to look out for your brother while he settles in?'

'Would you?' Shifa's heart swelled with gratitude that Ailish seemed to have decided to take her under her wing.

Chirelle handed Shifa a strawberry, so perfect-looking that she doubted that it was real.

'Eat! We only get these on welcome days,' Ailish explained. 'You'd better have some before your friend here eats them all!' Ailish prised the bowl away from Yara.

Shifa raised the fruit to her nose and smelt for its sweetness but was disappointed that it didn't smell at all. She traced her fingers over the fruit's tiny dots, like pockmarks on skin. She pulled out the stalk and inspected the furry tip, the crown hat and the glossy shine of the fruit's surface. She placed the strawberry in her mouth; the explosion of sweetness she'd anticipated turned out to be a watery, tasteless mush.

Ailish leant in close and whispered, 'You have to try them before they're sprayed. But don't get caught, or you'll be working off your debits for ever. Do as we say, not as we've done!' she joked.

Jermaine approached their table. 'I hope you're sharing all your *positive* experiences with our new recruits, Ailish,' he said, a twisted smile playing around his mouth.

Ailish ignored him, tapping her fingers on the table nervously. Jermaine hovered over them, seemed to want to add something further, but after a moment changed his mind and walked away.

'Ah! Here she comes! "The freak of Pollination Farm!"' Chirelle announced, following Shifa's gaze up through the clear roof of the food hall to a long misted window built into the back wall of the farmhouse – there a shadow loomed over them and by its side a smaller shadow crouched low.

Yara trembled and edged closer to Shifa.

'Give over, Chirelle!' Alilish elbowed her friend in the side. 'They call her Lona,' Ailish explained. 'We reckon this was her farm once. That's our theory anyway. When we first came we sometimes used to see her hobbling along with her dog around the edge of the farm, talking to herself, but she hasn't left her room for years now . . .'

'Tell her why,' Chirelle interjected. 'She might as well hear the truth.'

Chirelle leaned across Ailish and whispered. 'She went missing once and they had us searching for her, and I found her hiding with her dog in the hollow of the survivor tree, chanting away like an old witch about some golden treasure being "lost for ever"!'

Shifa shrank away from Chirelle – there was something spiteful about her.

'That's enough, Chirelle!' Ailish mumbled.

'Better they hear it from us than listening to all the rumours, I say!' Chirelle shrugged. 'Or maybe you prefer this version – she actually died years ago and it's her ghost up there at the window!'

Ailish hit Chirelle hard on the arm.

Yara started sobbing and Shifa held her hand.

Not satisfied by spooking Yara, Chirelle now pointed to Themba, who was helping himself to another pastry. 'Tell your brother.' Chirelle lowered her voice as she raised her chin towards Jermaine. 'He sends the wayward ones up to the old witch to frighten the life out of them. One never came back.'

'We don't *know* what happened to Zakir, Chirelle—'

'We know he was taken out of here by Freedom Care and was never seen again!'

Shifa felt sick as the shadow figure of what Shifa now knew was a dog returned to the window, closely followed by a looming hand pressing a torch against the frosted glass. The light diffused into an enormous moon.

Shifa glanced nervously over to Themba who was now jumping up excitedly, pointing at the window.

'Can I see the dog?' His voice rose above the clamour of the food hall. Luca stood too, placed his hand on Themba's head and pushed him back to sitting.

Yara began to weep again.

An alarm sounded and the general buzz quietened. Shifa watched Ailish's face and jaw tighten. 'Good luck! See you in the tunnels later!' she called back to Shifa as she and Chirelle got up to leave.

As soon as the older recruits had gone, Themba stood up and shuffled over on to the bench next to Shifa and Yara.

'Why are you crying, Yara?' Themba asked. Shifa still had one comforting arm wrapped around her, but Themba removed it, replacing it with his own. Shifa smiled. Perhaps Themba would learn to make new friends here too.

Yara pointed up to the window.

'She's homesick, that's all!' Shifa cut in before Yara could speak. If she could help it, Themba would never have to hear the scaremongering about old Lona.

'Please can I have my artbook back?' Themba asked.

'If you promise to listen better!'

Themba pulled back his curls and did his waggle-ear trick in answer, turning Yara's tears to laughter as his lobes moved without assistance up and down.

'Here!' Shifa smiled and handed the book and his pencils back to him.

Yara sat mesmerised as Themba sketched the food hall and the hunchbacked shadow woman in the misted window above, her dog sitting faithfully by her side.

Chapter Seventeen

Jax stood at the front of the food hall and placed a small white case on the table.

'Good morning, recruits! To commence your induction to Pollination Farm, we need to run through a few simple procedures to help you in your work ahead.' She laid out a cloth and lifted out an instrument, something resembling Nabil's binoculars. Shifa turned cold as she caught sight of the gun-like handle – smaller than the stun gun the Crow had used at the station but somehow more lethal-looking.

'Introducing Eyequaliser lenses – our latest technology from Freedom Care will ensure you all have perfect vision,' Jax announced proudly. 'In fact, even if you've never had to wear glasses in your life before, these lenses guarantee to make your eyesight sharper and more precise.' Jax beamed at the group. 'No need to take them in or out. After a while they harmlessly dissolve. We'll replace them on a monthly basis.'

Shifa's mind cast back to Nita the hairtaker in the agora with her unnaturally blue eyes, and the advice she'd given her. 'Follow instructions, take everything in your stride, don't be too clever and you'll be fine.'

Themba's hand crept towards Shifa's. 'No thank you with the eye thing!' He shook his head and carried on drawing.

Jax pulled on bright orange surgical gloves and opened a sealed packet containing transparent lenses. She then unpeeled another packet containing tweezers and, with concentrated precision, carefully placed the lenses into the glass orbs of the binoculars.

'Credits will be given to whoever's sensible enough to set an example and go first.' Jax scanned the room.

Without hesitation Luca stood up and walked to the front.

Creep! Shifa thought.

'Pop your eyes up against the Eyequalisers here.' Jax tapped the top. 'You'll feel a little sting as the liquid squirts into your eyes – that's all, nothing to worry about.'

Luca flinched as Jax clicked the trigger.

'No rubbing your eyes. Just blink!' Jax ordered as she held his hands from his face.

Luca blinked and his eyes washed pink and watery-sore. Jax opened his top lids and dropped in a tear of eye solution.

'All clear now?'

Luca nodded, but he still gripped the table edge as he returned to the bench.

'Shifa, you next!'

Shifa felt light-headed as she walked towards Jax.

'I didn't read about this anywhere in the brochure,' she said quietly, as she sat down.

'Your carers were informed when they signed their contracts,' Jax explained.

Shifa pulled back. 'They weren't. I read it . . .'

'No arguments. Hold steady.'

Shifa felt the spherical orb inside the Eyequaliser pincer her lids open, as a jelly-like substance shot into her eyes. They watered and stung until Jax administered eye drops.

Shifa glanced down at the tattoo on her hand. Now she could pick out every coded seed dot in the centre of the sunflower. She peered into the distance, but the survivor tree had grown fuzzy, shimmering like a mirage on the horizon.

'I can see better close up, but far away is blurred!' Shifa complained.

'Pollinating work is all close up. You don't need long sight much here.'

Shifa felt a hot bolt of anger shoot through her. How dare they change the way she saw things. As Shifa walked unsteadily back to the table the chilling thought came to her that Freedom Fields meant to dismantle them all piece by piece.

Right at this moment Themba was attempting to disappear, to draw himself out of the room. He was in the process of scratching thousands of straight lines into the page to form the crop fields beyond the farm. Every time someone underwent 'the procedure' Themba glanced up and would dig so hard with his pen nib that he made a hole in his page. By the time it came to his turn he had shaped the hole into an empty eye socket.

'Themba!' Jax called out.

'No! I need to see far for my art.' Themba carried on drawing and released a high-pitched whistle.

'Don't start with that!' Shifa implored and attempted to catch hold of his hands, but he pushed her away and his whistling grew shriller yet. She had not heard him panic whistle like a steam kettle for so long.

'What's all this racket about?' Jermaine growled as he came striding in and made a quick assessment of the situation. 'Where's Hannah when you need her!'

'Everyone's had their lenses fitted, but Themba's point-blank refusing,' Jax explained.

'Is he now! Well, I'll handle this. Is that loaded?'

Jax nodded and passed Jermaine the Eyequaliser. He took a pair of gloves out of the case and as he did so Themba slid under the bench and hid.

'Please let me persuade him,' Shifa said and joined Themba under the table.

'Get up, Shifa! I'll deal with this.' Jermaine yanked Themba out and dragged him to the table ignoring his wild jerks and thrashing legs.

Shifa sprang to her feet. 'No! You can't. You promised

you'd look after him!' she shouted.

'Luca, *hold her*!' Jermaine barked the order. Luca hesitated for a moment as Shifa lunged forward. 'I said restrain her, Luca!'

Shifa held her hands in the air. 'Don't you dare touch me.' The words hissed like venom from her mouth. Luca stood back.

Shifa was frozen. Clutching her locket against her heart she closed her eyes. *Help us, Nabil. Help us, Daisy. Help!* Shifa screamed inside.

'Hold his head firm, Jax!' Jermaine hissed.

Themba's whistle grew shrill enough to break glass. His fear ripped through her – she imagined the molten lava flow of her anger forced to travel underground, flaming and spreading across the Kairos Lands till it reached Nabil on the Flower Tracks.

'STOP! This has to stop!' Housecarer Hannah stood in the doorway. At the sound of her voice Shifa opened her eyes.

Jermaine released Themba's arms. He flopped to the floor and Hannah bent down to comfort him. Shifa too knelt down and cocooned Themba in her arms, rocking him back and forth.

'They changed me, Shifa.' His lament wracked his whole body and hers too, shaking her to the core.

When he had finally grown calm, Jermaine bent down and patted him on the shoulder, ignoring Shifa's glare. In her mind she was scratching at his face and eyes with sharp drawn claws. If he had known how dangerous she felt at that moment he would not have dared to come so close.

As Jermaine coaxed him up, Themba gradually began to uncurl from his foetal position on Shifa's lap and stand up shakily, flanked by Jermaine on one side and Luca on the other. *Like a Crow patrol*, Shifa thought.

'Dry your tears now, Themba, and you'll be able to see perfectly well,' Jermaine said, a note of impatience creeping into his voice again. He glanced at Themba's sketch of the shadow woman and her dog. 'That's Barley! He's a friendly old soul. Would you like to meet him?'

Themba nodded.

'Well, if you behave yourself and work hard I'll let you walk Barley. How about that?'

'Thank you!' Themba whispered through trembling lips. 'Want to see what else I've drawn, Jermaine?'

Luca walked over and offered Shifa his hand to help her up. If she could have spat at him she would.

'I don't want your help, *ever* for anything!' She jabbed the words out.

The tears rolled down her cheeks as she was forced to watch the bullying unfold – Jermaine's satisfaction at the hopeful expression on Themba's face as Themba offered him his artbook. Themba was such easy prey.

'Interesting!' Jermaine scoffed. 'See you like hares! Now, Themba, you do what you're told from now on and I'll let

151

you keep this and your art things, OK?'

'Thank you Jermaine!' Themba whimpered, as he took the book back.

Trusting Themba – he fitted his name so well. He was the most forgiving person Shifa knew, always willing to trust people even when they'd betrayed him, which is why she had never felt as afraid for him as she did now.

'Right then! Shall we get on, Luca?' Jermaine turned and nodded to Shifa as if his little show of strength had been intended to put *her* in her place as much as Themba. Had he spied a glimpse of the secret places of rebellion planted inside them? Was he attempting to stamp it out before the spirit contained in them spread like wild flowers?

Chapter Eighteen

'Orientation!' Jax announced. A giant screen that ran the whole length of the food hall slowly lowered, revealing a screensaver of a map of the farm.

Despite the minuscule writing, Shifa was able to read every word of the key at the side.

'Your daily schedules will be posted up here on the screen,' Jax explained. 'Simply click on your face and your schedule will appear.' The holding image of the map disappeared. 'Your debit and credit tally will show to the right of the schedule and will be updated daily.'

Jax invited each of them to practise. Shifa clicked on the image of her face.

```
Shifa Aziz

7 a.m. — Breakfast

8 a.m. — Polytunnels

2 p.m. — Lunch

3 p.m. — Recreation

4 p.m. — Polytunnels

6 p.m. — Laundry

7 p.m. — Dinner

8.30 p.m. — Recreation

9 p.m. — Sleep Barns

1 credit: Leadership skills recognised from
   transit behaviour
```

'What about school?' Shifa asked.

Jax sighed deeply. 'School has had to be suspended for the time being, due to emergency quota demands.' As she spoke the corner of her eye twitched. 'We don't usually have too many complaints about that!'

'But it's our right!' Shifa felt breathless with outrage. 'In the brochure it said it was ARK law that we have—'

Jax's face grew stern. 'As you seem to have a keen interest in the law, Shifa, we could put you forward for that . . . *if* you graduate from service with honours.'

'How's that going to happen if we don't get any schooling?' Shifa retorted.

'I think you'll find that each farm has the right to adopt their own rules on a needs-must basis. You might also like to muse on the difference between an intelligent question and disrespect, Shifa.'

Shifa clamped her mouth closed.

A boy she recognised from the Skylight carriage, still cuddling his teddy, tentatively raised his hand. 'When can our carers come?'

'That depends on you, Bilan,' Jax muttered, 'but you'll need a hundred credits to trigger carer communication, so you've a way to go.'

'But how do we get credits? It only says about debits in the rules,' Bilan said.

'Not by bringing teddies to work with you.' Jax removed his toy from his arms.

Shifa cast her mind back to the vague answers to FAQs – what did 'carer communication' mean? A call? A visit? Shifa was about to put up her hand as Jax clapped to quell all further conversation, signalling that the time for questions was over.

Their group stood outside the food hall facing the survivor tree. Shifa felt some comfort in its ancient presence. If only it could speak and tell of all that it had seen here. She took a deep breath as a sudden breeze chased through the corn field, setting in motion a giant golden wave. She had the urge to run and follow its gliding path. *This* was the Freedom Fields spirit that had been promised. A khaki-uniformed cadet drove a yellow harvester slowly through the crop, its sharp blades glinting in the hot sun.

Themba stuck close to Shifa now. She offered him a reassuring smile and looked into his eyes, where she could just make out the rim of a transparent lens around the iris.

'The recreation field is to your right. Barge ball and the like is played there.' Jax indicated a piece of dry flattened ground with goalposts and nets stacked under a shed at one end. They followed her now along the central path, to an area with young trees planted either side.

'We call this Hope Avenue.' Jax pointed to the line of spindly trees, each with a curved windbreak attached to its side. 'Imagine what this could be like one day, if even a few of these survive!' She smiled as she touched one of the sapling stems, and for the first time Shifa caught a glimpse of who Jax might be beyond a Freedom Fields leader.

'What kind of trees are they?' Shifa asked. 'How long will

they take to grow?'

'Ash, I think. I don't know. Jermaine and . . .' Jax peered up to the farmhouse window where Lona's shadow was trailing them. 'Jermaine planted them – ask him.' The idea of Jermaine caring enough to plant anything seemed unbelievable to Shifa.

'Now, as you can see, to your left are the polytunnels and if you continue along you'll find the walled garden of our very own orchard enterprise. Those of you who receive enough credits might get to help out in there one day.' Jax pointed into the distance. 'And beyond the orchard is the River Ore.'

Themba's eyes widened. 'Can we go down to the river now?'

Jax shook her head. 'You have work to do first, Themba. Fulfil your quotas and we'll think about taking you on a weekend trip.'

With that, Jax strode off along Hope Avenue towards the survivor tree. Shifa steadied herself by looking down at her feet. If she attempted to focus too far ahead she felt dizzy.

'We have plenty to keep us occupied here, as you can see,' continued Jax. 'The Farm cadets are in the process of harvesting our corn.' Jax walked them to the edge of the field where a deep trench ran to her left and right as far as Shifa could see.

'Our sensors keep predators off our land,' Jax explained, picking up several strands of corn, scrunching them into a ball and lobbing it towards the ditch. A constellation of fire-red embers sizzled and died.

'Try it!'

A few recruits followed her example, throwing handfuls of grasses at the invisible border.

'A bit of fun! But of course it's important to remember that *anything* that crosses that trench gets frazzled. Take a closer look!'

Themba covered his mouth and nose with his hand as the group stared into the trench where all manner of putrefying animals lay prone in the ditch. A host of flies blackened the body of a rabbit. Shifa's stomach heaved. She had never seen so many flies in one place before.

'Look what they've done to the hare!' Themba whispered.

'It's not been there long, poor thing. Let it be a warning to you.' Jax sighed.

Shifa's legs buckled and Themba held out an arm to steady her. *A hare, not a rabbit.* Shifa held her stomach and had to work hard not to vomit up breakfast.

'You feel sick now too?' Themba asked.

'I'll be OK,' Shifa whispered, but poisonous thoughts flowed through her. *The hare is not in the moon, Nabil, shining kindness over all the world, like in your fairy stories. It's caught in a trap right here and reeking of rot.* She stroked Themba's bruised face and squeezed his hand. She didn't care now what she had to do. She had been too 'clever' today, asked too many questions, but from now on for both their sakes, she would work to get Jax and Jermaine on side, earn those one hundred credits in record time so that she could speak to Nabil.

As they walked back across the field Shifa felt the last vestiges of hope drain from her. They could not stay here for four whole years. It would kill their spirits.

Chapter Nineteen

'Welcome to the hot house!' Jermaine pressed his face against the milky-white partition distorting his features against the milky film. His odd greeting seemed to amuse him, at least.

Inside, the sweat gathered on Shifa's forehead. She was relieved to find Housecarer Hannah at the head of a long white table lined with benches, a bowl containing blue liquid laid out in front of her. The table was set with small domes, the kind Shifa had seen in the agora nail palace.

Jermaine indicated to the group to sit. 'Boys on the right-hand bench, girls on the left!'

Luca walked around the table to collect Themba from Shifa's side. Her spine bristled as he drew near. *Is this what it feels like to hate?* Shifa asked herself as she stared unflinchingly at Luca.

Themba sat opposite now as Shifa inspected the interior of the nail domes and discovered grooves in the shape of fingers.

'Hands inside the manicure unit,' Jermaine ordered.

Shifa inspected her own nails, bitten to the quick as usual. Complaints erupted but with Jermaine's 'no nonsense' demonstration followed by his steely gaze, the recruits complied.

'Is it like the opposite of a pencil sharpener?' Themba asked.

'Exactly!' Shifa nodded across the table. 'It's just like using the nail clippers at home.'

'*My* nails, yes!' Themba nodded. 'But not yours!' Themba shot his hand up.

'No, Themba, don't—?' Shifa whispered, too late.

'Excuse me Jermin, my sister . . . !'

As Themba explained, Shifa saw Jermaine's eyes sparkle, relishing this little bit of extra power.

'"Jerm" like a germ that can make you ill, and "maine" like a lion's mane, Themba, remember that! Get on with it, both of you. I would hate to see *either of you* on night shift because of disobedience,' Jermaine warned.

'Just do it,' urged Luca.

'I was going to anyway!' Shifa glared at him and placed her hands in the nail dome.

Themba began his nervous whistle. Jermaine pressed a remote control and a quiet whirring sound buzzed inside the nail domes. Shifa clenched her jaw tight. *Do not flinch, do not give Jermaine the satisfaction.* The tips of Shifa's fingers shot through with pain, like someone had pulverised them under a heavy stone. Themba stopped whistling abruptly as relief lit his face. 'Didn't hurt!' he announced, fluttering his precision-cut fingernails in the air.

Shifa slowly removed her hands and inspected her throbbing fingers. The skin of every tip cut to way beyond the quick, was grazed and bleeding. At the sight of her blood Themba vaulted over the bench, but Jermaine grabbed him by the collar of his uniform and forced him to sit.

'I'm fine. Please don't make a fuss, Themba!' Shifa warned.

'You're not my friend, Jermaine! You hurt my sister.' Themba flushed beetroot as the outrage tore out of him. He jerked his neck backwards, butting his head into Jermaine's chest and sending him off balance.

'You two should have been split up on different farms. From now on . . .'

Jermaine was incandescent with rage as he steadied himself and signalled for Luca to get Themba out.

Luca obeyed and struggled to keep hold of a screeching, whistling Themba through the entrance to the polytunnels.

'Shifa, see Hannah for your treatment!' ordered Jermaine. He clapped his hands. 'The rest of you look sharp. Boys to the right, girls to the left. We've wasted enough time here.'

Hannah smiled sadly at Shifa. 'This is going to sting. Take a deep breath.' Shifa allowed Hannah to hold her fingers in the Chemisan. Needle-sharp pain shot through her nails as she watched the bloodied tips turn blue.

'The dye will fade as your bruises and scabs heal,' Hannah reassured her, dabbing Shifa's hands dry and gently massaging in a clear liquid. 'This will soften the pain a little,' Hannah soothed. But Shifa had succeeded in floating away to sit for a moment in her Flower Tracks haven with Daisy on her lap.

Tears rolled down Shifa's cheeks and she did not open her eyes as Hannah dabbed them away. *We're going to come home, Daisy, soon. I promise you, when Nabil finds out about this . . .*

Calling on Daisy seemed to restore a little courage. Following Hannah's expression closely, Shifa removed her hands from the table and cupped them into the shape of a skep-heart. The colour rose in Hannah's cheeks and her eyes blinked rapidly. Hannah's hands were shaking now as Jermaine appeared out of nowhere, swooping in like a drone.

'If you're done here, Hannah, Lona needs you.'

Hannah sighed deeply, nodded and stood up.

'Right, Shifa!' Jermaine bellowed. 'If your manicure's over! Let's get to work!'

Jermaine led the group through the entrance to the tunnels, where the path split in two directions. The section Shifa stepped into was ten times the size of the polytunnels they had practised in at school. The heat and the milky walls made her feel as if she'd been swallowed and was now straining to breathe inside a giant lung. Dewy sweat coated her whole body. The lights were dazzlingly bright and the drone of machinery deafening.

The raised beds on either side of the path contained

plants in various stages of growth and, above them, vine tendrils spread over the roof, reaching for natural light. From where she stood Shifa could clearly see that the tunnels were separated into three zones: planting, pollinating and harvesting.

Every few minutes, jets of water spurted from sprinklers in the walls, misting the vast expanse of seedling counters.

The older recruits were already working and Jermaine paired them up with the new girls to show them the ropes. Ailish walked over to Shifa and led her through to a changing area. Her fingers were too sore to unzip the sleeves and trouser legs off her uniform to adapt it into shorts and T-shirt as everyone else had already done.

'Poor you!' Ailish sighed, grimacing at the sight of Shifa's scabbed fingers and she reached out to help her. 'It happened to me too but that plant liquid Hannah puts on makes them heal fast.'

Shifa nodded, swallowing back the tears. She followed Ailish out and stepped up to the conveyor belt moving slowly around the surface area of the polytunnel. Jermaine appeared behind them logging their progress on a screen book, pulling up graphs and entering data as he followed them around silently.

'Monitoring work speed,' Ailish whispered. 'Just copy what I do.' She held a toothbrush in one hand and a paintbrush in the other. 'What's your instrument of choice?'

Shifa chose the fine-tipped brush. 'Themba thinks it's

best. In the polytunnels at school he always used to imagine he was painting instead of pollinating! Helped him get through,' Shifa explained.

Ailish raised her eyebrows. 'He's a case, that brother of yours! He'll have to learn to keep his ideas to himself. Best not to think too much. In fact, best not think at all!'

'What about at school?' Shifa asked, keeping her voice lowered.

'This is the only school you'll get around here!' Ailish laughed.

Shifa swallowed down the knot of indignation lodged in her windpipe.

'Don't be nervous!' the older girl said as she watched Shifa peel back the trembling leaves, touch the tip of the brush against the bright-yellow pollen of the stigma and transfer it to the stamen of the next plant.

Ailish smiled her approval. 'You're expert!'

'I love lilies.' Shifa leaned forward to smell the rich perfume of the perfect white flower.

'Say that in four years' time! I can't stand them. Sickly sweet!' Ailish fake gagged then laughed at the sight of Shifa's nose. 'You've got pollen stain! Hold still!' Ailish held Shifa's chin and blew the orange dust away. 'Now these are the ones I love!' Ailish moved on to a section of statuesque plants. 'Bird of paradise. Not usually a job for a novice but you'll rack up some credits if you get the gist of this! Paragons will pay a fortune for a bunch of these.' Shifa gasped at the pointed beaks and ruffles of orange petals and blue plumage. 'Think you're up for it?' Shifa nodded.

'Here, take this.' Ailish handed her a long-tipped, quill-tailed brush. 'You've got to be a little hummingbird, balancing at an angle, resting exactly the right weight or you won't find the centre of the flower.' She leaned over Shifa to help her. 'That's it! It's like you've found the key to a secret door when you get it right! Now dip your beak in there on the green bract . . . that's it!' Shifa felt the same sense of satisfaction she had at school in learning just the right technique for every flower, all so different from each other. If becoming a specialist at these could get her more credits she was determined to impress.

'Carry on! I'll be back in a bit!' Ailish said and stepped off the conveyor belt and disappeared.

Shifa sighed, stretched out her back and reached under her overall for her locket. As soon as she was alone the ache for home grew like a great empty cavern inside her. She fought hard to stem her tears, reaching again and again for her locket and . . . Daisy, willing her close. After a while her old friend heard her call and came prowling through Shifa's mind . . . her tinkling bell sounding her arrival. Shifa could see her now, peering out at her through the lush leaves. *Are you dreaming of me when I'm thinking of you, Daisy?* Shifa followed her path as she continued on her way. *No hunting birds, Daisy. They're too precious.* As Shifa stepped off the conveyor belt, her eyes misted, blurring the orange and blue heads. *What kind of song would these flower birds sing? They don't belong here either, Daisy.* They had flown from ancient tropical rainforests and jungles and deserved to be set free. The great flock seemed to hear. They turned their heads, spread their wings and rose through the polytunnel roof.

'A groit for them!' Ailish jolted Shifa out of her reverie.

'I was just thinking they look like they really could fly!'

'What have I warned you about thinking too much?' Ailish laughed.

There were so many plants here she had never seen before. She felt the pocket of her overall, where her seed packet lay against her chest. Maybe, if she was careful, she would manage to start a collection from the polytunnels.

Shifa peered into a deep-purple rose, bred to perfection except for its lack of scent. *Give me a wild-flower meadow any day, Daisy.* Shifa sneezed three times, joining the mini orchestra of sneezes all around her. *Pollen fever.* As she slowly worked along the line she realised that the roses were too uniform, like clones of each other. Her Flower Tracks would never be planted like this. One day they would contain hundreds of different species of flowers, each one celebrated for its own distinctive beauty. In her garden the wild flowers and the birds of paradise, the lilies and dandelions would all live happily side by side.

Ailish placed a warning hand over Shifa's. 'Don't stop!' she said, nodding towards Jermaine, who was eyeing Shifa suspiciously. 'Keep your botanical appreciation for when you've earned enough credits to work in the orchard – if you like gardens you'll love it in there!'

Shifa smiled gratefully and moved on.

Every half hour a buzzer sounded and they were permitted to step off the conveyor belt to drink water from hydration stations evenly placed along the polytunnel.

Shifa felt a stabbing pain behind her eyes and with it Daisy's mournful wail set Shifa's nerves on edge, accompanying her now as an anxious companion.

Five breaks later and her head throbbed, heavy as a bass drumbeat. Her back ached and her shoulders were in a constant state of tension. If *she* was finding it this hard, how was Themba managing?

'Not long to go now,' Ailish encouraged her, then quietly added, 'Just giving you the heads up! Your brother's only gone and earned himself two debits for stopping to draw flowers. Jermaine's confiscated his artbook. He's planning to charge Themba's debits to you! What's the matter with your brother, anyway?!'

Shifa hated that question more than any other. Themba was just Themba. Shifa took a deep breath and attempted to keep her irritation from her voice. Ailish had gone out of her way to befriend her and she needed friends. 'He's frightened! We've never been apart, that's all.' As she carried on working Shifa wondered how Ailish had managed to find out so much.

Were there were ways of communicating with the boys'

tunnel that she hadn't found out about yet? The world of the farm was as full of secret codes and ways as Kairos City, only here felt more dangerous because she had no handle on the rules.

The buzzer sounded and they stepped off the conveyor belt, heading straight for the nearest hydration station.

'Seriously though. You'll have to find a way to get through to him or he'll get himself thrown in confinement.'

Shifa gulped water greedily and began to choke.

'Steady!' Ailish warned, patting her back.

'What's confinement?' Shifa asked when she'd finally got her breath back.

'A storeroom cellar at the back of the polytunnels,' Ailish explained.

'Is it dark in there?' Shifa asked.

Ailish nodded grimly. 'Pitch black. Darker than anywhere I've ever been.'

'Why did you go there?'

Ailish waved away the question.

'They can't send Themba there. He's terrified of the dark.'

Ailish shrugged. 'Me too!'

Shifa worked in the harvesting section now and tried to focus on the task in front of her, allowing the rhythmic picking of small yellow, orange and red tomatoes to calm her. Shifa had the overwhelming urge to eat one but Ailish had already pointed out the roaming opticare monitoring their progress in the absence of Jermaine or Jax. Shifa sighed and carried her box of tomatoes to a collecting area, through a doorway at the back of the polytunnel, as Ailish had done.

She placed her box on top of the existing stack that reached level with her waist. Shifa bent down to read the label on the side of the trays. Kairos City agora. Shifa's spine stiffened. It seemed a lot longer than two days ago that she had been at the agora fooling herself that she could pass for a Paragon! It felt so wrong that this box would travel back to her home on the Skylight, but she and Themba were caged here – if only there were a way to hide among the crates and stow away. As she examined the stacks her foot edged over a red line on the floor that ran the length of the storage area.

A searing alarm sounded and immediately the opticare drone swooped in front of Shifa, emitting a bright ray directly into her eyes. Her vision blurred as she staggered back into the polytunnel, arms outstretched, to find Ailish waiting for her.

'What took you so long?' Ailish placed a supporting hand on Shifa's back as she clocked the roaming opticare. 'Crossed a red line already! Are you and your brother going for a debit record on your first day too? Take it from me. Don't even think about flying home on the Skylight!' She lowered her voice. 'Why do you think I was in confinement? Kiki tried so many times. She spent a whole month there once and look what it did to her!

Tears stung Shifa's eyes when she remembered Kiki's once playful nature. It seemed there was nowhere to hide here.

Ailish handed Shifa a misting gun. 'They have us spray the strawberries with it to make them stay perfect for longer,' Ailish explained. As she worked the chemical residue settled on her tongue. Shifa wrinkled her nose and pursed her lips.

Ailish laughed. 'Watch the wind doesn't turn or your face'll stay like that! You'll get used to it!'

That would be the most dangerous thing I could do, Shifa thought, *get used to it*. The sense of injustice that had been growing in her since she'd entered the agora was burning ever fiercer now. She cast around her fellow recruits. *I'm a child, we're all children*, she reminded herself. *Hot and exhausted from long hours of work and far away from home.* She thought about the Paragon children who would eat these perfect strawberries, decorate their homes with birds of paradise and would never know the conditions they were grown in. If the cost of a beautiful life for one child meant enslavement for another. how could you call it freedom? Lottie had been right to have no faith in the system. The whole concept of Freedom Fields was a lie.

The molten lava swirling inside Shifa hardened into a boulder of determination. She wasn't going to let Freedom Fields control her, or Themba. She wouldn't be broken like Kiki and she wouldn't be made into the next generation of leader either, as Luca was shaping up to be. Even if Ailish and Chirelle had survived it, and perhaps she would too, Themba would never get through unbroken. As soon as she'd got enough credits to speak to Nabil she would tell everything, not holding back on a single detail to spare him the worry as she'd done sometimes at school.

Jax patrolled the tunnel now, monitoring the workers. She stopped by Shifa and glanced at an alert on her screen book.

'Shifa Aziz. You arrived at the farm with a credit from your journey, and had earned half a credit today, but I see now you have a debit point against your name for loitering in the storage area and you're also taking a hit for your brother's debits. We're hoping the double impact persuades him to behave himself!'

'If we could be together—'

'Not happening,' Jax snapped, raising a flat hand to Shifa. 'Make sure you familiarise yourself again with the rules. Five debit points and your whole shift goes without supper. That sort of popularity you and your brother can do without, understand?'

Shifa nodded. After only one day she was beginning to understand the way this place worked all too well.

'You can start to make up for it now. A bumper order of sunflowers just came in from the Freedom Fields Careers Fair.' Jax pointed at Ailish. 'The fair that *you*, Chirelle, Zeb and Kiki are missing out on till you work out your debits! You'd better have a last push and get yourselves over the line or all the best jobs will have gone!' Jax handed a pair of scissors to Ailish and another to Shifa. It seemed like they had no choice but to stay. Ailish sighed deeply and demonstrated where to make the cut in the sunflower stem.

Chirelle joined them and they filled box after box of sunflowers. Shifa watched their tattooed hands repeat the same motion over and over again. *They've turned us into machines*, Shifa thought.

'Tough first day?' Ailish asked, feeling Shifa's weariness.

'I'm OK. I'm going to earn a hundred credits as fast as I can so I can speak to my carer.'

Chirelle and Ailish exchanged a hesitant glance. Ailish placed a hand on Shifa's arm as she wrapped the long stems in the silver insulating blankets.

'You've got to stop hoping for that, Shifa. Carers don't come here. I thought everyone knew that!' Ailish shot her a sympathetic smile.

Shifa twisted a sunflower stem so hard that it snapped. 'I *can* speak to him though?' she spluttered.

Ailish shook her head. Shifa began to cough violently. Chirelle ran over to a hydration station and returned with water.

Ailish gently prised the broken-stemmed sunflower from Shifa's hand and quickly wrapped it, her eyes flashing around warily to check that the break had not been recorded. 'By the time they find out it's broken, it'll be too late to blame

173

anyone. No harm done,' she reassured Shifa.

But there had already been so much harm done. She could already feel it building up as the elaborate system of locks and bolts slid into place inside her. She and Themba might not be twin brother and sister but they were the product of everything Nabil had shared with them; their story hive, their Flower Tracks, time spent in the warehouse with Lottie . . . The image of Nabil standing before her, arms outstretched, pleading for her to forgive him swelled a whole new wave of emotion in her. *I should have told him I love him no matter what.*

'Chin up! Eat up!' Ailish attempted to placate Shifa all through lunch. She chewed on some bread with little appetite. The cold, hard truth of what she had learned was so much worse than she'd feared. She couldn't let Themba know that Nabil would never visit, that they would not even get to speak to him.

The memory of Nabil finally telling her about finding her on the night of Hurricane Chronos echoed through her mind. Suddenly nothing seemed as clear-cut as it had, and her anger at Nabil for not telling the truth was already beginning to wane. After all, she had already decided to lie to Themba to protect him, just as Nabil had lied to her.

After their chores, Shifa, Chirelle and Ailish approached the courtyard, but their path was blocked by Jax. Ahead of them Crows patrolled, stun guns at the ready. A van was parked outside the gates, headlights on.

As Jermaine escorted Housecarer Hannah across the yard towards the van, Shifa caught snatches of their intense conversation.

'Lona's violent outbursts are getting much worse. She's a danger to herself and others too! She needs special care, and she's not the only one. That child Themb—'

'You would do well to remember the gagging clause you signed, if you want a reference!' Jax yelled across the courtyard.

'I need to say goodbye to her.' Chirelle lunged forward and a Crow raised his stun gun in warning.

Chirelle backed off straight away, holding her hands in the air.

Hannah lowered her head, exited the gates and was assisted into the car by a Crow.

'Is she under arrest?' Shifa asked.

'It's nothing personal. As of today all housecarers' contracts are terminated,' Jax explained.

Hannah waved through the back window and attempted a smile. Had Shifa been so desperate to find the hare in the moon that she'd imagined their skep-heart code? What if Freedom Fields had discovered that housecarers did after all leak information about what was going on in farms across the Kairos Lands? But in heart Shifa knew it was such a faint hope, a grasping at straws. Even if she had read a hint of recognition in Hannah's eyes, she now seemed so fearful that Shifa doubted she would ever speak out against the regime here.

The three girls crossed the courtyard in silence. 'That's it then! You lot had better get your acts together when we're gone. You're on your own now with the bad apples!' Chirelle sighed. When they went off to shower, Shifa hovered by the door, listening.

Ailish's voice drifted through the shower water's flow. 'I feel like we're abandoning a sinking ship. It was nothing like this when we got here. It's only when I see it through Shifa's eyes that I realise how bad it's got. It's like a whole new regime. I don't know how we survived it.'

'We had each other! Shifa's not our problem now. We're out of here!' Chirelle said as the shower water cut out.

After waiting anxiously to see Themba, Shifa finally spotted him after supper, walking to the sleep barn with Luca and the dog Barley. Once inside her own barn she showered and fell into bed, not even bothering to move Yara's feet. The first day at Pollination Farm had been the longest and hardest of Shifa's life. Every part of her ached but the greatest pain was in her mind. The memory of Hannah's warning about Lona took hold. What if Lona tried to set fire to the place? What if . . . Shifa forced herself to stop the questions scrolling through her mind. She summoned Daisy to her side and imagined lying by her side on the bed at home.

Hannah was the only adult who had shown a hint of kindness. If only she could get a few words to Nabil to make him know how awful this place was, she knew exactly what she would say. *The hare in the moon is dead, Nabil. The hare in the moon is dead . . .*

Chapter Twenty

In the morning Shifa was first up and ready, shifting from foot to foot, waiting for the girls' barn to open. She nodded to the cadet as he unlocked the door, and hurried up the slope to the courtyard, banishing the grim vision of flames taking hold in a bolted barn. She was the first out. It seemed ages before bleary-eyed recruits gradually emerged from the boys' barn, squinting into the bright morning sunlight. She scanned and scanned the rows. Finally Shifa spotted Luca but Themba was not by his side. Shifa searched his face but could read nothing in his blank expression.

In the food hall she ate her bowl of oatmeal, forcing herself to finish it. She waited for Jax to walk through to the kitchen then took her chance. Striding over to the screen, she tapped on Themba's picture and only just had time to read, 'Night shift + change of duty (care shift)' before she felt Jax's hand on her shoulder.

'You have no business perusing anyone else's record.' Jax clicked on Shifa's face. 'This is you!' Shifa's timetable was unchanged and her credits had been adjusted back to zero.

'I just want to see how my brother's doing,' Shifa explained.

'Badly! He's on nights. He'll be sleeping now.' Jax turned around abruptly and walked into the kitchen. Shifa followed her.

'What's a care shift?' Shifa asked.

'Like I said, none of your business.' Jax placed her hands firmly on Shifa's shoulders and marched her back through to the food hall.

Shifa wondered if they had changed Themba's shift to teach him to survive without her, so they wouldn't bump into each other at meal times or recreation. At school, teachers had always split them up too. Principal Daviala told Nabil once that 'twins needed to be separated to grow into their own skins.' He must have wanted to argue with her. But twins by birth or not, Shifa had always known that the special bond they shared threatened people.

She sat on a bench at the long dining table and felt the hunched shape of the shadow woman Lona above. Her dog pawed at the glass. She felt sorry for it trapped in there when it could have been wandering freely around the farm. *Nothing's free here*, Shifa thought.

'You think Lona can see us?' Shifa asked Ailish, who came to sit beside her.

'I don't see why she'd make that her perch if she couldn't.' Ailish gazed across the field. 'Maybe, if this place was once hers, she thinks she's keeping an eye on us!'

Shifa remembered Hannah's parting words – '*She needs special care*' – and felt a deep sadness for this woman shut away upstairs. But her compassion was also mixed with fear. In Kairos City she had once tried to walk a frail old Forager to the warehouse and halfway there received a barrage of abuse for her troubles. Without Hannah, who would look after the old woman? Take her food? Themba was to be given a 'care shift'. Surely they could not be so cruel as to give Hannah's duties to *Themba*?

The morning in the polytunnel dragged. It felt as if she had been working all day by the time they sat down for lunch. She inspected her tender hands – the fingertips hurt more than ever today. Her shoulders and the bottom of her back twinged too and her eyes were pollen-sore. It was not the monotony of the work that she hated most but the oppressive heat and constant surveillance. Ailish was right, the pungent smell of lilies had already lost its sweetness.

At recreation Chirelle and Ailish had tried to persuade Shifa to join them in a game of barge ball, but she'd made the excuse that she had a headache and needed to be alone. As she wandered around the food hall hoping for a sight of Themba, she wondered where the best place would be for her to write her letter to Nabil and carry out the pressing plan

180

that had formed in her restless head last night. In her wakeful state it had dawned on her that her only hope was to persuade one of the older recruits to get a message to Nabil.

But she needed somewhere private to compose her thoughts. The bowing branches of the survivor tree seemed to beckon her from afar, its glinting leaves appearing through her blurred distant vision like a halo. She had never in her life been near a tree as majestic as this and as she walked towards it down Hope Avenue it came more fully into focus.

She knelt and touched its dark bark as if asking permission to enter the deep hollowed out trunk. *A tree hive! We could snuggle up inside here together and hide away, Daisy!* She felt slightly foolish speaking to faraway Daisy as if she was by her side, but she was not willing to let the comfort Daisy's imagined presence brought her slip away. *I need you and this is our kind of hideaway!* The tree hollow was just about large enough for her to crawl into without knocking her head. Tiny mottle-backed creatures crawled over and tickled her hands – *bark beetles.* Shifa strained her neck upwards at the complex map of thick labyrinthine branches.

'Who should I send the message with?' she whispered. It was not Daisy who answered but the urgent bright call of a bird. *Ki Ki Ki Ki.* Shifa smiled as it dawned on her that Kiki would know where Nabil lived, and even though she didn't live on the compound any more, she could return to take him a message. Once she'd been brave enough to try to break out of Freedom Fields, but that defiant Kiki seemed long gone. It

181

would be hard to get through to her. *No! Stick with your plan!* Ailish was Shifa's trusted friend – she would be the best person to carry the message to Nabil, Shifa reasoned with herself.

Scanning around to make sure her movements were not being recorded, she reached up to the first branch to do what she had dreamed of so many times. *You and me climbing a real tree, Daisy!* Shifa pictured Daisy's once agile movements as she made her way through the thick lower branches, twisting, reaching, steadying herself and balancing. The Feetskins were perfect for climbing, *almost like paws*! As she climbed higher she tested the weight of each branch. Once securely enveloped inside the leafy canopy, her heartbeat steadied a little and she relaxed. She straddled a thick branch, found her balance and then lay back, stretching her spine along it. Close by, the tiny brown *Ki Ki* birds continued to sing and Shifa felt heartened by the brightness of their song.

If only she and Themba could simply fly far away from here. Turning her head to the side, she caught sight of the orchard beyond the polytunnels and spied Luca working there with some cadets. Shifa felt a sharp sting of resentment. There was no way Luca could have earned so many credits that quickly. She guessed that being chosen for your leadership qualities came with its rewards and if she could fully earn Jermaine and Jax's trust she might reap those rewards too. Why Luca had nominated her as a potential leader she could not work out, but maybe she should watch and learn from him. He seemed to know exactly how to play the system for his own benefit.

Beyond the orchard was a river but Shifa strained to see anything beyond a sludgy green and silvery shimmer. It seemed she had reached the limit of her Eyequaliser-controlled vision.

Shifa scoured the farm once again for Themba but there was no sign of him. She would search him out as soon as she had written her note to Nabil. She took her pen and seed packet out of her pocket and carefully unfolded the origami flower into a plain flat piece of paper.

Dear Nabil

The hare in the moon is dead.

They're not going to let you visit us, ever, or tell you where we are. You'll have to come and find us, save us from this. The train is called the Skylight because the only window it has is a tiny strip of Solarmirror on to the sky. We didn't see anything of the Kairos Lands so I can't tell you what we passed along the way, but I know we got off at the last station – stop 12, Pollination Farm.

Me and Themba are separated all day and night. He's started his chanting and whistling again. You should see the list of rules and punishments. There's something called 'confinement' – it sounds like a dungeon. I'm frightened, Nabil. Really frightened, especially for Themba.

The people who run the place are called Jax and

Jermaine. The only other one from our school's an ARK Freedom called Luca – and he's a real bully. They've put him in charge of Themba.

There was a housecarer called Hannah but she left. If you know her, try to speak to her. She saw everything.

There's a huge tree in front of the farm. They call it the survivor tree. It's a cathedral oak like the one you showed us in Baba Suli's book once.

The last thing I know is there's a river that runs near the farm called the River Ore and, from what the older recruits say, I don't think the ocean's that far away.

Please come and find us. I'm sorry I wouldn't say goodbye.

I'm making plans to leave, stowing things away to make a survival kit in case you don't come and we have to go it alone.

We're trying to be brave, hold true, dream, believe, but you can't even imagine how bad it is here, Nabil.

You and Daisy saved me once and now I have to save myself and Themba.

I love you,
Shifa X

P.S. The strangest thing is that it feels like Daisy's by my side all the time.

As she wrote Daisy's name her mournful miaow meandered its way into her heart. Once she had finished writing, she folded the origami flower containing her desperate plea back along its grooved lines. She tucked it into her pocket and cautiously climbed down, her legs dangling before she made the final leap to the ground.

Three days passed. Each night she stood on the toilet seat and kept watch for Themba. Once she caught sight of him walking Barley and another time entering the polytunnels but much later than the others on the night shift. Both times he had been accompanied by cadets and she dared not call out to him. To be so close yet far away from Themba was torture, but it shocked Shifa how quickly she'd learned to put on a blank expression like Luca to get by.

Shifa was on laundry duty, folding uniform after uniform, when Themba appeared at the door. She dropped a pair of overalls and rushed over to him, opening her arms for a hug, but he shied away, peeking warily back at the cadet. 'He says we can have just a moment together because I've done what he said.'

Shifa bit the inside of her lip as her pent-up fears threatened to overwhelm her. She breathed deep and forced herself to smile. 'Remember, I'm never far away, Themb. You might not have seen me but I've seen you walking the dog at night. Look up there to the barn and I'll be waving to you from the window every night,' Shifa whispered. A faint smile played at the corner of Themba's lips. Shifa stroked his sallow, sunken cheeks.

'Is it a friendly dog?' Shifa asked.

'Friendliest creature here.' Themba nodded.

'That's good.' At least Themba was finding comfort somewhere. Shifa swallowed the lump in her throat. 'How are you sleeping, Themb?' She ran her fingers through his tangle of curls. 'Have you still got my hair?'

Themba shook his head, peering over his shoulder at the cadet and lowering his voice. 'Luca and Jermaine took it away . . . till I do what they say.' Themba set to whistling under his breath.

'What do they want you to do, Themb?' Shifa asked.

Themba bit his lip and raised his head towards the farmhouse.

'Look after the Lona lady, like Papa told us he looked after Baba Suli when he disappeared into his story-hive mind.' Themba knocked against the side of his head and set up a shrill whistle.

'Shut up!' the cadet hissed.

Themba shoved his fist firmly into his own mouth.

Shifa signalled her skep-heart but felt as if her own heart would break as the cadet led Themba away.

Chapter Twenty-One

'One hydration stop away from our last shift – ever! I never thought we'd get here,' Ailish announced, embracing Chirelle. They clung to each other, rocking back and forth.

Ailish had forewarned Shifa. If all went well she and Chirelle would definitely be leaving the farm today and travelling back to Kairos City. Kiki and Zeb would leave tomorrow. The thought of life on the farm without Ailish was grim, but it had also offered a new seed of hope. Shifa had decided to wait till the last minute before asking her to take the letter. If she didn't have too much time to think about it she might feel pressurised in the emotion of the moment. Shifa gathered armfuls of sunflowers and placed them in a stack. Chirelle came over and handed Shifa lengths of metallic insulation cloth that unravelled into large blankets.

'Keeps the flowers at a constant temperature.' Chirelle demonstrated, swathing the yellow heads tenderly as if they

187

were the soft skulls of newborn babies. 'We could have done with some of these blankets ourselves last winter. You wouldn't believe how cold it can get here with the ocean and river breezes.'

Shifa was determined – *Whatever happens, me and Themba will not be here by winter.*

Shifa helped Chirelle for a while and then went to the store to get another pile of insulation. From the cupboard she scanned for the opticare drone and spotted it hovering over Chirelle. Shifa stowed two blankets inside her uniform. If all else failed and she had to find a way to break out with Themba, she would at least have a means to keep warm at night.

During the end-of-shift tidy, Shifa waited until the opticare had passed then slid a pair of scissors, some hydration sachets and tweezers into the breast pocket of her overalls. She felt strangely elated; whatever happened she would not give in and let Freedom Fields control her. For now she would store her collection of survival things high up in the branches of the survivor tree.

'You'll come and find me before you go, won't you? To say goodbye?'

Ailish nodded. 'I'll wait for you by the survivor tree at recreation.'

*

The *Ki Ki* bird sang brightly as Shifa kept watch from within the branches of the survivor tree, waiting for Ailish. She held the seed packet letter in her hand.

To Shifa's surprise, it was Kiki who approached along the sapling path, watering the trees and humming away as she ambled towards the survivor tree. Kiki set down her can and curled up inside the hollow trunk. For a moment Shifa thought to call out to her, but as she began to climb down, Kiki's humming became words, words of a song like a nursery rhyme Shifa vaguely remembered Kiki singing to them once, but back then the tune had been sunny. Now it was mournful, not childish at all, just unspeakably sad.

'You see I love you dearly, dearly, and I want you to
    love me.
You are my honey, honeysuckle, I am the bee.
And he vowed just like the bee,
I will build a home for thee—'

Kiki broke off as Shifa dropped from the last branch to the ground.

'Ailish said I'd find you here. She gave me this – for you.' Kiki took a note out of her pocket and handed it to Shifa. Her heart sank as she took it from Kiki and opened it. In the envelope was a pass with the words 'Emergency Exit' written on it. Her hands trembled as she began to read.

Dear Shifa,

Sorry I didn't get to say goodbye. But remember what I've
told you. Just keep your head down and the time will pass.

And in case something kicks off . . . Hannah left this
under my pillow . . . a way out of the sleep barn through
her room. She hated us being locked in, and at least
you'd get everyone out if you needed to. Keep it hidden.

There's no escape from the farm so don't even think
about running away. I've known four who've tried and
none of us made it!

Maybe see you on the other side?

Ailish X

Shifa read over the note again and crumpled it in her hands.
Swallowing down her crushing disappointment, she studied
Kiki's face – maybe there was still one way.

Shifa crouched down next to Kiki. 'You do remember our
family from the compound, don't you? You used to sing us
that song to get us to sleep!'

Kiki shrugged and hugged her knees closer into her chest.

'I was hoping . . .' Shifa peered out of the hollow, checking
around for surveillance and that no one had snuck up on
them, then took the flower-shaped seed packet from her
pocket and offered it to Kiki.

'Paper flower? Is it for me?' Kiki asked.

'It contains a few seedlings for Nabil.' She smiled. 'You remember where we live? I know it's asking a lot but could you give it to him, when you get home?'

Shifa gently placed the flower in Kiki's palm, and for a moment her heart raced as she watched Kiki seal her fingers around it. Then, as if entertaining the *thought* of taking it had sapped all her strength, she let it slip from her hand and watched, mesmerised while the bark beetles crawl over it. She seemed far, far away again as she began to sing a song Nabil used to sing and hum on the Flower Tracks – 'Where have all the flowers gone?' Nabil called it *a song to make you question*. As Shifa listened Kiki's voice merged in her mind to become Nabil's. She could not give up hope. It was worth another try. As Kiki came to the last mournful line and took to humming the tune Shifa approached her gently, in an equally soft and fragile voice.

'I understand. It's too risky. I shouldn't have asked for you to take the letter, but will you find Nabil and tell him what you know? Tell him we can't stay here?' Kiki continued to blank her and an edge of desperation crept into Shifa's voice.

Kiki crawled out of the hollow on her hands and knees.

'Please? Or just say, "The hare in the moon is dead". Say that – can you tell him that, Kiki? You can't get in any trouble for that – no one else will know what it means,' Shifa pleaded.

But Kiki ignored her as if she could no longer hear her. *What has Freedom Fields done to this girl?* Behind her the *Ki Ki* bird called insistently.

Shifa flattened her hand against her locket. If no one ever took the risk of telling the truth, the lies would just go on and on and the life blood of more children would be sucked out of them. Shifa could not let that happen to her and Themba, or to Yara and the others without at least trying to do something to change things. She unclasped her hands and inspected the dried, bloodied crusts that had formed on her fingers.

Shifa sighed deeply and placed her seed packet back in her pocket. The strains of Kiki's songs refused to be blocked out – *And he vowed just like the bee, I will build a home for thee . . .*

What kind of home was Freedom Fields building? What kind of family? Her gut twisted and her mind reached out for Daisy, who she found prowling along an impossibly high wall. She crouched now, readying herself and building up the courage to jump. 'Be careful, Daisy,' Shifa whispered, but in her mind's eye Daisy turned to her, crouched low and leapt. Shifa held her breath. She too would hold her nerve, watch and wait until she could find a way to leap, break her and Themba out of here and return home with the truth.

Shifa crept out of bed and into the bathroom as she'd done at this time every night hoping to catch a few glimpses of Themba as he clocked on to his night shift. The day after laundry duty he had turned to the window and waved and she'd felt a little comforted – at least he knew she was thinking of him.

Tonight she held her breath as she clearly heard Luca's voice. She stood on her tiptoes and followed Luca, Themba and Barley's walk along the path below.

'Themba's too tired to work tonight. It's not fair! Why do I have to look after Lona *and* work in the tunnels?' Themba was crying. To hear him refer to himself by his name troubled Shifa deeply. Whenever he'd taken to doing this before it had always been a sure sign that he was feeling lost.

'Your chores shouldn't take you that long. What were you doing all that time up there anyway?' asked Luca.

'Just talking and drawing,' Themba said. ' "Don't leave me on my own," she bawls and barks at me! It wasn't my fault. She *told* me to hide under the bed.'

'Well Lona's not in charge here, is she? Jermaine gets angry too – he'll put you in confinement if you're not careful,' said Luca firmly.

Shifa heard Themba's voice rise in panic.

'I can't go into the dark,' he yelped.

'Then take the old woman her food, do the chores you've been told to, and don't be late for your shift. You should think yourself lucky that you're on a shorter shift than everyone else.'

They reached the polytunnel entrance and a cadet prised Barley's lead from Themba and walked the dog back to the house.

Their voices faded as they entered the polytunnels and

Shifa's heart began to race. Themba wasn't cut out to be the carer of someone in such need. What if he said the wrong thing and upset her? What had happened to the boy Zakir who went missing after he'd visited Lona? Had he been hurt, and Jermaine and Jax covered it up? She knew now for sure that she couldn't protect Themba here – time was running out.

Chapter Twenty-Two

Shifa had studied how Luca played the game of getting Jermaine and Jax's trust. The first thing she'd done was stop asking questions, but it had not stopped the endless days and sleepless nights dragging on, feeling more like months than weeks. She had collected everything she could think of that they might need, and doubted whether a single thing more would fit in her rucksack when she was ready to transfer the contents of her hideaway in the survivor tree. *I'm prepared but I still don't have any idea how to get out of here*, she thought. It was almost two weeks since Kiki had left and Shifa had to accept what she'd known in her heart all along – the broken girl hadn't had the courage to find Nabil. He would be here by now if she had.

Every day Shifa grew more vigilant and fearful of being discovered as she climbed up into the survivor tree. Over the last few days the song of the *Ki Ki* birds had ceased to sound sweet but had morphed into a new alarm that echoed

Themba's high-pitched whistle. *Fly, fly, fly*, they chorused. Her mind was set.

Her strategy of keeping her head down worked. By the next Friday her and Luca's names were at the top of the commendations list.

'Congratulations! You have Friday free and a week-long recreation pass to the orchard!' the screen in the food hall read.

'We need more workers like you and Luca,' Jermaine said, appearing at Shifa's shoulder – *so creepy*, the way he and Jax managed to sneak up on you without being seen. 'This is your reward! Here's your orchard privilege pass. Your efforts are repaid with real freedom in there. No opticares, nothing! Just tap the pass on the gate lock for access. If you admit anyone else it will be confiscated. And of course, should your excellent standards drop, it can be removed from you before the week's out. Understood?'

Shifa nodded. 'Thank you.' A genuine smile appeared on her lips, but then she quickly rebuked herself, feeling ashamed. She was already falling into their traps. That's what they wanted – to make her feel important so she'd help control the others. It was terrifying, even with her plan to escape as soon as she found a way out, how this crumb of kindness *did* make her feel good, like she mattered to someone, even Jax and Jermaine! She thought of how Nabil had made her feel valued every day, not through force but by care and love.

'Do me a favour, Shifa,' said Jermaine, 'water the seedlings in the greenhouse!'

The idea that Jermaine knew and cared about plants was so weird. How could she and Jermaine have anything in common?

'Oh, and if by some miracle one of those hens finally lays an egg, bring it back, will you.'

As Shifa walked past the entrance of the polytunnels and headed to the orchard, she felt a tiny bubble of anticipation grow in her. *Hens!* From the survivor tree, as her eyes had grown able to see more distance detail, she'd *thought* she'd picked out some small red creatures moving around in there.

She approached the green door encased in a high brick wall that looked ancient. *Just like the wall I keep seeing you walking along, Daisy!* Bright blue and purple flowers grew between the cracks in the mortar. Shifa tapped the card on a screen next to the door and the heavy lock clunked open. She breathed a sigh of relief mixed with guilt that she was to spend the day outside, but she had convinced herself that the more freedom she got, the closer she might come to finding a way out of here.

Tentatively she peered inside and was relieved to find that she was alone. She stepped under the brick arch, closed the door and leaned against it. The centre of the garden was crammed full of bushes with arching branches bowing low with purple and white flowers dancing with white butterflies – like the the bush she had managed to grow on the Flower Tracks and then worried that the masses of white butterflies would give their secret garden away. It sometimes made Shifa feel sad that something that gentle and beautiful was so short-lived. But watching them dance, surrounded by beauty, food and calm bolstered her. Themba's mama Tia and her own mama had lived short lives and no matter how hard it had been, at least they'd lived a free life they'd believed in.

Shifa pressed her sore nails and reminded herself why she was here. *You have to find a way out. And now's your chance to collect some seeds to take back to Nabil. Bring something beautiful back home – not leave it shut away for a few people. You can share your seed store with him and Daisy!* she told herself. Against the high wall to her left were two old-fashioned wooden-framed greenhouses closed in with Solarmirrors.

To her right was an oblong of freshly turned soil. A fork and a hoe waited for a gardener to till the earth. Shifa placed her hand on the wooden handle. Was Nabil at the Flower Tracks right now? Perhaps he'd taken Daisy with him, carrying her in Themba's carrier on the back of his bike? As she turned the fine soil she smiled at the thought of Daisy keeping Nabil company.

A pathway of tripod canes ran from one edge of the tilled soil to the other, waiting for the delicate shoots to grow tall and spread. She trailed the hoe along, forming a furrow, and laid it on the ground. Shifa took her paper flower from her pocket, scanning the garden for opticares. Strangely, she had believed Jermaine that there was no surveillance in here. Maybe everyone needed their own secret flower track, even Jermaine? She began her collection of pips, seeds and flower heads. She dug up a tiny bulb of a white star-shaped flower she'd never seen before. These flowers were nothing like the overpowering lilies or birds of paradise of the polytunnels. She felt a sense of pride that even in Kairos City she had managed to find some of the wild flowers and plants that were here, but there were a lot that she had never seen before too. Like this bright fiery-orange head, a little like a daisy but bobbing on a longer stalk.

Shifa walked further along towards a cluster of well-tended young apple trees. She strained her neck up at the high walls – perhaps they would protect the young trees when a new storm hit.

She bent down and picked up a fallen apple – a small green fruit, slightly bruised. She rubbed her thumb over the smooth skin, then took a bite, knowing it was only half ripe, but enjoying the bitter-sweetness of something that had grown in sunlight in the open air.

'Thank you, tree,' she whispered.

She removed the pips, placed them in her seed packet and walked over to a small brick shed. She peered through the milky windows to discover shelves with neatly arranged apples. Beyond the fruit trees she discovered a brick well, a bucket attached at the side on a chain. She twisted the handle and lowered the bucket down and down until she heard a hollow splash and felt it grow heavy as it filled. Slowly she winched it up and unhooked it, filling the watering can next to the well. She returned to water Jermaine's seedlings and made another journey to the well to fill the bucket. Next, she watered the young plants whose delicate tendrils clung to the canes. She paused to enjoy the warmth of the sun on her face but guilt surged through her once more. Where was Themba now? *Please don't let it be*, she willed, *that Themba is locked away in the dark while I am enjoying all this light.*

A family of rust-brown hens wandered past her, pecking their way through the orchard. How strange to be so close to them! How Themba would love to see all this. Enchanted by their plumped-up feathers, Shifa followed them past the apple trees to a low wooden coop – no sign of eggs. Shifa scanned the orchard – it might seem like a wildlife haven but maybe the hens could sense that this was not a safe place to lay. There were more *Ki Ki* birds here but as they flitted around their song did not sing of freedom in Shifa's mind. She followed the flight path of a bird that perched on the wall beside the coop. It was joined by another and another and another, as if they were leading her . . .

Shifa pulled back a heavy tangle of vines and discovered a door half hidden behind them, but otherwise identical to the one she'd entered through with her pass. This must be the way that led down to the River Ore. Judging by the undisturbed plant growth, it could not have been used for some time. She took out her privilege pass and swiped it around but did not find a keypad. *How will we ever get out of here?* she whispered. Above her the *Ki Ki* birds took flight over the high wall. Crouching in among the vines Shifa leaned her back to the door, closed her eyes and was hypnotised by the constant flow of the river that seemed to be calling her name.

Shiiiifa, Shiiiifa, Shiiiifa!

Chapter Twenty-Three

'Due to essential Kairos Land-wide economies we will not be replacing Housecarer Hannah. Instead of weekday recreation you'll be taking up some of her extra duties,' announced Jermaine. He was greeted by a general groan. 'From now on Luca here will be in charge of pastoral care and weekend supervision.' Jermaine pointed to the golden star that flashed from Luca's uniform. 'Luca's already proved himself, helping to settle some of our more *reluctant* recruits.' He briefly glanced at Shifa. 'I'm pleased to say there are those of you who are showing promise and working towards joining Luca in transitioning to prefect positions very shortly.' At least her plan of gaining trust was working. *The more freedom I have the easier it will be to get us out of here if and when I find a way.*

She had kept her eyes trained on the window above as she ate but saw no sign of Themba, Barley or Lona. After breakfast Jermaine informed them that this weekend they were free to wander around the farm but once again there was no offer to go down to the river that every day seemed to beckon her louder and louder. Today the sleep barns had been left open all day, and Shifa slipped inside the boys' barn when no one was looking. She crept among a few occupied beds in which blankets rose and fell as night workers slept soundly. She peered at their heads and feet but there was no sign of Themba.

'What are *you* doing in here?' Luca appeared from the bathroom, making Shifa jump.

'Came to see Themba!' she whispered.

Luca stepped closer. 'Well, that's his bed you're standing by and as you can see he's not here!'

'Where is he then?' Shifa asked, shocked to see her strand of hair on his pillow. She eyed Luca suspiciously. 'You gave it back then?'

You take it off him again and I'll have to let people know about you needing a baby blanket to help get to sleep. OK? was what she wanted to say, but she restrained herself.

'Thank you for that.'

Luca nodded. 'You should go.'

She ascended the survivor tree at speed, Feetskins padding and clinging to knots in the branches. *I'm almost as good as you used to be at climbing, Daisy!* She smiled as she climbed until she reached her favourite branch and was completely hidden by the golden leaves. But how long would it be before the leaves began to fall and her hiding place was exposed? She placed the torch and gas lighter from the kitchen into the nook that was now full of her 'finds'.

This is not stealing, Nabil. It's survival, she thought, hearing him lecture her about honesty. The nook contained a food store, hydration sachets, water holders, a small bowl and sunflower blankets . . . and now the thing she'd had her eye on, the kitchen gas lighter, a means to make fire. If she could find a way out, she and Themba would have enough supplies to survive at least for a few days.

She climbed higher and scrunched her eyes as the ground swayed below. At least her distance vision was improving a little. In the orchard the hens were decipherable as hens now and not soft brick smudges. The power of the Eyequaliser lenses was fading and as they did it felt to Shifa that her own power was returning.

Beyond the glistening river she could just make out a mountain peak that rose steeply from lush green ground. She closed her eyes and felt a light breeze lift the hair off her neck. It had been almost a month now since they'd been here. Had it grown a little already?

'Oi!'

Shifa's foot slipped, she tilted dangerously and had to cling hard to a branch to steady herself. Her legs flailed till her Feetskins finally found a thin branch to grip.

'That tree's protected. You're not allowed to climb up

there.' Shifa gasped at the sound of Luca's voice and peered down to where he stood with Themba. Had he been tracking her movements?

On her way down, she pressed her hand into the hollow, pushing her survival store deeper into the nook.

'What are you? A cat or something!' Luca snapped.

She ignored him, jumped down and reached out to hug Themba but he pulled away and crawled into the tree hollow. Shifa stared at his face and the new purple egg-shaped bruise on his forehead.

'You and me need to talk,' Luca said, beckoning her to move out of Themba's earshot. 'You've got to find a way to get through to him. He keeps being late for his shift. He's getting obsessed with old Lona upstairs and I can't get him away from her.'

'Where did he get that bruise?' Shifa asked.

Luca shook his head. 'I don't know – he won't talk to me and he won't hear a word said against Lona. But you've got to make him understand. If he carrries on like this it won't just be confinement for a day or two . . .'

'Is that where he's been?' Shifa whispered.

Luca nodded gravely.

'Now they're turning me into a Crow, having to guard him!'

In her mind Shifa kept her fist firmly in her mouth but longed to spit the words out. *Can't you see! That is exactly what you're going to be one day – that's what they're training you up for!*

'I'll talk to him,' Shifa said, hating the fact that Luca knew more of what was going on with Themba than she did.

'Do something to make him start behaving, and stop his whistling and chanting, or things are going to get a lot worse for him,' Luca snapped and strode off.

Shifa saw red. 'Is that a threat? You'll make a good Crow!' Shifa called after him, cringing at herself as the words flew from her. Why did she have to be so hot-headed?

Luca paused for a moment. 'You think *I'm* in charge here, Shifa?' He shook his head and walked on.

Shifa crept softly to the hollow that was already echoing with Themba's voice. He sounded strangely disconnected, like Kiki. *How many children in need has this tree sheltered?* Shifa wondered as she laid her ear against the ancient trunk and listened.

'Lona says the River Ore's pure gold and beauty can't be bought or sold. Lona says there was once a wood, and in that wood flew all that was good. There the sheltered hands might store the precious species of the land – the ash, the oak, the beech, the pine. You think they're all locked in my mind, but Themba, there could still be time.' He recited lines, taking on the strains of old Lona's voice as if he'd memorised every word she said.

'Lona says Papa grew skep-heart hives to keep the sweet memory of bees alive.'

He took a stick and began jabbing and scratching at the ground.

'Themba!' Shifa knocked on the trunk. 'Can I come in?'

When Themba didn't answer she crawled in anyway and sat a little way from him.

'Does Lona always talk in rhymes?' Shifa asked.

Themba shook his head and drew a picture of a boat in the leaf mould covering the ground.

'It's Themba who makes the rhyme store, so I can remember more and more.' Shifa snuggled closer.

'Themb? What do you talk about with Lona?' Shifa asked gently, peering at his bruise.

'Told you! Golden memories.' Themba did not look up but drew sails on his boat. 'Once beyond the orchard door, there's a boat to sail on the River Ore . . .'

Themba dropped the stick and reached out to Shifa and she held him close.

'I'm doing like Papa did for Baba Suli when his memory store leaked out, listening to Lona's old stories. Lona's lonely. Themba too.' Tears welled in Themba's eyes.

'I miss you, Themb.' Shifa's chest ached. How good it was to feel him close, to hear his voice. She placed her hand over her heart and found the locket.

'You need to tell me, Themba. How did you get that bruise?'

Themba jabbed at the boat and scored it out. In its place he drew a face with angry eyes and a mouth twisted in rage.

'Who is that?' Shifa asked as he stabbed the image in the eye. 'Luca?'

Themba withdrew into himself again and began whistling and scratching at his arm. Above her the *Ki Ki* birds set up an inconsolable screech.

'Shifa! Themba!' Luca called, appearing a little way along the path. 'Jermaine wants everyone to assemble in the sleep barns. Someone's been stealing.'

Shifa's breath came in sharp, dark, shards – had she been spotted taking the gas lighter?

'Got a message for you!' Themba whispered as he crawled out. 'Lona says to tell your sister, the secret key to the river door is hidden in the apple store.'

'Hurry up, you two! Run, Themba!' Luca ordered and Themba did as ordered.

Shifa's head spun. *What! What did you say?*

Chapter Twenty-Four

A stony-faced Jermaine and four cadets were lined up in the food hall, arms crossed, waiting for Themba and Shifa. When they were seated Jermaine ordered Luca by his side.

'It has come to our attention that Freedom Fields property has gone missing,' said Jermaine solemnly. 'Unless the culprit owns up right now, we will conduct a thorough inspection of the sleep barns.'

Shifa stared straight ahead, willing her face not to betray the panic that was rising in her. Had Luca been watching her all this time as she built and hid her survival store?

As they filed towards the sleep barns, Shifa desperately searched her mind for a way to hide the seed packet before Jermaine found it. Then it struck her. Now a thief was suspected and Luca had seen her climbing the tree, she had to find a new hiding place for her survival kit straight away – maybe in the orchard?

Luca and the cadets rifled through shelves and under mattresses and placed banned items in a tray – mainly food.

Under Miri and Blessing's bed a cadet discovered a torch but they refused to say which one of them had taken it. Shifa had watched their friendship grow stronger every day. They stood together, chins jutting forward, refusing to give each other away.

'Right! Now empty your pockets, all of you!' Luca stood and watched as Shifa felt inside her uniform. The seed packet was fairly flat – she might get away with it.

'I haven't got anything!' Shifa said, holding her breath.

'Nothing except this!' the cadet said, removing Shifa's seed packet.

Luca stepped forward and held out his hand. 'I'll take that to show Jermaine.'

The cadet handed it to Luca and carried on her search. Shifa desperately tried to contain her rage as the cadet took a photomemory of Soraya's family. From Pooja a hand-sewn patchwork piece of material and from Yara her miniature doll. *Why are you taking those? They're allowed their comforters – why do you have to be so cruel?* Shifa wanted to scream and grab the doll back as she watched Yara crumple.

'These will be returned to you when your dorm-mates own up to who's been stealing!' a cadet explained calmly, shooting pointed looks at Miri and Blessing. Miri's chin began to shake and she stepped forward.

'It was me!' she whispered.

'Glad you saw the light! Come with me!' a cadet snapped and led Miri out of the dorm. 'Check their wardrobes too!' the cadet ordered Luca. 'Give them back their comforters before she deafens us all with her blubbing!' The cadet gestured to Yara who was face down, sobbing into her pillow.

Luca left the tray on the bed and signalled for them to take back their things, but as expected Shifa's seed packet was not amongst them. Shifa returned Yara's cloth doll to her. 'Shh now,' Shifa soothed, watching Luca's every move as he approached the cubicle where Shifa's daisy dress was stored. As he unfolded it, Shifa felt an uncontrollable wave of nausea rise in her at the humiliation of Luca's prying and she ran to the bathroom, reaching the sink just in time. Her whole body shook as she clung to the edge of the basin and Yara came through to comfort her, placing a hand on her back.

'You're all right, Shifa. It's OK. Luca and the cadets have gone now.'

Shifa cleaned the sink and walked through to the wardrobe to find her daisy dress scrunched on the back of her shelf. She lay on her bed and Yara climbed in next to her. *If I don't get out of here soon, there'll be nothing left of me.* The tears rolled down her cheeks and Yara placed a comforting arm around her shoulder.

'You want to cuddle my Ya Ya?' Yara asked, offering Shifa

her doll. Shifa shook her head.

Her mind was wracked with questions. Would Luca open the origami flower and find her letter? How long would he take to use it as ammunition against her or Themba? She felt like a tiny *Ki Ki* bird with a broken wing that, for a fleeting moment, had dared to believe that she might one day fly.

Chapter Twenty-Five

Themba's chant had whirled around her mind all night. *'The key to the river door . . . hidden in the apple store.'*

How is it that ideas that burn so clear and bright through the darkness of the night can fade into dying embers by the morning?

Here she was now, desperately clinging to truth keys in Themba's rhymes. Chants committed to his memory from stories of an old woman who had lost her memory. *And I told you off, Papa, for dreaming up the hare in the moon and all your hive and skep-heart stories.*

A faintly glowing ember of hope was better than nothing. She supposed that was what Nabil had tried to instil in them, and like it or not, it had worked.

But if Luca revealed her letter folded in the flower packet, she would never get another pass to the orchard, and she would never know for sure . . . So when the others headed for the food hall she carried on along the path and scanned her pass in to the orchard where, along with the sun, the butterflies had not yet risen.

Shifa ran her fingers along every shelf of the apple store and found nothing but a few wizened old cores. She bashed the empty shelves in frustration at her own naivety. The shelf collapsed, sending the apples cascading and loosening a brick in the wall. Shifa bent down to fix it but as she tipped the shelf upright . . . a large rusted key fell into her hands.

Dream, believe, imagine, dream, believe, imagine, dare to dream, dare to believe, dare to imagine . . .

Holding the old key in her hands, her heart racing, she pulled back the vine tendrils that led to the river door and Daisy's insistent wail rose up from behind it.

Every nerve ending was tensed as Shifa placed the key in the lock and twisted it with all her might. It would not shift. *Daisy, Daisy*, Shifa called and Daisy cried back bold and true. Shifa pulled and twisted the old key until the rust turned to powder in the lock and something gave. The door creaked on its heavy hinges and opened.

Daisy! Shifa whispered, but Daisy and her piercing voice were gone, replaced by the insistent call of the river whispering her name.

Ahead of her was a meadow of dry yellow grass, dotted here and there with splashes of wild flowers – cornflowers, daisies and red— Were those poppies? Here was a meadow like the ones she had dreamed she and Themba would run freely through every day at Freedom Fields. Her eye followed the incline of the land upwards to a small rise. *And over that hill is the river Ore*, on which Themba had drawn a boat. Shifa could almost smell the fresh rushing water. She felt her legs jittery and ready to sprint. If it was not for Themba she would make a run for it right now. But one thing she had learned from Freedom Fields was that there would be no freedom for her if Themba was not free too.

Pushing the heavy door closed she locked it with difficulty, pulled back the vines and made her breathless way across the orchard to the apple store. She had just replaced the key behind the brick when she heard the orchard door open and Jermaine and Jax walk in with Barley. Shifa crouched down but had no time to fully close the store-shed door. Her legs cramped but she managed to remain hidden as Jermaine and Jax moved quietly among the beds, watering and tending the plants.

Shifa held her breath as Barley began sniffing close by. She shrank away but the dog brushed its nose against her face and licked her cheek.

'Come, Barley. Don't you go bruising those apples!'

Now Jermaine and Jax were nearby she could see them through a crack of light in the wood and hear every word they said. Her heart drummed heavy in her chest.

'Feeling a bit calmer now?' Jax asked Jermaine as she linked arms with him.

'How can I be?'

'The whole place could have burned down. We still haven't found that gas lighter either,' Jax said, sifting soil in a sieve over the seedling beds. 'Make sure you and the cadets tell the ARK Government straight. We can't carry on like this. Why are they calling the cadets back anyway?'

'Outlanders getting out of hand, apparently.'

'Well we can't cope without them. You tell them the recruits are working night and day as it is. It's getting dangerous – they all need a break. I feel like we're all in prison. I need some free time!'

'You're not the only one,' Jermaine snapped and banged the orchard door behind him.

Chapter Twenty-Six

At breakfast a whisper of excitement caught at one end of the table, quickly growing in volume and force like a wave. Yara ran up to Shifa and wrapped her arms around her neck. 'We've got the whole morning off chores! Jax says she's taking us new recruits to see the river!'

Shifa hugged Yara close. It was so good to see her smiling after watching her night after night wracked by nightmares.

'She looks nice today!' Yara said as Jax breezed in. She wore her hair loose and her shiny black curls cascaded down her back. Shifa felt a sudden pang of jealousy as she reached up to her own cropped hair.

'What are you waiting for? Grab a packed lunch from the kitchen and a towel, and line up!' Jax called to them over the din.

Shifa had never seen or heard such excitement on the farm before. Was it always like this when Jermaine went away? But any momentary joy she felt vanished when Luca strode over and sat down opposite her. No sign of Themba. Was Luca going to choose this moment to use his power?

Luca's eyes were pollen-sore and he had dark circles under them. He lowered his voice to almost a whisper. 'Themba lashed out again when we tried to get him to leave Lona but ... He's been placed in confinement for the whole weekend.' He pointed to the window above but there was no sign of Lona. 'Because he missed his whole shift.'

Shifa nodded slowly, attempting to take in the horror of this news. Now she knew for sure that she could not wait another day. She had to take that leap beyond the river door, break into confinement and spring him free. She eyed Luca – she would have to try and get him to trust her.

Luca cast around and reached into his pocket, took out her flower seed packet and slid it to Shifa under the table. As far as she could tell it had not been unfolded and the flower head was still full of her finds. 'You know you're not supposed to collect seeds,' he said before walking away.

'Smile!' shouted Jax, taking a photomemory of the line-up of recruits outside the food hall. The anticipation of freedom made their faces glow and genuine happiness was captured as the new recruits anticipated a day off work. Shifa refused to smile and formed her hands into a skep-heart. If Nabil was ever sent this, he would find no Themba, her sadness, and their signal of love and longing to be back together on the Flower Tracks.

Her heart ached at the thought of Themba alone in a dark

cellar while everyone else was to go on a picnic outing. The grateful excitement of her fellow recruits continued as most of them were discovering the orchard for the first time. Yara clapped her hands in joy when she spotted the hens.

'Fulfil your quotas and you'll get to come and help us garden,' said Jax. 'Luca and Shifa have gained the first passes this week.'

'Luca!' Jax called. Shifa turned around sharply.

'Who's with Themba?' Shifa asked as he passed.

'No one!' he muttered. 'I need a day off too! I'm not his carer! Why don't you volunteer. He's your brother, not mine!'

Shifa ignored the accusatory tone in Luca's voice. The thought of Themba trembling and alone in the dark of confinement made her all the more determined. She must be alert to every possibility, sharpen her wits, form a strategy. Her job today was to make sure she staked out an escape route.

'I haven't done this for a while!' Jax smiled as she held back the vines of the river door, like a curtain. She loosened a brick and scanned a panel hidden inside. So the rusty key must once have belonged to Lona; perhaps in the secret crevices of her mind she had remembered placing it there long ago – a secret key locked away even from herself, until Themba had somehow sparked memories of it.

Their group quietened as they took in the sweep of the grassy meadow. The sound of the river's flow grew louder as they reached the brow of the hill. The sky beyond was a cloudless powder blue. Jax clicked away, making photomemories as the recruits scattered.

At that moment the bright midmorning sun shimmered off the water and welcomed them all with its dazzling golden light. There was a loud splash as someone threw a stone in, sending up a cascade of laughter, squeals of delight.

The river curved in a wide arc as it ran along the bottom of the meadow, but the water was low and had shrunk back from the steep banks. Through the shallows the sandy base of the river was clearly visible.

Shifa began to stroll along the bank, testing where the boundary lay, but jumped backwards as she picked up a powerful clicking, fizzing energy.

'Stand back immediately, Shifa! You too, Luca, or you'll get a shock!' Jax warned. 'We're on the boundary of the farm here where the sensors are at their most vicious. Now listen up everyone. The beam follows the line of the ditch straight over the river, so don't stray too close to the line in the water either.'

Shifa backed away from the carnage of hares and rabbits that lay on their backs.

There must be some way out of here . . .

'Wear your Feetskins for paddling – they'll keep you dry and warm. The river's low but still wade in only to calf height, everyone. Yes! That's even for swimmers! I don't care if you're a Kairos Lands champion!'

The recruits quickly unzipped their sleeves and trouser

legs, making their uniform into the shorts they wore in the polytunnels.

Shifa cautiously waded into the shallow water. The grip of her Feetskins allowed her to feel her way over the shingle and stones without fear of slipping or being cut. She tremored as the ice-cold water flowed against her ankles and calves. Shifa closed her eyes and imagined Nabil taking one hand and Themba the other and wading peacefully away.

A chill cry cleaved the air. Shifa's head jolted towards the sound. She gasped in panic to see Yara in the middle of the river, the current rippling fast around her. She jerked her head wildly, as if she was being pulled under.

Without thinking Shifa waded in up to her waist, then felt Luca rushing past her and diving into a deep dark pool. Now both Luca and Yara were being tugged along, barely staying on their feet. Shifa gazed beyond them to where she caught sight of a flash of red on the water's surface, floating closer. A boat, hidden in the reeds. As it bobbed it tugged Yara further underwater towards it. Whatever she was caught on was attached to that boat. 'Luca Freedom! Shifa Aziz! OUT of the water now!' screamed Jax.

On the shore, the sensor fizzed wildly as Luca emerged on the other side, closer to the boat. In his arms he held a spluttering, panic-stricken Yara. Luca trod water and struggled to keep her head above the surface. 'It's not even that deep. I can feel the bottom but her legs are caught in a net!' he shouted, his face contorted in panic.

Jax stood on the bank barking orders into her watch screen. 'Yes! It's an emergency. Just get here NOW! Hold on! Stay where you are. Help's on its way!' Jax yelled. But once again Luca ignored her and dived back under the water. As he did, Yara too disappeared. Shifa held her hand over her mouth – *please let Yara survive.* It seemed like an age before Luca reappeared on the near side of the sensor, propelling Yara up and out of the water. Her mouth gulped air and spurted out water.

'Move!' Shifa swung round to see two Crows from the front gates wading into the water, shoving past her. She stood frozen to the spot as they dived into the river, showering water in every direction, grabbing a sobbing Yara out of Luca's arms and carrying her to safety.

Shifa clasped her hands against her locket where it lay ice cold against her heart. Rough hands now grabbed her by her collar, dragged her to the bank and finally she began to breathe again as she knelt down to her friend.

'The net caught me, Shifa!' Yara spluttered. 'It was pulling me under.' She pointed to where she had emerged on the other side of the sensor.

The Crow glared at Jax. 'What were you thinking, bringing them here when we're so short-staffed? It's not safe. She could have died and then you'd have had the ARK Governmnent to answer to.'

The colour drained from Jax's face. 'I thought . . .

The river's so low . . .' Jax pulled her hair from her face and her hands shook uncontrollably. She seemed in shock herself.

The Crow placed his hand over his wrist screen to muffle his voice. 'Install opticare in the orchard. Permanently seal that door. OK. First thing tomorrow.'

Yara clung to Shifa all the way back to the orchard. Shifa held her close and trembled too as her mind and heart surged with one idea – *Tonight is our only chance to make a bid for freedom.*

'This should help you sleep, calm your nerves.' Jax pacified Yara as she administered medicine and instructed Shifa to keep Yara company till she fell asleep. Yara was already growing drowsy as Shifa helped her shower and change into her pyjamas.

'When you were under the water, Yara, did you get stunned? Is that what made you panic?' Shifa asked, as they curled up together.

Yara shook her head. 'I had my feet on the bottom but then the net caught me. I was drowning . . . Luca saved me.' Her eyelids were growing heavy as she spoke.

Yara's lips still trembled and retained a tinge of blue from the cold. 'Yara, I'm going to try and get out of here tonight, with Themba!'

Yara's eyes shot open and she clung to Shifa's arm. 'Can you take me?'

Shifa bit her lip. She'd known this question would come. 'We're going under the water sensor.'

'Can you and Themba swim?' Yara whispered.

Shifa shook her head.

Voicing her plan made it seem a thousand times more desperate.

'No . . . but I think I know a way.'

Yara closed her eyes and the tears streamed down her cheeks.

'You're my best friend and you're going to die,' she whispered.

And with Yara's words, Shifa's resolve began to slip away from her. Today, standing helplessly watching her friend drown and being unable to do anything to help had been one of the worst moments of Shifa's life. And now she was going to risk not only her own life but Themba's too. If Yara had panicked in the water, Themba would be a hundred times worse . . .

'I've got to try, Yara. This is the key to the door in the back of the barn. It was Hannah's – in case you need to get out and the barn's bolted.' When Yara did not respond, Shifa tucked it under her pillow. 'Keep it hidden.'

Shifa stroked Yara's hair over and over but was not sure who needed comforting most.

'If we make it out of here, Yara, I'm coming back for you,' Shifa promised, taking a last look around her dorm-mates' empty beds, their comforters laid out on their pillows. 'I won't forget any of you.'

Her blood surged with a heady cocktail of fear and adrenalin.

She had never felt so alive or afraid as she made her way along Hope Avenue, on the alert for roaming opticare drones and Crows who might be on hyperalert after today's events. She climbed the survivor tree. She unzipped her uniform and began to stuff her backpack with the contents of her survival kit. 'Thank you for being my shelter,' she whispered, clinging to the branches as she scaled back down.

Now was the most dangerous time, her backpack visible for all to see. Spine trembling and dreading the shot of a stun gun in the small of her back at any moment, Shifa headed swiftly to the orchard, sighing with relief that Jax and the Crows had not thought to confiscate her pass yet. She stowed her full backpack in the apple store, checking once again for Lona's rusty key and finding it tucked where she'd left it behind the brick.

She was making her way back out of the orchard when she heard the door click. She held her breath. What if one of the Crows had come to install a new lock? She cast around wildly for somewhere to hide as the door swung open and she stood face to face with Luca.

'I saw you heading this way,' he explained. 'How's Yara?'

Shifa attempted to steady her voice. 'Shocked, but sleeping now.'

Luca bent down, picked up some soil and let it sift between his fingers.

'Jax said she doesn't want the tunnels working tonight but as you've signed up for the night shift you can take Themba his dinner and keep him company . . . That's why you volunteered, isn't it?'

Shifa nodded.

'Well, there's a bed in there I've been using so you can sleep there. I have to help Jax with Lona tonight.' He sighed.

Shifa eyed him warily. Was this some kind of trap?

'Anyway, I can't stand another night with his stupid chanting.'

That sounded more like the Luca she knew. 'OK!' she whispered, breathless, readjusting her plan to free Themba in her head.

The food hall was rowdy. Shifa peered up at the window as a strange sound emerged from above. A few recruits mimicked Lona's howls, like a wolf baying at the moon. Along Hope Avenue the survivor tree was bathed in eerie blue moonlight. Shifa girded herself for the test ahead.

After stopping to collect the dinner tray, Luca led Shifa through to the boys' polytunnel. Beyond the storage area was a camp bed blocking a low cellar-like door.

'I let him out for the toilet and a walk around but last night he refused to come up. He's all right – I've heard him moving around down there . . .' Shifa took a deep breath and prepared herself for the state of her brother.

'Themba! It's Shifa!' she called gently.

No reply.

'I'm out of here!' Luca handed her a torch and she climbed down the steps, balancing the tray and avoiding the dusty walls. She listened for a moment till she was sure Luca was gone. The air in the cellar was stale and hot and stank of urine. She swung the torch to the right; the walls were lined with narrow shelves containing hairy tubers, their knobbly growths forming grotesque faces with bulging eyes, twisted noses and mouths. Shifa let the thought settle that these roots were storing nutrients, readying themselves as she had, for the first opportunity to bud into life. *Like me and Themba – in the dark, searching for the light.* It was a long way down, twenty steps or more. Around halfway she heard a gentle whimpering and followed it to a curled-up bundle.

'Themba!' she whispered, sinking to her knees. 'It's me . . .'

Shifa gathered Themba in her arms, gently shining the torch over his face. Shifa licked her fingers and wiped them over her brother's forehead where he had drawn a large circle. Inside the circle sat a spindly creature with long legs and ears.

'It's my hare – easier to feel your way to make art in the dark,' Themba explained.

'Hare in the moon!' Shifa whispered. 'Papa told *you* that story too!' Themba nodded. His eyes were wide with fear

227

as he squinted into the torchlight. Shifa's own belly was a furnace of raging fire. How could Jermaine and Jax do this to Themba? To anyone?

He twisted his fingers around and around Shifa's plait of hair. 'When I told him roots grow into ghosts in the dark, Luca brought my hair to me,' Themba whispered.

'Themba!' The raging fire in Shifa flamed higher. 'You won't have to sleep here ever again if you listen to me.'

His weeping subsided a little and he clung tighter to Shifa.

'Old Lona was right. I found the key to the river door,' Shifa whispered.

A flash of recognition lit Themba's face. 'In the apple store?' he asked.

Shifa nodded, her breath coming hard and fast. 'We have to leave now. We have to get home to Papa.'

Themba clung tighter to Shifa's arm as she shoved the food in her pocket. 'I'm so hungry!' he groaned.

'Eat later, talk later, we have to get your things together and go now. If Luca comes back—'

'Follow my art – I know the way!'

'Shh, Themba!' Shifa scrambled around for his inks and pencils and shoved them with his artbook in his overalls pocket. 'There's no time for stories now!' Shifa grabbed his arm and Themba crawled up the stairs on his hands and knees, counting the steps.

'Shh!' Shifa whispered, opening the cellar door to check that the coast was clear. No sign of Luca.

Once outside they ran in silence. A gust of wind caught in the branches of the survivor tree, and it lifted and bowed in a low salute. Shifa scanned her pass and headed straight to the apple store.

She grabbed hold of her backpack before reaching for the key. Themba had released his fist from his mouth and gasped at the sight of the orchard.

'Lona spoke true! The secret key to the river door is hidden in the apple store,' he whispered.

'Yes, now come on, Themba!' She frantically tugged him, scattering the hens. Every sound was amplified. Shifa's own heart drummed so loud that it echoed in her ears. Her fingers trembled in the lock as she attempted to open the river door, twisting the key harder till finally it gave.

'We're going to have to run for our lives!' Shifa grasped Themba by his shoulders.

He held the torch and clasped her hand as they raced towards the crest of the hill.

'Run, hare, run, hare, run, run, run!' Themba chanted at the sight of the long ears appearing and disappearing above the meadow grass.

'Shiiiiiiiifa! Themba! Wait!'

Luca! They were over the brow of the hill now when Shifa heard his voice calling them. Why hadn't she stopped to lock the river door behind her?

Themba turned back at Luca's call and tripped. Shifa grabbed his hand and, ignoring his protests, dragged him down to the river's edge.

He stood frozen in fear as he stared at the ice-cold water running black as ink.

'Themba. You must do exactly what I say. We have to cross the river, in the middle. It's not deep – you can feel the bottom – but we have to duck right under the sensor. I'll hold you, OK?'

From his stunned expression, Shifa was not even sure that he'd heard her speaking. She could hardly breathe herself now. Her backpack had grown heavy and the nerves in her jaw pulsed. But she could not show Themba how terrified she was of drowning.

She grabbed Themba's hand and pulled him into the icy water. His whistle pierced the silence and was matched by a deafening alarm, sounding sharp and clear over the now brightly floodlit farm. Shifa's fear pulsed through every vein in her body as she dragged her brother further into the river.

'Can't swim, can't swim, can't swim!' Themba chanted between his screech whistle.

'We don't have to swim, Themba, we've just got to dip under the sensor. See! There's Lona's boat!'

'Once beyond the orchard door, there's a boat to sail on the river Ore . . .' Themba chanted.

'That's right, Themb – keep chanting! Watch the surface!'

Shifa took a deep breath and forced her head underwater and her eyes to open as she thrashed around with her feet and hands on the silty riverbed, clouding the water, grasping for the net and dragging it to the surface. She gulped air greedily as she surfaced, hauling and yanking the net towards her, and with every effort the boat upstream drew closer.

Themba's back was turned from her as she reached out for him and caught the flash of Luca's torchlight looming closer, his shouts growing urgent and accompanied by angry barks. Crows and their patrol dogs were silhoutted against the brow of the hill, backlit by flares.

'We've got to hide now. "Bold, Brave, True", Themba!' Shifa reached out and grabbed for his wrist. 'Don't let go. Hold your breath.'

Shifa pulled him underwater and tugged hard on the net, feeling the weight of the boat draw closer, but Themba beat about wildly, slowing her down. Shifa struggled to haul them along with the weight of her backpack and Themba's flailing arms pushing her down. His fist caught the side of her head as her Feetskins slipped and her mouth opened in shock. Water streamed into her as she grabbed at underwater reeds, clinging on and propelling herself and Themba back to the surface. Coughing and spluttering, they found Luca looming above them, grabbing their arms and drawing them close to his face.

'I've seen the way. You go down with me or you don't stand a chance. One breath, NOW!' Luca pressed Themba's head under then Shifa felt a hand pressing her own head under too. Themba struggled but Luca had tight hold of him and pulled him along. Desperation cleared Shifa's mind and she clung to the net, tugging the boat ever closer as their underwater faces distorted, hair floating, chest burning. *Time is not here*, Shifa felt . . . for thoughts were slipping far away . . . with her ebbing breath.

Soft grasses meandered past as water filled her ears, eyes, nose. Themba's eyes glowed amber in the dark, shining wide and bright as moons.

A golden light shone, beckoning her closer, lulling her away. Then a hand shoved her hard in the back. Her hands and Luca's grabbed at the net and the boat drew closer still. Luca pointed upwards and she felt herself being compelled to the surface, mouth wide, gulping for life.

Shifa reached for the edge of the boat and with her last ounce of strength, hauled herself over the side. Next Themba's face appeared, Luca forcing him up from below. Shifa grabbed hold of Themba and dragged him into the boat. Luca's hands appeared over the edge but he struggled to pull himself up, his strength spent. Shifa gritted her teeth, using all her power to haul him into the bow of the boat. Torch beams flashed all around them, reflecting off the water.

Shifa fumbled in her backpack for the small knife she'd taken, her frozen fingers struggling to unwrap it from its cloth binding. The plug of water in her ears cleared and a cacophonous howl of animals, humans and rushing river water filled her ears. Crows waded into the water accompanied by the baying of wild-eyed dogs, teeth bared, rearing away from the crackling noise of the border sensor and its metallic stench of death.

Shifa hacked frantically at the net, severing the last strand as the current took charge of the boat, sweeping them away.

The three of them lay flat, limbs aching, breath intertwined as they sped along, listening to the barks and voices fading and watching the bright flares explode overhead.

Shifa pulled Themba close. Their hearts pounded as one as they clung to each other. The boat was thrusting, tilting, surging wildly forward now. A blast of icy water lashed their faces as it surged faster again.

The voices of their hunters had long faded and now the flow of the current slowed.

Shifa attempted to snatch a look to where the surface of the wide river ahead flattened, grew eerily calm and still as glass.

'Make a wish in the silence, before the weir's water roars,' Themba whispered, his eyes wide with fear.

'I wish for us to live,' Shifa shouted back as the bow tilted and the boat lurched over the precipice through the night air.

Were they flying or falling?

PART THREE
RIVER

Chapter Twenty-Seven

Time slowed. Water rushed in where air once flowed . . . Breath came sapphire, sky blue, reed green, foaming silver water white. Arms were water weeds, bodies driftwood bashing against rocks. Reaching for daisy chains, calling, catching, miaowing, clawing for Daisy, holding her close, head against heart, *together again*. Locket opening, daisy chain floating, caught in the turn of the tides. Skep-heart beating slow and slower. Sinking to the river bed. *'Papa, Papa!'* Themba chanting, whistling, Lottie's flute drifting water music, dancing, dancing. Themba floating away . . . Skep heartbeat, beat, beating. Fight, fight, fight for life drawn towards a distant light.

Shifa woke to a sky swelling with sweet birdsong. Beyond their chorus the river flowed calm and serene. She rubbed her eyes and stared up at the sky; dark grey and pink wispy clouds stippled the dawn. She propped herself on her elbows and tentatively surveyed the riverbank.

'Themba!' she called, but her voice would not carry.

She crawled on her hands and knees across the sandy shore to a figure curled in on itself. She reached for a shoulder, willing it to be Themba's, but it was Luca's head she turned towards her. He opened his heavy eyelids. *Let Themba be alive too.*

'Themba?' she croaked, frantically casting around for him. Luca pointed downriver, whispering, 'I held on to you both for as long as I could.'

Shifa stared into the calm, clear water reflecting the dawn sky. They must have been lying on its banks for hours. Tears coursed down Shifa's face and she made no attempt to stem them. She had only dream-memories of how they had been washed up on this shore. Her mind blasted her with one question. How could she return to Nabil now without Themba? She was meant to care for him, to save him, just like Nabil had saved her. If he had drowned, then it was her fault for leading him to a watery grave. It could not be true . . .

Shifa stumbled to her feet and began to follow the river, calling Themba's name. She climbed over a piece of driftwood and navigated her way through a bed of lush green water reeds in the shallows. Ahead, the *thrum, thrum, thrum* of water lapping to and fro against an object, caught her attention. She parted long rushes and there, caught in a bed of reeds, she discovered a flash of red – their boat. She paused, hardly daring to take another step, when a small voice rose from the stern.

'Lona didn't say I'd be left alone, without Shifa, without a home . . .'

'Themba!' Shifa lunged forward and held out her arms, sobbing uncontrollably with relief and joy.

Themba stood and hurled himself at Shifa, almost toppling the boat.

'You're not alone, Themba,' Shifa said, when words finally came. 'We're together and we're free!'

'But where's Luca?' Themba asked when they finally drew apart. Shifa pointed through the reeds, but Themba was already wading ahead of her.

'Wait! Themba!' Shifa paused to secure the boat firmly, knotting the rope and net around the thick reeds and placing a large rock on top of it to make an anchor. Following her beaten path back to the sandy bank, Shifa was amazed to see Themba running into Luca's arms, as if he was greeting an old friend.

Just then the earth vibrated and a low engine rumbled on the bank above. Luca caught Shifa's eye and nodded up towards the riverbank. Taking Themba by the hand they retreated into the reed beds for cover.

The vehicle came to a stop and a door opened and banged closed again. Feet came running towards the riverbank.

'Anything?'

'It's the boat all right but it's empty!'

The three of them crouched in the icy water holding their

breath as the reeds trembled.

Just ahead heavy boots splashed into the river and hauled their boat ashore.

'They'll have been caught in the weir. This is all Freedom Fields needs! What's this, some kind of . . . necklace?' Shifa reached up to her bare neck and pushed her fist into her mouth to stem her cry. Themba took hold of her other hand and squeezed it tight as the tears washed her eyes.

'They must have been desperate. Two of them couldn't even swim. They nearly drowned trying to get under a sensor that's never even worked over the water!'

'It's a miracle no one's tried before.'

'They'll wash up on the banks soon enough. Only the ARK Freedom had a chance. We'd better take this evidence and the boat back to the farm and file a report.'

They stood shivering in the reeds long after the engine had faded into the distance.

Finally they waded back to the beach and Luca began pacing up and down. 'It's good they found your necklace. Now they think we've drowned, or you two at least. But we can't stay. We need to get as far away from here as we can in case they come back.'

Shifa slumped on to the sand, holding the place where her locket had lain against her heart. She closed her eyes and attempted to call on Daisy but no matter how much she willed it, she could not draw her close. 'Daisy's gone, Themba. Daisy's left me.' Shifa sobbed. Themba crouched by her side and held her head on his lap.

'Daisy didn't come with us, Shifa! She's safe at home.' Themba leaned in close. 'Sorry about your birthday present from Papa,' Themba whispered. Shifa held her brother close and released the howl of abandonment, hurt and confusion that had been building in her since the day Nabil told her how he'd found her on the night of Hurricane Chronos.

'Quiet! It's only a bit of jewellery, Shifa!' Luca reasoned. 'You're alive, aren't you? We've got to go.'

Tears coursed down Shifa's cheeks, their flow as unstoppable as the river's. Luca and his words meant nothing to her, for her mind had flown to Nabil's side, and her heart was breaking as she pictured her papa being handed her locket – and given the news of their deaths.

Chapter Twenty-Eight

Shifa felt numb inside as Luca led the way, wading through the reed beds. Themba screeched as something black and sleek slithered through the water under their Feetskins.

'A water snake!' he shouted, frozen to the spot. Luca waded back, picked Themba out of the water and carried him away. Shifa trailed behind. Her legs felt as heavy as lead and her heart heavier still.

They must have been walking for several hours. The morning sun had grown stronger and brighter, breaking through the clouds. The River Ore widened again at this point, its banks producing large sandy-coloured boulders.

Themba clambered on to one and sat down.

'We can't stop here! Themba,' said Luca, 'I told you. We've got to get as far away from the farm as we can before night-time.'

'But I'm so thirsty and hungry,' Themba complained.

Ignoring Luca, Shifa sat down next to him, unpacking from

her backpack some of the food that had been intended for his supper. A bread roll, some oat bars. Themba grabbed them off her and shoved them greedily into his mouth. Shifa reached into her pocket and took out her precious seed packet. *At least I still have this to hold on to*, she thought as Luca reluctantly sat down, opened his bag and took out an energy bar.

Shifa glanced at his supplies. 'You planned to escape too?'

'Not exactly,' Luca mumbled. 'I've been watching and waiting . . . and' – he pointed to the origami flower in her hand – 'I read the letter hidden on the inside of that.'

A tornado of resentment twisted Shifa's gut. It was all falling into place now. So it had been a set-up leaving her alone in the cellar with Themba. Luca must have been lying in wait, watching her every move. Shifa inspected the flower.

'I was careful to put your seed collection back,' Luca said.

A lump formed in Shifa's throat. She remembered the words she'd written to Nabil almost off by heart, and the thought of Luca having read them made her trust him even less. Now he would know from her words exactly what she thought of him. She had no reason to hide her contempt as she gathered up their things. The cold stare she shot him sent him striding ahead.

'Come on! We can't hang around here!' Luca hurried them on.

'Don't be mean to Luca. He's my friend!' Themba announced as he leafed through the pages of his artbook.

'Like Jermaine was your friend!' Shifa scoffed. 'Luca didn't talk to you about anything that was written in a letter, did he, Themba?' Shifa whispered, the thought of Themba discovering that they were not brother and sister in that way filling her with dread.

Themba shook his head. 'What letter?' he mumbled as he swallowed down a mouthful of bread.

'It doesn't matter now. It never got sent!' Shifa sighed. Perhaps Luca was keeping that piece of information back, ready to use it when he needed. 'Can I see your art?'

Themba handed her his book. There was the Skylight with wings, a picture of children walking in moonlight through fields, the courtyard and the farm and a shadow at the window. Shifa paused on a picture drawn in dark charcoal, where grotesque creatures glowed in the dark. She hoped in time Themba would tell her of the monsters he'd had to face without her.

She turned the page to find the survivor tree with Shifa, Themba and Luca standing at its trunk. She scanned the image of Luca's face for signs of cruelty, but found in his drawing a soft smile of kindness, head tilted to one side, listening. If he was one of Themba's monsters she saw no sign of it in this portrait that looked like a group of friends . . . or siblings.

'Slow down, Luca!' Themba called out to him, gesturing for him to draw close. 'I want to show you something!' Luca slowed his pace.

Themba flicked to a page in his artbook, pointing out a painting of Lona lying on her bed, Barley at her feet. Shifa peered into the picture, realising that for her it was the first time the shadow woman at the window had taken a human face. Lona was ancient and wrinkled. In the drawing she was gesticulating with her hands but her eyes were closed.

'Listen! Lona knows this land! And by my art and memory words I've got to make her old voice heard.'

Luca sighed heavily but came to hunker down by Themba's side as he leafed through the sketches in his book. Themba became more excited with every turn of the page.

'See! Here's the golden key to the apple store, the river boat waiting on the Ore!' Shifa and Luca peered closer. There was the red boat that saved their lives. Themba turned the page. 'Look! There's the weir we had to fear.' Within each drawing or painting he had written a rhyme.

'Those are Lona's words of wisdom,' he explained, pointing to the swirly writing.

Luca's face contorted in frustration. He stood up and began pacing up and down again. 'Themba, we can't waste time with this now.'

Themba's face crumpled in disappointment.

Shifa inspected Themba's painting of the weir.

'Wait! Luca, did you tell Themba about the boat and the weir?' Shifa asked.

He shook his head. 'How could I? Didn't know what a weir was until we went over it.'

'Exactly!' Shifa nodded. 'Neither did I.'

'Believe me now? Lona knows this land, like the back of her hand.' Themba nodded excitedly and carried on turning through the pages. 'How long is three days rowing in walking time?' he asked Luca.

'How should I know?' Luca grimaced. 'Why?'

Themba showed a page on which he'd drawn an old station house. 'That's how long it takes to get to the station . . . and this is the trail we've got to follow.'

Shifa smiled. 'I don't know about you, Luca, but that's where we're heading – to the station.'

'Yep! We just follow the art trail to find the golden treasure!' Themba added.

Luca scoffed and grabbed Themba's artbook from him. 'Treasure? This isn't a game, Themba! No time for your stories now.' Luca prodded the almost washed-away hare in the moon Themba had inked on to his forehead. 'Enough time-wasting. We need to move NOW!'

Shifa grabbed Luca's arm and pushed him away. 'Don't touch him!' Luca stomped away. 'What's the matter with you? Give his book back to him!' Shifa shouted after Luca. 'We're not at Freedom Fields any more! You can't tell us what to do! No one asked you to come with us.'

Luca paused and turned back. 'You would never have got out without me! Lona couldn't even remember that Jax and Jermaine were her grandchildren so how's she going to help us?'

'Lona knows! I had to draw the way to the golden treasure before it's lost for ever and ever.'

Luca brandished Themba's artbook in the air. 'It's all in your head, Themba!' Luca made off with it again along the bank. 'If you want your artbook you'll have to come after me! Stay here any longer and we're all dead.'

'Lona was telling the truth,' Themba complained to Shifa. 'It's why she got angry when no one listened to her.'

Poor Themba, what he must have been going through. Shifa took Themba by the hand. 'Tell me what happened, Themb. Where did you get all those bruises?' She raised her chin towards Luca. 'Was it him?'

Themba pulled a face and tugged free of Shifa's hand. 'No! I keep telling you, Luca's my friend. Not talking about the farm any more.'

Shifa nodded and smoothed Themba's hair back from his temples. There was no use forcing him.

'Best not to talk about art trails and treasure in front of Luca.' Shifa wrinkled her nose. 'He doesn't understand about story hives or Flower Tracks, does he?'

'That's true. Poor Luca.' Themba sighed. 'OK! Just follow the landmarks in Themba's art. The first should show themselves before dark,' he called to Luca and ran to catch up with him.

Walking in peace for a moment Shifa took in the river for the first time. It was not lined with trees dipping their overhanging branches in the water as she'd imagined, but it was not as barren of life or bleak as Freedom Fields had made the Kairos Lands out to be after Hurricane Chronos either.

She watched Luca bend down and pick something up to show Themba. Now, away from the farm, Luca did not seem like the monster he had grown into in her mind. To tell Themba that she was not his sister would have been cruel, but Luca had not done it. Perhaps people, like land, could regenerate? Shifa stared at the water – it had been a sandy colour but now, with the afternoon clouds overhead, it reflected silver-grey. The river might not be golden but it seemed to be painted with as many colours as existed in the world and who knew what other colours flowed under its surface?

Chapter Twenty-Nine

After a while, the sandy banks of the Ore turned to shingle and the boulders to rock escarpments. The mountain Shifa had seen from the survivor tree came looming closer. The rocky banks were becoming too large and slippery to climb over. As they picked their way between the rocks, a green slimy creature leapt from beneath a large leaf. Shifa jumped sideways, grazing her knee. But Themba seemed more amused than alarmed and began copying its guttural croak.

'Frog!' Themba laughed. 'One like that's on my river page with your hair in it! Want to see?'

'I forgot about that!' Shifa said – their birthday seemed like light years ago.

'Not now, Themba!' Luca snapped. 'It's getting too steep to stay at the river's edge. We'll have to walk further inland.'

Luca climbed up the rocky bank, setting off at marching pace across a wide-open meadow. Shifa got the impression that he was as irritated by her as by Themba.

Now forced by the terrain to walk in the open land above the river, Shifa saw Luca's back tense and his pace quicken. She felt exposed too, her eyes constantly scanning in an arc, alert for strangers or hunters. *What would they do with us if they caught us now?* Shifa dreaded to think. Still, when she spotted a few red poppies fluttering in the long grass she paused, bent down to pick one up and placed it in her seed packet, for luck. The poppy had been her first survivor flower. *Let it not be our last.*

In a fenced-off zone at the end of the river meadow a large sign loomed over them, reminding Shifa of the advertising hoarding behind the Flower Tracks.

'Farm Land Requisitioned by Freedom Fields.'

Shifa looked into the clear stream, hypnotised by the underwater dance of grasses, and more insects than she had ever seen settling and floating on the surface, glittering wings opening like tiny boats. Shoals of silver fish glinted, moving like hundreds of dancers swaying together. A jewel-like, orange-and-turquoise winged bird hovering over the water looked to Shifa like a bird-of-paradise flower. So much movement, so much life . . . Here on this water meadow there was more wildlife than she had seen in her whole life. The further they walked the louder nature began to hum.

As the afternoon bled into evening and the sun set pink in the sky, they fell into a rhythm and there were times when Shifa almost forgot that they might still be hunted. Luca swatted a mosquito on his neck and a flick of blood splatted on his skin. Why was it that the most irritating creatures seemed to survive? The insects now began to dive-bomb their ears. As Luca walked ahead his square shoulders tensed, hands swatting around his head. When they slowed Luca down, Shifa thought that he would have liked to swat her and Themba too.

A blast of air buffeted the water and Shifa lifted her face to the cooler breeze, and the mosquitoes rose in black clouds from the water. The weather had been sultry and dry since they'd left Kairos City. It had to break soon but these tiny gusts had come before and turned out to be false alarms. Shifa closed her eyes and a piece of rainbow cloth came floating towards her, swirling, gliding, twisting, turning, lodging in her mind.

Dare, dream, believe, imagine . . .

She felt sorry for Luca as he marched ahead, hardly pausing to take in the wonders of the countryside that surrounded him. Occasionally Themba would catch up with Luca and they would walk together for a while, talking, oddly companionably. Shifa sighed with relief when Luca finally handed Themba's precious artbook back. Luca's strategy had worked though, as Themba had kept pace by his side until it was returned to him. Themba waved his precious book in the air, jumping up and down in triumph.

Luca clearly thought they had now put enough space between them and the farm to afford to slow down a little.

'Now you'll see! I trust you, and you trust me, sitting under the survivor tree! I made that up.' Themba giggled.

'Tell Luca what *Themba* means. Tell him, Shifa!' Themba grabbed Luca's hand and forced him to walk back towards Shifa.

'Trust! It means one who trusts.'

Luca nodded. Shifa wondered if Themba was trying to forge some kind of friendship between her and Luca. Perhaps he did achieve a kind of truce because for the first time the three of them walked side by side.

'Underneath the weeping willow tree where I found you and you found me . . .' Themba began to sing as he pointed to a tree with trailing green branches sweeping the water. 'See!'

Themba knelt down under the tree, whose leaves fell like a waterfall – *Like my hair used to flow,* Shifa thought as she watched the soft branches dance. Themba flicked through his artbook till he came to the painting of a similar tree with the word 'willow' written above it. He had stuck and folded his river page carefully on to this page too. 'See, there's the frog, there's the willow!'

Luca itched obsessively at the top of his arm where a bite was now swelling. Themba stopped, clapped his hands and started counting on his fingers. 'Apple store, red boat, weir, willow tree! Why aren't you more amazed! Are you even alive? See! This proves it! Lona's landmarks are true.'

'It's just a picture of a tree, Themba.' Luca shrugged.

'Underneath the weeping willow tree, I found you and you found me.' Themba glanced between Shifa and Luca and suddenly started giggling. He grabbed their hands and pulled them towards the trunk and there, scored into the bark, were the initials that were also in his painting.

S. A.

L. F.

'Stands for Silas and Lona.' Themba peered into his book. 'She couldn't remember her old name, before she was married. Said something about how they were friends for ever! That's funny! Letters are the same as Shifa Aziz and Luca Freedom!' Themba laughed. 'Maybe you're the chosen ones too!'

Shifa traced her fingers over the letters.

'No one's chosen, Themba! But I have to admit that is weird!' Luca pondered.

'Believe Lona's way now?' Themba challenged them both.

Luca shrugged as if he had no way of answering that question, but he did not look as disparaging as he had before. 'So you think Lona's shown you these landmarks as a kind of escape route? But when was the last time she left that farm?'

A smile broke over Themba's face. Shifa had not seen that glowing smile since they'd left Kairos City. Themba turned the page in his artbook to a new portrait of Lona. In this drawing he had captured the face of a proud woman, with deeply grooved smile lines. He began to speak in her voice. Themba had always been a good mimic.

'They treat me like an old fool. Memories of today and yesterday just slip away but I remember long ago when I was a girl, swimming the Ore, catching fish and sitting by the shore.' Themba broke off and pointed to the carved initials. 'Silas was Lona's husband. She misses him, like we miss Papa. Like Papa misses Mama and Baba Suli.'

Luca nodded towards Shifa. How strange it felt that he knew that Themba's mama was not her own. Daisy's bell sounded. Shifa peered around then realised what she had always known in her heart to be true. Daisy's bell, her love, was deep inside her. She carried it with her for ever just as she did Nabil's love. *What does it matter now who my mama is? Themba's right – if the daisy chain's made with love, that's what matters.* Shifa raised her hands to join Themba in a high five.

'You two are lucky! I don't miss anyone.' Luca spoke the words in a flat voice and his face returned to an unreadable blank.

Themba raised his head from his book. 'You would miss me . . . in a way!' Themba said without a whisper of irony.

'In a way!' Luca admitted and smiled at Shifa. 'I would.' His smile softened his face so much that for a moment Shifa forgot how much she hated him and smiled back.

Luca peered up at the darkening sky where the sun now filtered thinly through the cloud. 'We might as well shelter here for the night.'

Themba smiled and took out his art materials. As Themba drew, filling in the detail of the river, bird life, fish and vegetation, Luca and Shifa walked a little way upriver. Shifa collected some edible hips from the trees where wild roses had once grown, ate one, smarting at its sharpness, and offered one to Luca.

'You sure you're not trying to poison me!' Luca said, spitting it out.

'On the farm I wanted to,' Shifa admitted.

'Not now?' Luca asked.

'Like you said, I don't know you,' Shifa answered, attempting to rid her voice of the coldness she still felt for Luca in her heart.

'I don't know me either,' he mumbled. Shifa did not know how to respond to this new Luca who seemed to want to reach out to her. She wandered along the bank pretending to be concentrating on foraging finds.

By the time they returned, Themba was sleeping soundly, wrapped in the silver insulating sheeting, beneath the shade of the willow tree, occasionally twisting his fingers around Shifa's hair-strand. The constant flow of the river and an owl's distant call had seemed to have a hypnotic effect on all of them. They spoke in hushed voices.

Luca winced as if his head ached. 'But Themba knows who he is.' Luca picked up Themba's artbook.

Shifa scowled at the effort it was taking to piece together this boy with the monster she had known all her life. *What does he want from us?* Shifa wondered.

Luca paused on Themba's drawing of the winged Skylight. 'You shouldn't humour him so much. I've spent ages trying to get him to face reality. And now you're encouraging his fantasy treasure stories again.'

Shifa felt a deep, burning resentment towards Luca. 'What's so great about reality?' Shifa retorted, glancing over at Themba. 'His stories and art have kept him going in the dark. That's the way he knows himself. Through the stories he tells. If you don't like it you can go.'

As soon as she spat the words out she wished she could have swallowed them back down. She knew in her heart that Luca was right. They never would have escaped without him.

'Where would I go, Shifa?' In the darkness, quietened by the river's flow, Luca sounded lost and desperate. For the first time Shifa heard the heartbreaking strains of Lottie's flute in his voice. 'Anyway . . . Themba's right. I would miss him.'

'What's your plan?' Shifa asked.

'Haven't got one. Never did. Just took my chances . . . I'm sorry I read your letter but I thought if you and Themba were getting out I'd make a break for it. Have *you* got a plan then?'

'Only to find a station, hide away on the Skylight and make our way back to Kairos City and Nabil . . .'

Shifa felt all twisted inside. It had been so much simpler to hate Luca. Great silences opened up between them, filled only by the river's constant flow. The owl's call drew closer and louder . . . now Shifa looked up to see a small brown owl land on the branches of the willow tree above them. Shifa placed her finger over her mouth . . . too late. At the sound of Luca's voice it flew away.

'I know you don't trust me but you have no idea how lucky you are.' Luca let out a deep breath. 'After I read your letter I couldn't stop thinking that you could have ended up being just like me. How different would you be to me if you'd known nothing else – been told who to be, what to think, how to walk, even?'

Shifa stayed silent

'The way Themba talked about you and Nabil . . . it made me want to be part— It made me think I could learn how to be free one day.'

Luca took the soft blue blanket out of his bag. 'A neighbour handed me over wrapped in this blanket and I've never known anything except Freedom Fields Family ever since.'

Shifa flinched. So this was the 'blanky' Themba had told her that Luca could not sleep without.

'The locket I lost in the river was the only thing I had of my mama,' Shifa whispered into the dark.

'Sorry.' Luca sighed.

Shifa took out her seed packet and held it between her palms.

'Thank you for not telling Themba . . .'

'I'm not the monster you think I am,' Luca said, shivering with cold. Shifa took the insulation sheet and unfolded it to share. He nodded and wrapped his blanket around his shoulders too as they lay with their backs against the rocky bank.

'Do you think you could ever trust me, like Themba does?' Luca asked into the dark.

Shifa opened her mouth several times to try to answer, but could not find the words.

'There's my answer,' Luca murmured.

Shifa lay awake listening to the ebb and flow of the river. Luca was a bully, hard and sometimes cruel, but maybe that was what an ARK Freedom had to learn to be. Jermaine and Jax had seen in him a leader, but then they had seen that in *her* too. He had taken her letter, but not used it against her. He had been Themba's jailer, but he had not locked the door. He was an ARK Freedom . . . but what did that mean? She'd always thought of them as being given everything – better food, better lessons, better opportunities – but Luca had nowhere to go, no family he cared for to seek out or return to. What was the point of being free if you didn't belong anywhere, or care about anyone?

Luca's legs twitched in his sleep and Shifa remembered how Themba had said he was a restless sleeper. Themba's bruised face on his first day had probably been an accident.

Above them the willow tree waved in the wind and a branch floated towards her, brushing her hand with its feathery leaves. How strange that their initials were the same as Lona's and Silas's, as if this tree was sharing a message with them. The owl that she had been told was extinct had come to sit here too. *But what is this all meant to mean?* Above them she heard the sound of light-footed animals racing through the grass. The night was alive, with running hares darting in every direction . . .

'Look for the hare in the moon, Shifa – look for kindness.' Nabil's voice filled her mind. *In the morning I'll find a way to answer Luca's question – tell him that I want to trust him but that trust takes time to build.* Shifa watched Luca sleeping – all the hard lines in his face were smoothed away by sleep. He was right. She was lucky to have been found and given a home by someone who could truly teach her what trust and love meant.

She cupped her hands together in a skep-heart. *I love you, Papa.* For now she knew she had been given a truly golden gift that Luca had never known – love.

Shifa stared into the water. In her rippled, distorted reflection she froze as she turned her head sideways to see a bony white wolf, head poised, teeth bared, watching her with ice-cold silvery eyes. Never losing sight of it, she edged backwards, away from the sheer edge, and as she did the creature drew parallel and looked straight into her eyes.

'Shifa!' Themba called from above.

The wolf raised its head and sniffed, before bending low and licking a trail of blood clean from the rock.

*

Shifa jolted awake, gashing her head against the rock. She felt the back of her head where a small trickle of blood seeped from her scalp. Her head swirled as Themba pummelled her chest.

'You made him go! Luca was my brother-friend. He looked out for me. We have to find him. You were so mean to him!'

Still reeling from her wild dream Shifa stirred herself and held Themba's hands to fend off his blows.

'Wait! Themba, I have to wash this wound.'

Shifa's head pounded as she bent down to the river to wash the blood from her head. As the river water ran pink she quivered at the haunting, bloody memory of her dream.

Themba followed her down to the river.

'Is it bad?' he asked. Shifa shook her head.

'Just a little cut.'

She pressed hard against her scalp until her blood stopped flowing. Shifa wondered if the dream had come to her for a reason. Maybe it was the kind of premonition that Nabil said he'd had since childhood and signalled great danger ahead?

'Luca! Luca! Luca! Where are you?' Themba called.

Chapter Thirty

Themba called out for Luca till his voice was hoarse, refusing to heed Shifa's warnings that there might still be hunters around. He insisted on peering over the increasingly steep riverbank and scanning the seething waters below.

With every step, Shifa's guilt grew as Themba told of how Luca had been his hare in the moon in more ways than she could ever have imagined. Themba demanded to know what they had talked about while he had slept, what she had said to him to make him leave. There seemed no point hiding the truth from Themba.

'Papa always says you should tell people you care about them before you go to sleep! Never wait for the morning!' Themba reminded Shifa.

Themba was so set on finding Luca that he refused to stop to eat or drink, accepting only a few biscuits and slices of dried fruit as he searched for Luca. Shifa was dismayed to find that their water supplies had almost run out. The mountain now loomed over them, brooding in the grey afternoon sky. Eventually Themba's shoulders slumped and his insistent calls for Luca ceased.

Shifa breathed deeply as she knelt down to inspect a red trail of . . . She reached out and touched the rich ruby colour – it *was* blood and it led into the water. Shifa gasped, grateful that Themba had gone off to pee. She leaned into a pool and washed the trail away. The river ran pink as it had with the blood from her own head wound. *The river runs the same colour with our blood*, Shifa thought. She made a skep-heart of her hands and willed Luca to be alive, that they would find him and show him that there were people in the world who cared for him. Themba could not know about the blood but the wild-eyed wolf of her dreams now prowled through her mind as a constant companion.

'I've been thinking!' Themba said as he returned from peeing. 'Luca could already be at the station house because I showed him my landmarks.'

'He could!' Shifa nodded in encouragement as the thought seemed to lift Themba's spirits.

Ahead of them the land rose steeply and the ridges and plateaus grew gradually smaller, and narrower.

'I've seen this before!' The light of recognition shone in Themba's eyes. He got out his artbook and flicked through the pages, tapping on words.

'Told you! Lona knows the land like the back of her hand.' Themba mimicked Lona's croaky voice.

'*Where the land rises up like the tiers of my wedding cake, then you'll have a climb to make!*' Themba began chanting Lona's rhymes; some Shifa had never heard before but these last words channelled through Themba's mouth revealed the confusion in the old woman's mind and left Shifa with a sense of deep forboding.

And when the time comes,
When the light fades
And it's time for the trusted to make their mark,
Don't be afraid to climb out of the dark.

The current of the blackening water sped up dramatically, rushing and surging through narrowing rocky banks. Fresh waterfalls scudded across rock as the gorge turned a sharp corner, changing its course straight towards the mountain.

Themba began punching the air and raised his voice above the river's shout.

'Golden key – apple store! Red boat! Weir! Willow tree! Tiers of a wedding cake! Wait for the watermill, the old farm and then the station to take us home to Papa . . .'

Themba was silenced by the insistent crack of gunshots puncturing the air. By instinct Shifa and Themba dived to the ground, hands protecting their heads. Shifa's heart thudded hard against the ground. She reached for Themba and pulled him close.

'Oi! I swear I saw one run that way along the bank. The beggars can swim, you know! I think I got a hit!' came a gruff voice just above them.

Shifa's blood ran cold. Had Luca been shot?

'I don't know, I didn't see. One skinny hare! That's all we've got to show for a dawn hunt! Hardly worth waking up for!'

The voices of the hunters receded but the sound of their gunshot fired raw fear through Shifa long after they'd gone. Nabil's hare story had followed them all the way from Kairos City. She stroked Themba's forehead where the hare in the moon he'd inked on his skin had now faded without trace. *Is this a message for me?* Had she forgotten how to see Luca's kindness when it had been staring her in the face and now . . . maybe it was too late.

Chapter Thirty-One

Fear spurred them on and they hurried along a narrowing river path. Luca's question, 'Do you think you could ever trust me, like Themba does?' haunted her. *If I had answered his question and given him some hope, would he have stayed?*

Themba stopped abruptly. In the hollowed-out earth was a baby hare not much bigger than the size of Shifa's hand. Its heartbeat was clearly visible, pulsing furiously through its soft grey fur. Themba approached cautiously.

'Hare, not in the moon, on the ground!' Themba whispered in amazement. Creeping towards it, bending low he whispered, 'What are you doing here? All alone? Waiting for your mama and papa to come home?'

Shifa crouched low next to Themba. The hare looked so small and frightened, its amber eyes wide. 'Our friend Luca's somewhere on his own. Will you help us find him?' Themba whispered the question. 'I know! Find the hare, find Luca!'

Themba announced, his eyes brightening with a resurgence of hard-to-fathom Themba logic.

Shifa was amazed that the hare allowed Themba to stroke it. As he did, Nabil's words flowed through her: 'The hare's a survivor. When threatened it stays stock still in its form.'

'What if its mama's coming back for it?' Shifa whispered. A cloudy ghost of a woman with long, dark hair and Daisy's shrill cry filled Shifa's mind. She pushed the intensity of it away.

'No!' said Themba decisively. 'Hare's too thin. Maybe the hunters shot her.' Themba gently squeezed his hands under the hare's soft belly and scooped it up. 'A baby hare is a lev— lev— leveret! Lev needs saving, Shifa!'

'Come on, Themb, we've got to go.' Shifa attempted to wipe her eyes but more tears replaced the last in a constant stream that the tiny vulnerable heartbeat of the hare had brought to the surface – tears for baby Shifa, for Daisy who she might never see again, for Halonah and her Honey, and baby Luca wrapped in a blue blanket handed over to Freedom Fields, for grown-up Luca who had no one, for Yara and Kiki and Anton and for her papa and Themba's mama Tia, for the mama she would never know.

'Be brave, hold true,' Themba whispered and placed the hare in his pocket. It squirmed against him but did not attempt to leap away.

'We'll press on till it gets too dark,' Shifa said, dragging them into a run, relieved that, with Lev to distract him,

Themba hardly seemed to notice now that dusk had turned to night. As the moon rose higher in the sky and the light dimmed through shades of grey to ink and a few stars scattered the night, Themba came to a halt.

'I'm thirsty and Lev's too tired to go any further,' he announced, sinking to the ground.

Without Luca's supplies they had run out of water. Shifa walked to where a stream cascaded down a rock that ran from the mountain above. She bent down, cupped her hands and cautiously sipped. It tasted earthy but clean. She offered a little to Lev in Themba's pouch and he sipped thirstily.

'If it's good enough for Lev . . . !' Shifa nodded to Themba to drink from her cupped hand. He pulled a face at the taste then glugged thirstily as Shifa replenished her water holder.

Shifa searched the underside of the bank and found a wide cave-like overhang where they could shelter for the night. They finished what scant supplies of dried biscuits and apple they had left, and Themba discovered some tiny button mushrooms under a tree.

'Safe earth treasure?' Themba checked in with Shifa as Nabil had drilled him to do when foraging.

'Safe!' she said, savouring the soft creamy taste.

Shifa kept watch while Themba curled up with Lev, wrapped in the insulation blanket, and slept fitfully, twitching and calling out for Luca in his sleep. No sign of the owl tonight.

Now that it was just the two of them and Lev, Shifa felt the need to keep alert. Her dream of the wolf licking blood off the rock refused to leave her. *What if there are wolves here and the trail of blood in the water belonged to Luca?* Shifa shuddered at the thought. *You cannot sleep,* she told herself. In an attempt not to doze off, Shifa picked up Themba's artbook and flicked through the images and words by torchlight, pausing on the rhymes and images that had so far proved to be true.

The secret key to the river door is hidden in the apple store.

It's the water's roar you've got to fear . . . surging water's called a weir.

Underneath the willow tree where I found you and you found me,
In the bark we scored our love,
The willow branches swayed above.

Where the land rises up like the tiers of my wedding cake, then you'll have a climb to make!

No matter how confused Lona was, it seemed that from somewhere deep in the caverns of her mind she had remembered the old landmarks. Shifa flipped through the pages and paused on Themba's picture of the gorge, recognisable as where they now rested in the shadow of the mountain.

At the turn of the watermill's hands, head inland.
At the turn of the tides, run away from the river
Where it rushes too strong.

She turned the page to discover what, according to Lona and Themba, lay ahead.

Beyond is the barn.
Look out for the red roof of the old farm
Where the old plough can be found
Sticking out of hilly ground,
Where hares run free over grassy mounds
If my memory hasn't died
There the station house lies!

Chapter Thirty-Two

For the first time in her life Shifa had lain awake all night and watched the rainbow colours of dawn rise. Halfway through the night the hare stuck its head out of Themba's pocket and she gently eased it from him, holding it in her hand as she stroked its soft fur. Together, its beating heart in her palm, its bright amber eyes shining, they witnessed nature's painting of the sky, showing her something she would never forget in her whole life – that every new day brought new miracles . . . If Lona's rhymes proved true, soon they might reach 'the turning of the tides', but by the freshness in the air Shifa was sure that the weather was finally turning too.

Placing Lev in her pocket, Shifa watched the surface of the river surge brightly, throwing up curls of white surf. Small gusts of wind tugged at her hair and the clouds grew brooding.

'We've got to make it to the station today, Themba!' Shifa nudged him awake and handed over Lev, hurrying Themba along as he insisted on seeking out new plants to tempt the little hare to eat.

As she peered into her dull reflection, Shifa was transfixed for a moment by the dance and sway of bright yellow flowers, their green tendrils tugging this way and that in the current. She bent down, pulled one free and held the flower under Themba's chin. 'Like a water buttercup!' Shifa smiled as Themba's skin shone golden.

'Try it on Lev!' Themba grabbed hold of the flower and placed it under Lev's chin. 'Doesn't like butter!'

Shifa felt Nabil's smile, as if in a flash he could see them there.

'Why wouldn't you say goodbye to Papa?' Themba broke into her thoughts.

Shifa sighed as she picked another water buttercup, dried it and placed it in her seed packet. 'I was angry with him for sending us away,' she answered.

Themba nodded, before carefully lifting Lev and placing the hare back in his pocket.

'I'll carry you, Lev. I'll look after you for ever,' he promised, with such love it made Shifa's heart ache. Sometimes she wished that someone would carry her too, take away all the responsibility. Why had she been so slow to see that Luca had taken care of Themba too – and that Nabil had loved and carried her all her life?

They came across a bike lying on its side, its spokes whirring in the breeze. She gestured for Themba to hang back and crept forward slowly, but as she did her foot loosened a trail of shingle and she cascaded with it down the bank to the water below. There was frantic splashing, and a stick and line lashed towards her. She automatically grabbed hold of it and a sharp metal hook stabbed her hand in the skin between her thumb and finger, right in the centre of her sunflower tattoo.

Shifa yelped and reeled from the pain, her body braced with pulsing panic.

'Shifa!' Themba called, his voice full of fear as he leaned over the edge and reached for her, then froze as a muddy figure climbed up the bank towards him, filthy and limping, icy grey eyes peering out of a ghostly, blood-smeared face.

'Luca!' Shifa whispered.

'Luca!' Themba shouted. He slid down the shingle and launched himself at Luca. Themba's whistle, Luca's yelps and Lev's squeals merged into one.

Shifa took in a large sodden rag of red cloth wrapped tightly around Luca's hand.

'I knew you were alive,' Themba shouted. Luca disentangled himself from Themba and walked towards Shifa, taking her hand where a hook was firmly embedded at the end of some line attached to a stick. Blood trickled steadily from the wound. For the first time Shifa read in Luca's eyes the honest, compassionate, steady gaze of a true and trusting friend.

'I'm sorry,' she whispered, looking straight into Luca's eyes.

He nodded slowly, taking in all that was held in her *sorry*. 'I need your help now, Themba. Will you be my right hand?'

Luca asked. 'Help me hold Shifa's hand steady. Best to look away!' he whispered.

Shifa turned her head towards the river and caught a flash of white on the bank above. She looked up where a white wolf sat and watched.

'Wait!' Shifa pulled her hand away and pointed. 'See that!' But when she looked back the wolf was gone.

Luca gently eased her back towards him, taking her hand in his.

'Trust me!' He smiled sadly and gently, slowly removed the hook that had caught in the centre of her sunflower tattoo. 'Sorry,' Luca said, every time she winced with pain.

'I'm sorry! I'm sorry,' she whispered through her tears. 'For all the things I didn't understand.' Shifa nodded towards the sodden red cloth. 'What happened to *your* hand?'

'I had to cut them out of me.'

Luca held the sharp metal hook. The seed centre of her sunflower tattoo was smudged in blood.

'Cut what out?' Shifa asked.

She leaned down and held her hand in the river's flow.

'Freedom Fields,' came Luca's answer. 'With Jermaine's penknife.'

Themba had his arms wrapped firmly around Luca's shoulders. 'Why did you run away without saying goodbye? I thought you were my forever friend.'

Luca bit his lip and looked up at Shifa.

'If you asked me again I would say yes,' she whispered.

As if he had been waiting all his life to be seen for who he truly was, a tortured cry emerged from Luca's chest and Shifa recognised in its strains her own unfettered howl. Themba sprung into his arms and hugged him close.

'It's OK, Luca. You're not on your own any more. We're here now!' Themba soothed.

'I've got a story to tell you now, Themba!' Luca's words emerged slowly through his sobs. Shifa and Themba listened in amazement as he told them how he'd run away because of his feeling inside that he belonged nowhere, was wanted by no one and had nowhere to go.

'See!' Themba nodded at Shifa. 'You should have been kind!'

'It wasn't her fault. It was hard to know me,' Luca admitted and carried on with his story of how he had convinced himself that while he was branded with the tattoo he would never rid himself of Freedom Fields. He had taken the penknife he'd stolen from Jermaine and cut the sunflower out of his skin. He'd had to cut deep; the seed code had been implanted much deeper than he'd imagined. He had watched his blood flow over the rock turning the river pink.

Shifa's hand trembled as she felt the scabbed wound on the back of her head. So the trail of blood she'd seen had been Luca's.

'I don't know if I saw or imagined it, but a white wolf came to sit by my side and licked away my blood. Have you seen anything?' asked Luca.

'*Some say the Moon Wolf lights your way.*' Themba smacked his own hand, irritated with himself. 'I thought Lona was making things up that day! Tell me what it looked like and I'll draw it!'

But how is this possible? Shifa cast a wary look up the bank. They would have to keep vigilant . . . but *the white wolf had been trailing them.* She had thought it was vicious but Luca had dreamed of a kind and caring creature. Here on the river, following Lona's trail, Shifa couldn't be sure any more what was real or imagined.

'Anyway, wolf or no wolf I fell backwards into the river and got carried away by the current. I kept bashing my head on boulders, then it all went dark. The next thing I remember was a boy hauling me out of the water, holding my hand and bandaging it with a piece of rag. Then I slept – I don't know for how long, but I woke by a fire with a cup of oat milk next to me. They left the bike and a fishing rod too.'

It sounded to Shifa like the kind of thing Lottie did. 'Foragers?' Shifa asked.

'Think so! You asked me if I had a plan, Shifa . . . I would have stayed with them if they'd waited around for me to wake up.'

'You should have stayed with us. We didn't stop looking for you,' Themba said. 'Then we found Lev and I knew you were alive!'

Slowly Luca raised his head and wiped his tear-sore eyes as Themba gestured to the hare in his pocket that had listened intently to the whole story. Luca's survival tale was eclipsed by his laughter as they watched Lev hop around. 'You were right! I *have* missed you!' Luca patted Themba on the back.

By the time he had finished telling his story Luca looked truly exhausted. Shifa wrapped an insulation blanket around his shoulders and insisted he rest. Inspecting his ribs and concave stomach, Themba announced he would attempt to catch a fish 'to fill their empty bellies'.

'I know how to do it!' Themba said, referring to his river page.

'Good luck to you. I've been trying all day.'

'You caught a big Shifa fish!' Themba joked.

Shifa and Luca locked eyes and laughed.

Themba concentrated hard as he hooked the fly bait the foragers had left and cast the line out. The first time it tangled, but he practised and practised until he had done a final graceful cast that landed in a dark patch of water.

As she watched Luca sleep and Themba fish, Shifa felt a golden glow flow over her. They were equal now, the three of them, no longer shadows of themselves, forced to breathe the stale air of the polytunnels. Whatever happened to them now, they had tasted true freedom. She leant against the riverbank wall and closed her eyes letting the sound of the water lull her.

'Help!' Themba's shrill shriek brought her to her feet.

A tail thrashed the water, the fishing line pulled taut and a golden-scaled fish jumped clear of the water and attempted to twist free. Themba leaned back but slid forward at speed on the muddy bank towards the rushing water. Shifa grabbed him while Lev squealed, still snuggled in Themba's pocket.

'Watch Lev! Don't crush Lev!' Themba yelled.

Shifa took the line from Themba and felt the surprising power and tug of the fish on the end of it. Her hand pulsed where the hook had entered her own skin, but something deep inside her would not let go. Her arm ached as the fish pulled at the line. The commotion had woken Luca and he and Themba were behind her now, encouraging her, and for a while she was completely absorbed in the battle until she felt the fish tire and give up. Tears fell from her eyes as she watched it gasp for life, thrashing its tail one last time. She pulled the golden-scaled fish from the water and it lay gasping for breath on the rock, its glassy eyes leaking life. Shifa dropped the rod and stared at it, her hands clasped over her own mouth.

'I hooked it. So I'll kill it. I'm going to feed everyone tonight when we get to the station house!' Themba was saying with a puff of pride. 'But how do you kill?' Themba's words grew into a panic whistle.

Luca stepped forward, took a rock and let it fall; a wet thud rang out. The fish was instantly still. Themba grew silent. 'We need to eat,' Luca whispered as they stood over the fish.

'Sorry, rainbow trout!' Themba said. 'Like the one on my river page. Thank you!'

Luca shrugged. 'It was teamwork.'

Shifa smiled. She had been wrong about Luca. They were not so different. All he had been doing at the farm was following his instinct to protect himself and survive.

Chapter Thirty-Three

Shifa wrapped the fish in leaves and they placed it in the pannier basket on the back of the Forager's bike.

'They must have thought it was too much of a risk to stay with me. It was good of them to leave me the bike but I've never ridden one and . . .' Luca clasped his hand and winced. 'Not sure I could anyway with this hand.'

'What do you mean you can't ride a bike?' Themba laughed as Luca attempted to balance.

'It wasn't something Freedom Fields taught us!' Luca shrugged.

Shifa's mind cast back to the day that Nabil taught them both to ride one of the bikes at the warehouse. It was so tall that their feet couldn't touch the ground . . . the long way to fall had concentrated their minds on staying upright. Nabil had laughed and clapped as they took turns to pedal, and in the absence of brakes or fear, they had always trusted him to slow the bike and hold them when it was time to stop.

Shifa and Luca watched Themba trundling over bumps on the increasingly flat river path as they approached the base of the mountain. He was intent on searching for the watermill he'd drawn as the last point on the river before they were to turn inland.

'We'll be forced to stop soon, anyway!' Luca reasoned, staring up at the vast outcrop of sandy-coloured rock.

'Maybe when your hand's healed you'll be able to balance,' Shifa commented as they walked through a meadow scattered with leggy blue flowers and large star-like heads that bent in the wind.

Shifa picked one and stored it in her seed packet.

'Or maybe I just can't ride a bike!' Luca grinned. He glanced down at the seed packet. 'You know, it was Jermaine who told me to give you that back! He got your thing about seeds and flowers. It was his orchard – he planted it!'

Shifa pulled a face at the unwelcome reminder of Freedom Fields and a picture of Jermaine she did not recognise.

'He hated the polytunnels as much as we did.' Luca shrugged.

'Do you really believe that Themba can lead you to the station through this?' Luca stared up at the steep mountain directly above them where the river gushed through. 'Have you even once heard the Skylight going past?'

'No,' Shifa admitted, allowing doubt to creep in again.

'But I have to believe we'll get home, to Papa.'

'I'll come with you and say goodbye. Then I'm going to find the Foragers and join them. There's no papa waiting for me in Kairos City.'

Themba's cry of delight punctured the air. He pointed inland and they followed his gaze to a red-roofed barn and hilly mounds of earth. 'It won't be long! It won't be long till we get there!' Themba danced along like a river sprite.

He hopped back on the bike and began to pedal at full speed.

'I admire how sure he is of everything.' Luca laughed.

Shifa and Luca attempted to catch up as Themba rode around and around and finally brought the bike to a skid stop. 'Lona said she was ploughing near a red barn when she was just a girl, but the plough got stuck and it's been there ever since, somewhere near the station.' Themba's confidence seemed to ebb away from him. 'But it's not here, or the station . . .'

'Don't get upset, Themba. The machinery could have been buried over time, when the river flooded maybe?' Luca's legs suddenly buckled and he fell into Shifa. She held him by the shoulders.

'I need to sleep,' Luca muttered.

'You're boiling hot and you stink!' Themba sniffed at Luca's hand.

'So do you!' Luca smiled weakly.

'Not sweat, or fish . . . Rot. You smell of rot!' Themba screwed his nose up. 'Serious, Luca. Got to kill the infection or it will kill you – like it killed Mama. Isn't it true?'

Shifa hugged Themba close. 'Luca's not going to die, Themba,' she reassured him, but a bitter smell entered Shifa's nostrils too. She inspected Luca's bandage. The material the Foragers had wrapped around it was still seeping blood and pus. Without even looking she was sure that the wound was infected. They needed to get Luca somewhere to rest and find something to kill the infection that had entered his blood.

Luca looked up at the sky, where the clouds were now chasing each other ever faster. The breeze whipped up again.

'Themba, stay here with Luca and Lev for a minute,' Shifa ordered. 'Let me see if I can find this station nearby.'

Shifa wobbled at first but finally got her balance and rode the rusty old bike along the path, feeling her hair lifting off the back of her neck. She had not been going for more than a few moments when a rock face rose steeply out of the land, taller than any of the high-rises in Kairos City, and more spectacular. Shifa gasped. In the distance, standing at the foot of the rock, was an old brick station house.

She rode back to Themba and Luca with a light heart. It would be slow progress on foot with Luca so weak, but at least they had found the way home. Returning to the Flower Tracks and Nabil felt less and less like a dream.

Chapter Thirty-Four

Shifa's heart sank as they drew near the long-abandoned station house and trampled over the faded sign for 'Ore Hill Station' half buried under long grass.

Themba pushed open the door cautiously – the hinges squealed and a few crumbling bricks fell from the lintel above their heads. Themba swerved, placing his hands over his chest pouch to protect Lev.

They found themselves in a small dingy room with a rubble floor, a half-rotten table and a mouldy sofa. Next to it was a stove with a chimney pipe that reached through the roof, where the tiles had been swept away, leaving only skeleton rafters penetrated by sky. On the far side of the room were steep stone steps leading to a high window. Shifa climbed them and discovered a broken chair by a complex collection of colour-coded levers and two large pulley handles. One was labelled 'Safe to cross', the other 'Danger'.

'So this is where Lona's rhymes have brought us.' Luca sighed and collapsed on the old sofa. Its legs buckled at one end and the seat crashed to the floor in a cloud of dust.

Themba clenched his jaw. 'This *is* a station house! Just not how she remembered it.'

Shifa stepped through the far-side door and yelped as she fell directly on to a track, catching her foot on upturned metal. Luca and Themba came after her, braking at the point where a collapsed platform now collided with track.

'It's OK, Lev – shhh, shhhh.' Themba comforted his hare as they climbed down, carefully making their way to Shifa, stepping sideways so as not to fall head-first down the rubble slope.

Shifa clutched hold of her throbbing foot.

'Train tracks!' cried Themba. 'Flower tracks, Shifa!'

'They won't get us back to Nabil though, will they?' she muttered, closing her eyes on her hopes.

'Is your foot OK?' Luca asked.

Shifa tested it, bending it back and forth and nodded.

'Bruised, that's all.'

Luca placed a comforting hand on her back. 'Look at the state of us!'

Shifa couldn't help but hear a note of relief in his voice and she felt sorry for him.

'Why don't we rest here for the night, eat that fish and see if we can find those Foragers who helped me?' Luca slowly made his way back up to the station house.

He was right. It was time to start facing reality and maybe the Foragers could be persuaded to show them where the nearest Skylight station was, the safest way to stay hidden and ride back on it? Lottie had told how Foragers sometimes travelled the lands 'hitching lifts' on the 'roof rack' or the undercarriage of the train. In any case, if she knew that Luca had found a place to belong, it would be easier to make their way home too.

Themba nudged Shifa on the arm and attempted to pull her hands away from her eyes. 'What's the matter with you, Shifa! Can't you see where we are?'

Shifa opened her fingers and let the light seep through.

The ground was covered in a sea of wild rainbow colours: blues, pinks, yellows and white lace flowers. Here was the most beautiful giant flower track – but it led nowhere.

Themba peered further along to where the tunnel bored through the foot of the mountain. The opening was almost blocked by a fallen boulder.

Themba sat next to Shifa and gently pulled a sleepy Lev from his pocket.

'Do you think Lev wants to run free?'

'There's only one way of finding out,' said Shifa. 'Hares like to stretch their legs, especially at night.' Shifa hauled herself on to her feet, tentatively testing her weight, and found no real damage done.

'It's OK, Lev, you don't have to stay with me,' Themba whispered as he lowered Lev on to the grass. The hare's ears flattened along its back and it skittered sideways a few times before tentatively sniffing around, then bolting.

Shifa placed a hand on Themba's shoulder and watched his eyes fill with tears as his hare disappeared along the tracks.

'There's plenty to forage here, for Lev and us,' Shifa said, but despite the fact that there were more varieties of plants here than she had seen on the flower tracks or on Pollination Farm or even along the river banks, she could not hide the disappointment and exhaustion in her voice.

'It wasn't right to keep Lev, if he wanted to be free . . .' Themba said, staring down the track.

'That's right, Themb!' A mustard-coloured butterfly landed on a flower next to her; its wings stilled and closed. It seemed like weeks rather than days since she'd watched the butterflies dance in the orchard. Shifa walked unsteadily along the track, brushing every plant with her hand, rubbing the leaves between her fingers and adding new seeds to her store.

Shifa sniffed at a plant and found Lev nibbling away. She beckoned Themba close and he knelt down, reached his hand out and Lev hopped on to his palm!

'If you *want* to stay with me, Lev, that's different!' Themba laughed!

'Lemon balm! This is what I was foraging for on the river.' Shifa picked a handful of the fresh, fragrant leaves and rubbed them over the wound on her hand. She winced at the sting. She would need enough to use on Luca's hand and for the bites, the bug sores they'd picked up on the farm and the mosquito stings from the river.

Shifa wandered further down the track and peered through a narrow gap between the arched roof of the tunnel and a huge boulder where a large clump of dandelions grew. She leaned in and tugged them firmly by the root. As she did she stared into the tunnel but could make out no light within that would signal a path through to the other side.

The wind lifted and gusted – Shifa turned to see a million tiny seed heads glisten and float towards her in the dusk.

'Dandelion clocks,' Shifa whispered; memories of her last night on the Flower Tracks of Kairos City came wafting back to her. She picked a seed globe and blew – 'One o'clock, two o'clock, three o'clock, four o'clock, five o'clock, six o'clock, seven o'clock,' Shifa counted, and on each count Nabil's voice floated closer. '*If a single aigrette remains you are not alone.*'

It felt as if she really was floating, not walking, as she returned to Themba. Maybe if she could find a way to cook the fish they would all feel stronger.

'Try Lev with this,' said Shifa, handing a milky root to Themba. Lev cautiously approached, nudging it, then sucked frenziedly at the milk.

'Hare's starving!' Themba smiled contentedly as Lev nibbled at the leaves. Then he winced and scrunched his eyes closed. 'My head stab-pained me. It's spinning hungry!' Themba groaned and hugged his stomach, slumping down where he sat.

Shifa began chewing on a dandelion leaf then handed one to Themba. It was the same old bitter taste as in Kairos City and both of them pursed their lips but carried on chewing. Shifa and Themba supported each other as they scrambled up the shattered platform back into the station house where Luca lay on the broken-down sofa, dozing fitfully. Shifa eased a milky dandelion root between his lips but he gagged and brushed her hand away.

'Come on Luca, you've got to drink this. We won't be going anywhere tomorrow if you get taken with the infection.'

Finally he relented and sipped a few drops of milk. Shifa unwrapped the bloodied cloth around his hand and as she did the pungent smell of rot grew stronger. Luca winced.

She drew a sharp intake of breath at the depth of the gouge. How could Luca have done this to himself? Shifa washed the cut as well as she could with water and lemon balm sap and wiped more of the dandelion milk over the gash. As she wrapped Luca's hand in the large spiky leaves, she felt him drift off to sleep. She made a leaf bandage, tying it with the string she took from the bottom of her bag to make a poultice as she'd seen Lottie and Nabil do many times before.

The air grew heavy and Shifa peered up through the rafters at a glowering sky. *No sign of stars tonight. Luca was right.* For now the station house would be the safest place to hide out, but tomorrow they would go in search of the Foragers.

Chapter Thirty-Five

The gas lighter Shifa had taken from the farm kitchen sparked only once but afterwards, despite her desperately clicking it time and again, it failed to ignite.

'Completely dead,' Shifa sighed and let it drop to the station house floor. Her stomach groaned. *No fire, no food. We killed for nothing.* She rubbed her hands over her face in despair.

'I've got Lona's flints if we need them,' Themba said, placing a pile of sticks and thin branches in the stove. He reached into his pocket, took out a handful of pencil shavings and spread them over his pile of combustible finds. Shifa was amazed to see him reaching into his pocket again and taking out two sharp brown stones that he began bashing against each other. 'It takes ages, but I made smoke once.' Themba's face clouded at the memory. 'Lona showed me. I nearly got a flame too – if Jermaine hadn't stopped me.'

As Themba rhythmically struck the stones, Shifa knew she could not give up on getting home to Nabil and telling him of their ordeal. The sooner she let the truth be known the sooner Yara and the rest of them could be out of danger. *If Themba's playing with flints had turned into a fire and spread to those locked barns . . .* Shifa shivered. Who would send their children away if they knew the truth about Freedom Fields?

Shifa had given up on the idea of fire after hundreds and hundreds of strikes of rock against rock; she closed her eyes and wished that Themba would stop. But smoke wafted towards her. She opened her eyes to a spark of light that smouldered, then caught on his pencil shavings and began to flame in the stove.

'My fire art!' Themba gasped as he watched the embers catch and glow.

Shifa squeezed his arm in excitement. Together they quickly placed more dry grasses and sticks around the shavings and coaxed the flame into life.

The smell of their trout cooking woke Luca. 'Mmmm.' Shifa helped Luca to prop himself up and as he did he dislodged the slimy leaf bandage around his hand. Shifa took hold of it and peeked at the skin beneath.

'The dandelion leaves are supposed to take some of the heat out of the wound,' Shifa explained, pulling more leaves from her pile. 'That's a bit better – cleaner.' She padded out the dressing with new leaves and bound them with string.

'Where did you learn this stuff?' Luca asked.

'Our family's known all about healing stuff for generations.' Shifa shrugged.

'Baba Suli, our great-grandpapa, told our papa and our papa told us!' Themba explained proudly.

Shifa smiled and Luca nodded with real kindness in his eyes. *Why could I never see that before?*

'Well, it feels a bit better and I haven't got a fever any more. So something worked! That smells so good.' Luca gestured towards the stove.

Shifa took a stick, dislodged the tray from the fire and began unwrapping the fish, pulling back occasionally to avoid burning her fingertips. The skin was crisp and the flesh had turned white and moist. *'And so the hare leapt for the fire, offering herself as food.'* Nabil's story played around Shifa's mind. The idea of eating something that had been alive and free repulsed her and yet her stomach groaned in anticipation.

The trout crumbled as Shifa divided it into three and served it on parcels of herbs and leaves. It tasted of river and the bitterness of dandelion, sweet thyme and lemon balm. Despite the unfamiliar fleshy texture and taste, she felt her whole body relax and warm from the inside as the energy it gave entered her blood.

After their feast Shifa huddled next to Themba and Lev in front of the stove and felt her eyelids grow heavy.

Shifa sprang back from the Flower Tracks as she heard the distant rumble of a steam train approaching. Passengers scattered rose petal confetti from the windows. An old man wearing a hat and a long coat opened a carriage window and waved her over.

'Baba Suli!

'Shifa, my child!' He smiled, handing her a skep. 'It's in your hands now!'

Chapter Thirty-Six

Shifa was blasted awake by the wild charge of a raging sky. The bike wheels whistled and whirred as the wind whipped through their spokes. She sprang up and a rat scurried off with a mouthful of fish head.

'Themba! Luca!' she called but her voice was a feathery wisp and neither of them stirred in their sleep.

There was no time. She grabbed hold of their belongings and stuffed them in her backpack, picked up the torch and switched it on.

Shifa raised her eyes to the black clouds and a swirling vortex above that was forming into a corkscrew of spiralling wind and torrential, lashing rain. Shifa nudged Themba awake and he shivered as he lifted a trembling Lev into the safety of his pouch.

The door on to the flower track creaked, flew off its hinges and thudded against the wall, narrowly missing Luca who was staggering up from the sofa. Above them the station levers clanked, stirred into action by the giant, angry hands of the storm.

'Head for the tunnel!' Shifa called, hauling her backpack on to her back. They pushed their way along the tracks, clinging to each other as they struggled to place one foot in front of the other. A flash of lighting zigzagged through the sky and lit an image in Shifa's mind of Nabil carrying home the golden hand of the Kairos City clock.

The wind raged on and on as they clung together, slowly making their way towards the tunnel's mouth. Now the lashing rain grew into hard pellets that picked up power and strength, forming into bullets of ice.

'The sky's shooting us!' Themba yelled.

The torch cut out and Shifa cast it aside. Thousands of wailing bats shot along the tracks, their screeches melding with Themba's as they flew past them to enter the dark shelter of the tunnel.

Shifa pushed Themba forward to be first to climb through the gap between the boulder and the tunnel roof. Luca yelped in pain and fell backwards as Shifa grabbed for his wounded hand. She helped him up and eased him forward as he scrambled through the gap. Her hands were numb and her head pounded as she pulled herself through the narrow crevice, the boulder grazing her back.

Once inside all three of them leaned against the boulder, too exhausted to move a step further. Shifa crouched low and felt for what was under her feet. It seemed like they were standing on some kind of lever that now creaked under their weight. Shifa felt the urge to jump off. Too late as the boulder shifted and a deep rumble swelled around them; the gale built to its crescendo. A lightning flash and a huge crash shattered the tunnel, bricks and boulders flew in all directions. They crouched, protecting their heads. Shifa felt the earth groan and crack under their feet. The second wave of the storm transformed the loosened boulder into a plug that now shunted them further into the tunnel. Shifa squinted up just in time to catch the narrowing crack of sky between the flower tracks and the tunnel roof close as the last bats shot in, their animal and human cries as one. They clasped each other's hands as they were propelled into the deepening darkness. The tunnel echoed with the screech of winged and human fear.

'Themba,' she whispered, peering into the darkness and touching a bulbous bruise on her forehead. She felt a small trickle of blood run down her cheek.

Shifa opened and closed her fingers. Dust and rubble filled her hands and coated the grazed skin on her face. She moved her head from side to side, wincing at the stiffness in her neck. She was standing in ice-cold water that rose higher by the second.

'Lev's alive!' Themba whispered and somewhere from inside the murky tunnels of her mind Shifa chased and caught the meaning of another name that belonged to her.

'Luca!' she called, reaching out and finding his shoulder close to hers.

Luca croaked her name.

Shifa shook as she felt the presence of millions of shrieking bats crowding in around them. Now Themba's high-pitched whistling rose above them all.

'Luca! Help!' Themba screamed.

'Themba! You'll have to be a bat and we'll follow your voice echoes – remember, like you did in the cellar,' Luca coached.

Shifa groaned. If only the bats could carry the echoes of their screams all the way along the flower tracks, across the Kairos Lands to Nabil. For the first time in her life she felt darkness envelop her heart. Was this how they would die?

'My whistle echoes. I need to whistle!' Themba shouted. 'Whistle and chant so you can follow me!' He began to shift closer, feeling around the walls, keeping up his piercing whistle so that Shifa could locate exactly where he was in the dark. She was amazed how patiently Luca urged him on, encouraged him as they felt their way around the walls while rubble poured from above, Lona's rhymes pouring from Themba's mouth.

'Look for the ladder to take you from night into glorious golden light!'

Despite the calmness of his voice Luca clung unsteadily to Shifa's side.

'Stay close!' Shifa whispered, her head still whirring.

'Keep going, Themba!'

Lona's rhymes echoed deep through the tunnel as the three of them edged their way around the walls, water rising rapidly. They would have to find a way to climb out of here or drown in the darkness. Themba's constant search for a ladder leading towards a light was their only hope.

The strangest sensation was to open your eyes wide and find nothing, not a single speck of light. As bats shifted and screeched around their heads, something cracked and fell from a cave ceiling above. They dropped to their knees into the ice-cold water and clung to each other, wailing into the dark, shivering and then lifting themselves out.

Shifa opened her dust-sore eyes and blinked hard. In the far distance she thought she discerned a star sending tiny shafts towards them.

Themba was wading ahead faster now.

'A ladder.' Themba choked on the word. 'I found the ladder!'

'Don't be afraid to climb out of the dark.'

There was no time to question Lona's words now – the water had reached waist height. Shifa felt for the ladder and attempted to rattle it, testing her weight, but it held firm.

'Climb, Themba!' Shifa called, her mouth full of dust.

The tunnel could cave in at any moment. Shifa lifted Themba's skinny body up, he let his uniform drain of water, and he transformed into a whistling, screeching, chanting, climbing bat, his voice echoing deep through the tunnel.

'I can't! My hand!' Luca moaned.

'Here! Wrap your blanket around it,' Shifa ordered, tugging it from her pocket, holding it above the water and helping him bind his hand. It took three attempts for him to haul himself free from the rising water. 'I'm behind you,' Shifa whispered.

By the sound of his whistling, Themba was way ahead. Every time Luca placed his hand on a rung he yelped in pain.

Shifa's body shook with the effort as she reached ever upwards, numb feet and hands grasping for each rung of the ladder. Their hands brushed the rubbery wings of hanging bats that squalled and hollered against their heads as they climbed. Once Luca swayed dangerously as he dropped his blanket and reached for it, howling into the dark. Shifa felt something soft fall on to her shoulders.

'I caught it!' Shifa called to him. 'Keep climbing.'

Themba kept up his panic whistle and chanting, with new rhymes that spoke of meteors, mountains, forests of flowers. Shifa too clung to his word-flints that struck and struck again until specks of light began to grow from dots into an orb releasing heat and gold. Light tendrils fell in shafts, cocooning their bodies.

A thick coil of hair dropped towards her and Shifa clung to it for dear life.

'Mama, mama, mama!'

Her screams morphed into Daisy's heart-rending parting cry.

PART FOUR

METEORE

(BETWEEN EARTH AND SKY)

Chapter Thirty-Seven

Time was a ghost that glided and floated. Shifa felt pads of tiny feet creep over her chest as she drifted in and out of consciousness.

Now something sweet was placed on her tongue – a strawberry jewel dissolved in her mouth . . .

From time to time she tasted fresh water and felt it wash her cheek. Bitter milk dabbed against her lip. Voices flowed back and forth, came and went, light sparked and faded and sparked again.

'Themba,' she murmured. There it was again – a gentle kneading on her chest . . .

'Daisy?' she mumbled and opened her eyes to meet the wide-eyed stare of a baby hare that now skittered away as she stirred. 'Lev!' Shifa raised her head to feel a crippling realisation shoot through her. Why would Themba leave his precious Lev?

Shifa clung to a filthy blue blanket that was wrapped around her. Her head burned hot with fever. She leaned forwards, crawling on her hands and knees and using the wall of the cave to ease her way to standing. Her backpack was strewn open on the ground, but there was no sign of Luca or Themba. She reached out for the blanket and remembered the shape of it falling towards her along with a strand of spiralling hair. *Please let it only be this that fell. Not Luca and Themba.* She called their names until her throat was gravel.

She searched the rock wall behind her but could not find the ladder she vaguely remembered climbing. In front of her the exit to the cave narrowed, forming an archway. Shifa unsteadily followed Lev out of the cave, her head cloud-floating somewhere above her.

She squinted at a lake that shimmered in bright sunshine, surrounded on two sides by steep golden rock. Her breath caught as she stood open-mouthed, staring at its sheer glistening beauty. Was this the treasured land that Themba had spoken of?

But where was Themba? Where was Luca?

She made her way to the water's edge and stared at her reflection, at her grazed, bruised, dirt-smeared skin. A memory-flash of a girl staring into a mirror in the agora returned to her from a lifetime away. *This* mirror of clearest crystal reflected a girl who had not known her power in Kairos City; a girl who had risked everything and maybe lost everything too.

Her mind was clearing. She made her way over to where a gentle spring gurgled horizontally down a crack in the rock, forming a waterfall. She carefully took off her filthy overalls, removed her Feetskins and stepped into the icy mountain water. Tiny fish raced over her feet. She stood beneath the stream, opened her mouth and drank the cleanest, softest water she had ever tasted. When her thirst was quenched, she began to wash the memory of the tunnels from her hair, face and body. Afterwards Shifa sat in the shallows, sifting sand between her fingers and staring at the iridescent lake.

Emerald dragonflies danced and shimmered, chasing each other over the water.

Please let Luca and Themba have survived to see this, Shifa willed as she washed Luca's blanket in the water, calling their names again.

Shifa removed her seed packet from her pocket and washed her overalls in the water. Though the uniform was instantly dry Shifa could not bear to wear it. Wherever this was, it had nothing to do with Freedom Fields. Shifa laid Luca's blanket over a rock to dry and set off back to the cave, followed by Lev. She removed her daisy dress from her backpack and though it was slightly damp, she put it on. Wearing the soft material against her clean skin flooded her with memories of the Flower Tracks and Nabil's stories. She placed her precious seed packet in the deep pocket.

Shifa crouched down when she spotted animal droppings and prints. Her heart thudded hard. To her right, through dense gorse and high grasses, came a flash of rust brown and the snout of a hairy, round-bellied creature with sharp tusks grunting at her. She froze as it locked her gaze, snorted and retreated at surprising speed.

'Luca! Themba!' she called, louder this time. *Can that be my voice?* Shifa wondered as the force of it echoed through the mountain but then boomeranged back unanswered.

She sat on a mound of spongy green ground and pressed her hands into it to leave indents. The velvety moss held her handprint for only a moment and then sprang back. It felt comforting between her fingers and toes. She had no name for the red insect with black dots that crawled over her arm, then shot its wings out and flew away.

Lev grew bored waiting for her and hopped away. Shifa continued unsteadily, keeping the hare in sight as she floated along the path. Finger prongs of light fell through huge, sturdy trees either side of her. Shifa's eyes were bright with wonder, but inside she felt again the deep ache of loneliness as she longed for her family to be with her right now, to share whatever this was with her.

Shifa moved through a wood in a trance, her bare feet treading lightly around every wild flower that carpeted the ground: buttercups, dandelions, pink, purple and white clovers, lavender banks, tiny yellow trumpets of woodland flowers she wished she had names for.

She rested her head against the warm slender trunk of a tall tree with silvery bark. Shifa strained to see through the rock hands of the mountain far above and remembered the tiny window in the Skylight. She knew now why Freedom

Fields had not wanted them to see outside the train. If nature's spirit existed here, it could exist elsewhere too, and if people knew that not everything had been destroyed . . . then who would be taken in by the lie of Freedom Fields ever again?

'Themba! Luca!' she shouted, willing them to respond. But only the song of the forest returned to her.

Lev ran ahead and when Shifa caught up with the hare, she found it rolling on its back in a bed of sweet camomile. Shifa picked some of the daisy-like yellow-centred, white-petalled flowers, breathed in their scent and lay on her back, attempting to take in the immensity of what she saw and felt. Here was a tiny globe containing the earth's beauty in one place, a forgotten secret with trees, flowers, birds and insect life she had never even dreamed of – and it had not yet been destroyed.

Shifa forced herself to keep moving, to keep searching. She followed the sun's rays, tracing a line between the trees until they led her into a clearing of golden light.

In the middle was a long seat carved from a wide tree stump. She drew closer and discovered words carved into the bark: 'Golden Treasure' and 'Meteore Mountain'. Words she remembered Themba chanting in the dark. *Has Themba been here?* But this carving looked old, as though it had been scored into the wood long ago.

High up in the branches she spotted nests, and heard the squabble of birdsong and other creatures that were hidden amongst the foliage. Then came a gentle buzzing in her ear and she opened her eyes, alert. Something crawled over her cut skin around her sunflower tattoo. She held her hand away as she stared at the black-and-yellow striped insect on her hand – *a bee. Not extinct. A bee.* Shifa froze and held her breath, but the jewel-like insect soon realised the sunflower was fake, that there was no nectar or pollen to be drawn from it, and flew away.

'How could *our* hands ever replace you?' Shifa whispered as her eyes followed the bee's journey from flower to flower, multiplying into many more bees dancing between flowers, seeking the nectar they craved. How could Freedom Fields have made the joyful bees' pollination dance into something as ugly as forcing children to work in airless polytunnels?

'Baba Suli said our beekeeping ancestors were famous for never once being stung!' Nabil's voice floated to her on the breeze as she moved fearlessly, wrapped in his protective words, towards a tree at the edge of the clearing. It had a small dip in the trunk where hundreds of wild bees had congregated. Her arms and dress were covered in bees now, but she did not flinch as she reached up into the hollow and discovered a hive containing . . . honey.

Shifa returned to the bench in shock and lay back in the sunshine. She felt Daisy pad to her side and lie on her chest. *Please, Daisy, when I wake, make Themba and Luca be here by my side to see all of this.*

*

Shifa lay on the carved-out bench, her head resting in Baba Suli's lap, Lona at her feet.

'I've been waiting for you. Lona here arrived today too! Have you met my Shifa?'

'Through your brother Themba,' Lona smiled.

'No time for pleasantries! Us beekeeping elders have waited all this time to share our golden treasure – to spread sweetness in place of poison. In Kairos time all things are possible, Shifa . . . If you live up to your name . . . Honey is healing, but you know that. I've handed you the skep and now it's time to take the truth home, for all our sakes!'

Lona took Shifa by the hand and touched the spot where the hook had entered. 'Just one thing! Shifa, you are brave as Themba is trusting and true, but if you leave here all together, this treasure risks being lost for ever.'

Wide-eyed deer ran in the forest all around her. One or two came close and nudged her with their soft, cool noses. Their graceful presences leaned over her, their kind expression of concern and the wondering dark orbs of their eyes gradually coming into focus.

Shifa felt breathless with wonder and then it struck her. She wasn't on earth any more. Her body was still in the tunnel and her soul had flown here with the ghosts of Baba Suli, Lona and all this extinct wonder.

Chapter Thirty-Eight

'Shifa! Shifa!' Themba called, peering down at her. 'Why did you leave the cave? We thought you'd been eaten by the wolf.'

Fever clung stubbornly to Shifa despite Luca's and Themba's tending. The days came and the days went, with rosy dawns and fire-sky nights, and the owls and Moon Wolf returned, calling to Shifa more urgently with every dawn and dusk. Though Themba and Luca never saw or heard it, the Moon Wolf stood guard over them every night, poised between the hands of Meteore Mountain.

All Shifa could think of was building her strength now that she understood why they had been led here. She was alive, and the bees and the beauty of the forest were real and she could prove it.

Themba and Luca gathered feasts of nuts, wild berries, almonds, pears and apples that they collected in the forest, but they were wary of the flying-insect world and were put off getting too close to the tree-hives after they had both been stung – Luca's sting on his cheek ballooned and the swelling closed up his eye. 'You won't get me going near again!' he announced.

'I'm braver than you with flying things! I'm braver than you, who knew!' Themba teased. But Shifa longed to see the bees again. As soon as she was strong enough she persuaded Luca and Themba to take her up to the forest to sit in the midst of the wild bees and watch them pollinating the flowers. Remembering one of Baba Suli's stories, Shifa set fire to some lavender and placed it in the tree hollow, making the bees sleepy enough to let her take a little honey. That night they sat by the fire dipping apples in it. Shifa persuaded Luca to smear some on his wound, which had begun to heal but was still hot and red.

Shifa slipped in and out of sleep as they sat around the fire each repeating their own distinct memories of their survival story. Themba insisted that he had known all along the name for Meteore Mountain but Lona had made him swear to keep it to himself in case it got it into the wrong hands.

Shifa lay in the sun and watched Luca instil in Themba the confidence to lay his body in the water. Patient hour after hour, Themba grew more self-assured floating on his back, until the moment that Luca held his hands in the air and called out to Shifa to watch. Themba, arms and legs splashing wildly, counted four independent strokes in the water and leapt for joy into Luca's arms.

'This place is paradise! I'm never leaving!' Luca laughed, swirling Themba around.

There was so much beauty and joy here but Shifa felt as if Lona and Baba Suli were at her shoulder, prompting her to hurry and get well. Shifa knew that what Lona had said in her dream was true. If they all went together and they were all caught, the truth about this precious globe of nature could be lost too. It was too great a risk. This wasn't only about them escaping Freedom Fields any more, or even returning to Nabil to plant a beautiful secret garden on the Flower Tracks. As the fever began to leave her, Shifa felt the purpose she had been charged with shining in her as clear and bright as the golden lake, and her promise to Yara to expose the truth returned to her again and again. In Lev she saw the innocent, pleading gaze of Anton and all the other children who could be set free.

In her waking moments Shifa's mind teemed with questions. How had Pollination Farm survived the storm? Was the survivor tree still standing? What if Yara hadn't found the escape key and Miri, Blessing and the others in her dorm had been trapped inside in the storm? Maybe it would be the safest place – but watching the flames that warmed their nights, Shifa's fear of fire haunted her. In the dream that finally broke her fever, Kiki came to sit by her side and sang.

'You are my honey, honeysuckle, I am the bee.
And he vowed just like the bee,
I will build a home for thee . . .'

Not the voice of the broken Kiki from the farm but the lively Kiki she and Themba had once known on the compound. If one more child was broken by the system, it was one too many. It was not the the great gliding white swans, or the sighting of a snowy owl, or the daily visit of a kingfisher bird that convinced Shifa it was time to go. One morning she had awoken to the song of a plain brown *Ki Ki* bird that had flown into the skep she'd been weaving in her waking moments – and that had decided her.

Wading into the lake, letting the hem of her dress trail in the water as she watched the long-tail birds dive and dance on the surface, Shifa found a dead bee floating. There was no reviving this one but as she held it in her palm the idea came to her – *this bee is evidence*. She carried it back to her skep and the *Ki Ki* bird flew. Shifa reinforced the skep by weaving in a few more strands of lavender stems, thyme, rosemary and sage. She would take home as evidence the bee and some of the honey she'd collected on a nest of whatever flowers, plant and tree life she could gather. Her seed packet was now full and the paper flower ready to burst into bloom.

It took many hushed arguments but Luca eventually accepted Shifa's reasoning – that if they all went together they risked everything being lost. But he was afraid for her, worried that she was not strong enough to risk her life again so soon after they'd faced the darkness.

'I actually thought we were dead down there in the tunnel.' Luca quaked at the memory.

'When I woke here I thought I'd died and gone to heaven!' Shifa sighed. 'Only it was a sad, lonely kind of heaven. How can we live happily in our own perfect little world if other people we care about are suffering?'

'But everyone I care about is right here,' Luca said, raising the hand where his sunflower tattoo had been. Smearing it with honey had healed it completely. 'I meant it when I cut this out. I'm never going back. And the tunnel's flooded so there's no way out that way.'

Themba, Luca agreed, should not know the plan till it was fully formed. Shifa and Luca spent the day exploring the most direct way out. They discovered that there was no other way in or out except by scaling the towering Meteore mountain and passing through its hands.

Shifa loaded her backpack with nuts, fruit and spring water.

'You've made up your mind, haven't you?' Luca said as Shifa placed the dead bee in a nest she'd made inside the skep. In hushed tones, she told Luca that she trusted him to care for Themba. She promised that she would return with Nabil as soon as she could. She would leave at dawn to take the bee and a taste of honey back to the city and prove that nature endured and could revive – that there was hope of a different way of life, not governed by Freedom Fields' lies and cruelty.

That night, when Themba was asleep, Shifa picked up his artbook and wrote a letter to her brother. She was interrupted by Luca.

'You've never felt how frightening it is to feel completely alone. What if you fall?' Luca whispered quietly.

'What if I fly?' Shifa answered.

Laying down the pen she found herself telling Luca the story of the hare in the moon. He lay on his back, hands cradling his head and listened. Lev jumped on to his chest and lay down, as if breathing in the story too.

'Seems like we've got everything we need right here.' Luca stroked Lev's soft ears. 'Why look any further? I've never seen a hare in the moon, but I've found friends and . . . a family for the first time ever. Please stay, Shifa.'

'I can't.'

Luca turned away but she had already seen the tears that now welled in his eyes. She reached out and hugged him close – he had become her brother-friend too.

'I didn't know how much it hurts to care for people before.' Luca covered his eyes with his hands.

As they sat by the glow of the fire Shifa realised that Luca had always been beautiful – it was Freedom Fields that had made him seem ugly, and if they weren't stopped, their ways would poison the whole of the lands.

She kissed Themba's head and laid open his artbook. It had taken her so long to write her goodbye. Tears had smudged her words and even after pausing over every word it was not exactly what she wanted it to say. But it would be something for him to hold on to, along with her strand of hair that he now grasped between his fingers.

For the first time since arriving at the Golden Lake, Shifa pulled on her Freedom Fields uniform, tucking her daisy dress inside. At first light she would slip away.

PART FIVE
OVER THE THRESHOLD

Chapter Thirty-Nine

Shifa's heart swelled with emotion as she made her way up above the cave. 'Swallows.' That was the name of the long-tailed, arrow-winged birds that flocked across the lake. 'As swift as a swallow,' she chanted to herself as she climbed upwards. *That is how I need to be – as swift and light as a swallow.*

Once in the wood she located the tallest tree nearest the rock wall. She stretched up and found the first foothold in the trunk. Now, she would climb as high as the branches allowed and then shift over to a level where the canopy met a flat rocky platform. From there she would need to navigate the face of Meteore Mountain, climbing towards the sunlight that streamed through the almost closed hands of the rock formation.

She moved steadily upwards, her heart thudding hard and hot in her chest. She made the mistake of looking down through the canopy only once, as the earth below her swirled in a rushing green whirlpool. Once level with the platform, the space between the branch and the rock face was wider than it had looked from the ground. If she fell here she could break every bone in her body.

Leap with me, Daisy, climb with me, she whispered as the branch bowed and dipped, forcing her to make a great bound towards a ledge. Her feet found the edge but for one heart-lurching moment she bent backwards, losing her centre of gravity. Her arms spun but she reached into her core and drove forwards, smacking her hands and knees on to the hard rock. She stilled her body but blood fired through her like the rapids on the River Ore.

At first it had been easy to find crevices to place her hands and feet in, but now she had climbed above the tree canopy the rock face was smoother than it had appeared from below. Her fingertips were red and swollen from clinging so tightly to shallow wrinkles in the mountain's side. Just when she thought there would be no way forward, another ledge offered itself up, this one just wide enough for Shifa to sit on.

She carefully took off her backpack, glugged some water and dared to look down once again. A small herd of deer trailed through the wood. Her heart swelled at the thought of Themba meeting those graceful, gentle creatures. She had done the right thing, she told herself. Themba would be safe with Luca, held in the hands of Meteore Mountain.

A shriek tore through the sky and a wide-winged shadow darkened the rock. She turned to find an enormous brown eagle with golden neck feathers and sharp hunting eyes swooping towards her, its talons splayed, ready to pluck her up. She flattened herself against the rock and the bird of prey flew past her. The slipstream of air from its flight path lifted her hair. Above her the eagle was skirting the rock close to where an enormous nest lay in an alcove. The giant bird's deafening cry rose up through the valley of Meteore.

'I'm not going to steal what's yours,' she whispered, but the eagle continued circling angrily above her. Finally, with a gut-wrenching cry, the huge bird soared back into the forest.

There was no other way but past the nest. She clung on to the rock and concentrated on finding the handholds and using her Feetskin grips to feel for a lip to propel her upwards. At last she was level with the nest. She edged past the carefully constructed cradle, where one large egg lay surrounded by a blanket of soft downy feathers. She was mesmerised by the sheer perfection of the mottled-white oval shell and the promise of a rare new beginning.

The faster she got away from the nest the safer she became. It was this thought that kept her going as she climbed the final stretch of rock face towards the welcoming hands of Meteore. Themba's chanting filled her mind, as did his excitement when she had shown him the words scored into the seat, words that tallied with the rhymes written in his artbook.

What golden treasure you have in store,
Held in the hands of Meteore.
Now it's time to uncover the lie,
In the mountains that rise between earth and sky

The world is full of things beyond my understanding, Shifa thought. As the slope flattened out to form the top of the mountain, Shifa felt her weary muscles tremble. She lay on her stomach for a moment, gathering her strength, watching the eagle circle below, and something else too – staring up at her from a rock ledge. The Moon Wolf raised its head towards her, opened its mouth and howled. *Like Lona's howl on the farm.* Was the wolf spirit of Lona guiding her through? Shifa watched as it made its way back down towards the forest. Shifa felt a strange sense of comfort that the Moon Wolf would stay close by Themba and Luca, but with its parting she felt a splitting, agonising grief of being alone. She was suddenly wracked with self-doubt. Why had she left the freedom of the Meteore forests to place herself in such grave danger?

As her doubt rose Shifa felt the strangest sensation of something buzzing against her spine, as if the single bee had multiplied and sprung to life. It was her answer.

From this high vantage point she could follow the River Ore back to Pollination Farm in the distance, and for the first time in her life, way beyond the farm, she spied the wide ocean. But Pollination Farm seemed oddly obscured by wide red pillars. The air smelled charred and stale. Her ears strained. In the distance the sky juddered as the great black eye of ARK AIR hovered for a moment over . . . were those upturned storm-barn roofs? The engines charged, revving louder and louder before shooting above the Skylight tracks. Shifa splayed her body flat against the rock and prayed that it would not detect her as it sped above Meteore Mountain and disappeared in a flash. She trembled with fear long after the aircraft was gone. Below her she imagined Themba staring up through the mountain, hands clasped over his ears in panic.

Yara's face loomed in her mind and a wreath of foreboding wrapped itself around her. An ARK aircraft signalled an official visit. What had happened to prompt such a rare outing? The River Ore flowed silvery grey in the midday sun. She scanned the sodden land below for train tracks and located where they ran well away from the river. They would never have found a station on the path they had followed. Shifa calculated the nearest station was about five kilometres from the foot of the mountain, across flat open countryside. She should have plenty of time to get there before nightfall, the time she'd observed that the train had always passed through. If she could board the Skylight there and hide on the roof or undercarriage, then she might not be discovered when it stopped at the farms to load goods and recruits. Her spirits rose. Finally it felt within her reach to be on her way to Kairos City.

Shifa reached in her backpack for water, her mouth dry with fear. When she replaced her water carrier she felt something soft inside and pulled out . . . Luca's blanket. He must have slipped it into her bag last night. This was his one comfort and he had given it to her. She wiped the tears of gratitude from her eyes.

She jogged across the rough rubble ground at the apex of the rock and discovered a steep but navigable path leading down the other side. As she slid on wet ground she realised how wrong she'd been to think that descending would be easier than climbing.

Part of the way was so treacherous that Shifa had to scramble on her bottom; the rest she navigated by sliding down sideways. Once she fell and gashed open her knee but doggedly carried on walking. Shifa's hips and knees ached as she ran down the last stretch of slope. Looking back up the steep mountain pathway it was hard to believe that she had descended so far, so fast. From above it had seemed easy to map a straight line to the station, but it was harder to keep the direction clear in her mind once on the flat ground.

The sky was blue and clear but something seemed adrift. Shifa looked to her left where the wheat fields opened out. Some crops had been cut and burned and were now blackening stubble – perhaps that was the charred smell that had clung to her as she'd descended the mountain. She looked beyond the blackened plots to uncut fields that had been flattened, like wet hair smeared against skin. Her

Feetskins sank deep into the mud. Every step was a struggle as the ground sucked her into ploughed furrows. As she pulled her feet out she discovered small objects and possessions – a muddy-faced teddy bear, bedding and insulation sheets floated through the air flashing fearful thoughts of what had happened to Yara, Bilan and her dorm-mates. Shifa's feet slid over a huge Solarmirror panel and she careered down it, spinning out of control until she came to land alongside a a harvester that lay on its side, spilling metal blades and guts.

Shakily she stood and carried on walking past a field where cracked trunks of young trees lay across her path. She paused to take in the devastation of the storm they had been cocooned from, sheltered by the protective arms of Meteore. *Please let Yara be safe*, she willed.

On the other side of the field, a new farmhouse came into view. This must be the next one before Pollination Farm. She picked up her pace – if it was anything like their walk from the station to the farm she still had a way to go.

Shifa stepped over a plaque – 'Welcome to Golden Fields Farm'. From there she progressed cautiously, alert to roving opticares and Crows, but the farm seemed destroyed and deserted. Once she got closer she realised that one side of the building had been blasted open – the contents of the rooms tumbled out like fish entrails. A row of dormitory beds hung halfway out of a room, clinging to the floor. *Where were all those chidren?* The further away from the mountain she walked, the more she was filled with dread. She followed a straight path away from the devastated farmhouse, keeping the eagle's fierce, protective eye in her mind.

A chill shot through Shifa as she heard voices. She instinctively jumped aside, but there was nowhere to hide on the plateau apart from the ditch – if the sensor was on . . . She held her breath, every nerve ending tensed as she jumped into the watery ditch. No shock came, no sparks flew, but she lay on her belly beside the watery grave of petrified animals: hares, rabbits and birds. Lev's sweet face shot through her mind. She covered her mouth.

The voices grew louder and a small procession of children filed past with their backs to her. Shifa counted twenty wearing Freedom Fields recruits' uniforms. She observed their hunched backs and the way they silently clung to each other, like ghost people still trapped in the stifling air of the polytunnels. At the back of the line she recognised a voice – 'Almost there now.' Jax. She held Barley on a lead. Shifa stared at the recruits to see if she could make out Yara's walk or any of the girls in her dormitory. But they were all silent and it was impossible to see them more clearly, keeping her head low in the ditch grave so as not to be seen herself.

Barley whined a mournful lament, straining his neck back towards Meteore Mountain.

'Come on Barley, Lona's gone now. Time to say goodbye!'

So Lona had died and her spirit had flown up to the forest. Perhaps Barley sensed her there too.

Once the recruits were ahead of her, Shifa scrambled after them, grateful to be out of the filthy ditch. Her hands and face were now smeared in earth and ditch water. Once again Barley turned, but Jax tugged at her lead, urging the dog on to the station.

Above the sound of the children shuffling along the platform, came a humming sound and a flash of silver as the Skylight drew into the station.

Why was the train here so early? A scattering of Crows stepped out on to the platform. Shifa felt her heart beat faster as she quickly assessed the safest place to hide.

'There's nothing left of our station,' Jax said to a Crow. Her voice broke on the words. 'The river flooded it completely. We saved who we could.'

'Jermaine?' the Crow asked.

'My brother died trying to get them out. Why did it take Freedom Felds so long to get help to us? It's taken us a week to walk here.'

Shifa felt the heavy hand of grief weigh her down as she manoeuvred herself on the opposite side of the track, desperate to see the survivors' faces.

'Sorry. So sorry. The hurricane zigzagged its way across the Kairos Lands. It was hard to predict where it would hit.' The Crow's voice cracked.

Shifa's heart sank. What if she made it back to Kairos City and found that her papa was— She could not bear to think of never seeing him again.

Carriages opened and the Crows walked calmly up and down the station, taking children's hands gently in theirs and registering them on their wrist screens. Shifa judged that this was her moment, while Crows ushered distressed children on to the trains. She stared at her mud-smeared reflection in the silver sides of the Skylight. Her eyes glinted fiercely and she looked barely human. The engine began its low purring. There was no time to hesitate.

Chapter Forty

Shifa crouched low and scurried under the train, ignoring the sharp stones penetrating through her overalls, until she came to the small space in between carriages. There she spotted a thin ladder leading to the top of the train. The last ladder she had climbed had taken her to a place she could only have imagined. She trusted this one would take her home.

On the top of the train were further rungs, to navigate horizontally across to the skylight above the carriage. She acted on instinct now, pulling her backpack off her back and strapping it to her front. She pulled out Luca's blanket and tied it tight to the rung on her right, wrapping it firmly around her waist, back under her spine and securing it to the rung on her left side. This blanket was Luca's gift to her – Luca was a survivor.

She hooked her Feetskins under another rung and clung to the bars by her sides.

A shrill alarm sounded and the Skylight revved into motion. Shifa felt a swelling, buzzing sound rising from her chest. It was as if the one bee, lying in its skep, had sprung to life and multiplied into a hive that now pulsed with energy.

I am not alone, she soothed herself, but as the train picked up speed, her body was slung to the side and, for a second, her feet dislodged from the rungs and her legs drifted in mid-air. She fought against the train's movements and clamped her feet back under the rung, every nerve in her body tensed, intent on survival.

Her hair streamed across her face and her cheeks indented, quivering with the force of the Skylight's speed. At first she kept her eyes closed but as the train settled into a steady rhythm Shifa dared to turn her head and finally view the Kairos Lands stretched out before her.

There were places of devastation where homesteads and communities lay broken and abandoned, but where they travelled now through a valley, there was no sign of recent devastation. There were pockets where the trees stood tall and proud alongside the giant turning arms of wind turbines. She was amazed to see small clusters of woodland where deer and wild horses grazed. There were inland lakes and rivers, and in small enclosures cows and sheep grazed. They were flying along a hillside, greener than any she had ever seen. Across the land small groups of people gathered in encampments of Foragers, fires lighting her through the night. There were forests, and sweet meadows – Meteore was not the only place that had survived Hurricane Chronos and was starting to regenerate.

She felt the molten hot anger course through her veins again. So many lies her life had been built upon, but now she would carry home the truth not just for her family either, or for their tiny patch of flower track. The land was fertile and if only things were organised in the right way there should be enough here to feed everyone, even without the bees.

She cautiously uncurled her fingers, reached under her backpack and unzipped the pocket for her precious flower seed packet. She cupped the paper flower head for a moment and imagined the lands strewn in a rainbow carpet of fragrant blossom. She opened her eyes wide, squeezed the flower head and watched the hundreds of seeds and specimens she'd collected fly out, spreading far and wide across the Kairos Lands. *Fly, hope seeds, fly!*

The train sped on all through the day and into a star-scattered night. Shifa's body and mind were wracked with exhaustion and her wind-sore eyes grew heavy. The Skylight veered sharply on a bend in the track and for a second Shifa's body was propelled forward so that her head rolled on to the window. Luca's blanket held her and stopped her rolling any further, and she quickly pulled her feet back and righted herself. It was a split second, but in that second she saw a girl and a boy below she recognised – Yara cuddled up beside Bilan hugging his teddy. The two of them lay on their backs staring straight into her eyes. Barley raised her head and barked wildly. Jax's eyes were wide with surprise as she pointed up to Shifa.

Shifa opened her mouth and silently screamed into the night. She'd been so close to getting back to Kairos City undetected. How could she have allowed herself to doze? Fear took hold as she waited for an alarm to be sounded.

The pulsing hive of hope had stilled in her chest long before they reached Kairos Station.

She was Lev, frozen in her form as the train began to unload and weary voices gathered together. She lay flat and unmoving, waiting for Jax and the Crows to come for her.

Time shrank to the beat, beat, beat of her heart.

The engine of the Skylight stilled and the hum of the station grew silent as the hare in the moon watched over.

Chapter Forty-One

Daisy's paws kneaded at Shifa's chest and her cry wrapped itself around her heart. Shifa woke, casting around for signs of Daisy. She looked down at her own body tied to the train in a blue blanket, and for a moment she had no idea who she was, where she was or how she had found herself here. Her legs and arms were numb, but slowly she unravelled herself, and crawling on her hands and knees her body began to prickle into life. She climbed down the ladder and felt for the ground, unzipped her filthy uniform and cast it aside.

She drank a long gulp of spring water and splashed some over her face. She wrapped Luca's blanket around the skep and secured it in her backpack. If the Crows who had found the boat had filed their report and returned her locket to Nabil, she was likely to be registered as dead, but there was no guarantee of that or anything. *Keep alert. You can't be caught now, when you've come this far . . .* she coached herself.

You're carrying more than your own future on your shoulders.
She pulled her backpack straps tight around her waist.

Who could she trust with the evidence she carried but Nabil and Lottie? What would happen if it got into anyone else's hands? It was eerily quiet as Shifa crept through the Garden Belt. The Paragons' gardens had not been spared from the force of the storm. Shifa climbed over debris and stuck to shadows, keeping her eye open for Crows and opticares. Shifa was amazed to see only one Crow, sitting on the pavement, jacket discarded. He shone his torch over her dress to her Feetskins and she thought for a moment that would be the end until she caught the look of disappointment in his eyes. He held a photomemory in his hand and flashed it at Shifa. 'Have you seen my son?' Shifa shook her head sadly and sped on, stepping over Freedom Fields signs that lay on the road.

Every stride she took along the empty Orbital Road, she felt stronger. The city was changed not only by this latest storm. She passed a Freedom Fields School entrance. The word 'Freedom' had been scored out and replaced by 'Prison'. The building was boarded up; bees and flower meadows were painted where windows had been. Walking past one of the warehouses she had visited once, music poured out. A woman sat on a ledge dancing her child on her knee. The baby waved at her and Shifa waved back. *That could be Honey.* Maybe Lottie was inside and she longed to see her but she could not delay for a moment.

She felt as if she was connected to Nabil and the Flower Tracks by an invisible cord that was now pulling her home. Almost every building she passed had grown Graffitrees; beautiful, colourful imagination trees had taken over the walls of the city. Each artwork spurred her on, nurturing her spirit bolder . . . *Dream, believe, imagine, dare*, she chanted as she hurried on.

Shifa's heart raced in anticipation as she approached the advertising billboard. In place of the Freedom Fields advert was a bright-pink blossom tree, identical to the one she'd seen on the compound on her birthday. She held her hand over her mouth in an attempt to contain her joy. It had been Nabil's gift to her after all, and now she was home.

She eased her body underneath the hoarding and entered the Flower Tracks that had shrunk to a tiny strip of ground. At the bottom of the steep slope was a green canvas tent surrounded by autumnal flowers. It looked a little battered but not destroyed. A stooped Nabil wore Baba Suli's coat. His hair was whiter than she remembered and he had grown a beard. In his arms he cradled something wrapped in a grey blanket – from inside came a faint soft cry.

'Papa, Daisy!' Shifa whispered, her voice floating as light as an aigrette.

Nabil turned slowly as if unable to believe his ears. 'Papa!' Shifa called again.

Nabil reached for her locket around his neck.

'There Daisy, seems like you've brought a ghost home to break my heart again.'

'Papa! I'm alive. Themba too!' she whispered but Nabil stood frozen, uncomprehending.

Gently Shifa placed a hand on his shoulder and took Daisy from him and unwrapped the blanket. Daisy was so frail and thin, she hardly had the energy to miaow or lift her paw. Shifa bent low to her head and kissed her over and over again. *You waited for me, Daisy. You stayed with me all the way. I never would have survived without you.*

'Are you real?' Nabil whispered. He took off his coat and dropped it on Shifa's shoulders as if he believed it would crumple to the ground. When it rested on her shoulders Nabil clung to Shifa and broke down as they sank to the earth together wrapped in the frayed lining of Baba Suli's coat. 'Themba's alive, you're alive?' Nabil repeated over and over.

The tide of their emotions flowed free, surging and swirling with deep undercurrents dragging them along. They dived together, gulping air, almost drowning in their tears until they were spent. Then they would build again on a new wave of telling of their journeys. As she approached the moment in her story when Baba Suli and Lona had been waiting for her in the forests of Meteore, Shifa felt a warm glow course through her as if Lona and Baba Suli had travelled with her back to Kairos City. Nabil placed a hand on her shoulder before she could tell of the golden treasure and he began to speak.

'They said the agora tree sculpture could never be uprooted – they were wrong. It had fake roots.' Shifa did not interrupt as his words slowly began to flow. He spoke of how Daisy had gone missing on the night they'd left. How he and Lottie had searched the whole of Kairos City for her, but had finally given up . . . until he'd woken that very morning to find her weak and crying at the top of the Flower Tracks steps, unable to leap down. He told of how the news of their deaths had been a catalyst for one housecarer to step forward.

'Hannah?' Shifa whispered.

Nabil smiled and explained how Hannah speaking out had prompted housecarer after housecarer to give evidence to the ARK Government of the cruelty they had witnessed on Freedom Fields farms all over the Lands.

The night after the storm he and Lottie had led a vigil through the city joined by thousands – Paragons as well as Foragers who had painted the city in too many Graffitrees to remove. The era of the Freedom Fields Family was over. It had lost the trust of the people. A new ARK Government was being formed right at this moment with representatives of all people in the Lands. Its first task was to form a truth council to make sure that the stories were recorded for ever in the hope that the atrocities of Freedom Fields would never be visited on future lands or generations.

Nabil turned to Shifa and smiled. 'Sometimes truth is stranger than fiction! You think my stories are far-fetched? Then listen to this. A Forager with ribbons in her hair called

335

Carlotta is rallying people from all over the Kairos Lands to work together and find a new way, for a new time.'

'Lottie!' Shifa laughed, but it didn't seem so far-fetched. Lottie's heart and caring spirit, her knowledge and care for the natural world was what was needed now, and who knows what she and her Forager friends could do with the information Shifa was about to share. 'Close your eyes, Papa! I've carried something back with me, a kind of miracle . . .' Shifa whispered, removing the skep from her bag. She took the honey she'd collected on lavender stems from the skep, dipped them again so they were well coated and placed them to Nabil's lips. He frowned, tasted, and tasted again.

'Sweet lavender?'

'Try again, Papa!'

Nabil took his time. Shifa knew he couldn't have tasted anything as pure and sweet since he was very young.

'Honey?' he gasped, opening his eyes as she placed in his hands a skep containing a nest of wild flowers, herbs and grasses – and cradled in the centre was a wild bee. On the train, in her dream Shifa had imagined the poor dead bee would spring to life and multiply into a whole hive flying across the Flower Tracks – maybe one day that dream would come true.

Shifa held Daisy and her heart ached with every weakening breath. Shifa traced back over all the times when she'd felt desperate and Daisy's love had strengthened her. She kissed her head over and over.

In the evening the moon shone bright and Daisy reached a paw to Shifa's tear-stained cheek and mewled weakly. Shifa followed the path of a silver aigrette as it floated towards her and landed on Daisy's mouth, where it lay still.

Epilogue

Welcome to
**SURVIVOR TREE
RESIDENTIAL
CONSERVATION
RESERVE**

Working to restore the balance between earth and sky

The cockerel weather vane turned steadily. It had been the busiest summer on the reserve for many years. Even at this early hour students skated up and down the row of ash trees that formed Hope Avenue. A delegation of specialists were visiting the polytunnels of survivor-tree forests that boasted the widest species store anywhere in the world. Some students collected fruit in the orchard. In the meadow beyond, they were tending hives and learning of the wildflowers, bees, birds, insects and animals most needed for rewilding the Kairos

Lands. As there was no forecast of high winds the boats on the River Ore set forth white-water rafting over the weir.

But our solitary adventurer sought a peaceful nook . . . She placed her hand on the ancient bark and peered up through the branches of the survivor tree, following the scurry of a squealing red squirrel. Above, hundreds of bright-breasted birds scattered and a cluster of daisies fell upon her hair. *Who would plant daisies halfway up a tree?* Bare foot by bare foot she climbed until she discovered a whole patch lodged in a nook. She reached in and picked a few flowers, threading a daisy chain and placing it on her head to make a crown. Out of the corner of her eye she caught something glinting silver. Reaching inside she found an insulation-wrapped parcel containing: a pale blue blanket; a dented golden locket; and an artbook with an origami flower tucked inside . . .

She placed the locket around her neck, picked up the paper flower and gently squeezed the head. It opened. On the inside she spied old-world writing. She delicately unfolded the paper flower along well-worn ridges until it was flat. With held breath she read a rescue letter from the times of the infamous 'Freedom Fields Family', words composed on the branch-spine on which she lay. Her own spine tingled to feel that bleak past, so close, in touching distance as she read the desperate plea for help of a girl called Shifa. Questions spiralled through the girl's mind and set her heart racing. Searching for answers she opened the book. Immersed in the chaos of Hurricane Chronos, the pages turned on a freshening breeze and a tiny hare etched into the bottom of each page sprang to life and ran like the wind dislodging a golden leaf.

Our adventurer followed the leaf's meandering path down through the watchful branches of the survivor tree to find that something else had fallen too. Wrapping the blanket around her shoulders, she hunkered in the tree's hollow. Dusting a bark beetle from the page, she began to read. A poem, like a riddle from another time.

It's your turn now to turn over the page
As we must do in every age
To plant the seeds
To have and to hold
If you're to discover
Where the river runs gold.

Acknowledgements

Books are an act of communal making. My first thanks go to my immediate book-growing family, without whom this story would not be in your hands!

Sophie Gorell Barnes of MBA Literary Agents, who is always so encouraging and never tires of reading the many drafts I present her with!

Sam Swinnerton (Senior Commissioning Editor), for being such a champion of my writing and this story and for her enthusiasm to come world-building with me in the Kairos Lands! It's been such a pleasure to work with her again. Our many conversations and insightful editorial work have helped to nurture this story into being. This book is dedicated to Sam's baby Ada, who was born around the same time as this book. I am immensely grateful to Tig Wallace (Senior Commissioning Editor) for casting fresh eyes over the final stages with such enthusiasm for the world and characters.

Thank you to the wonderful team at Orion: Sarah Lambert, Ruth Alltimes, Dominic Kingston, Emily Finn, Samuel Perrett, Rosalind McIntosh, Maurice Lyon, Helen Hughes and Joelyn Esdelle. Thank you to Evan Hollingdale for the beautiful artwork.

Thanks to my talented friend and artist Natalie Sirett, with whom I shared early drafts of the manuscript, for bringing forth beautiful drawings of Shifa and Daisy that I will treasure.

With immense love, gratitude and appreciation to my family who have shared in the world-building and roamed with me in these Kairos Lands! None of my book gardens would bud or grow without their patience and love.

The second group of acknowledgements are scattered wider, like Shifa's seed collection!

To the brave young activists around the world who are standing up to governments to demand urgent action to protect this planet. As my story comes to publication I cannot think of Shifa and Themba without also thinking of Greta Thunberg and fellow Climate Action activists she has mobilised worldwide. Their urgent call for change draws on the same source that spurred me to action . . . by writing this evocation of the Kairos Lands.

I was energised to complete final drafts as I walked beside fellow author and conservationist Gill Lewis on 'The People's Walk for Wildlife'. On a rainy day in 2018 young people presented a manifesto for wildlife to UK Parliament and I heard conservationist Mya-Rose Craig (Birdgirl) speak. I felt I had come face to face with my character Shifa!

A giant defender of the natural world since my own childhood, Sir David Attenborough's lifetime's work has chimed through me as I've written this book.

The character of Themba was inspired by Alex Harrison, my brother-in-law, who communicates through art as Themba does. Unlike Themba, Alex is a man of few words – watching him draw and paint is a constant reminder of the vital power of the arts to express our place in the world.

The creation of the Kairos Lands is indebted to the wild flower meadows, rivers, mountains and lakes of my Lake District childhood, 'Meteora' in Greece and a love of urban re-wilding spaces, flower tracks and walks where I've discovered 'Graffitree' artists at work.

The threads of art and storytelling in this book have been energised by working alongside illustrator Jane Ray at Islington Centre for Refugees and Migrants. In the art and writing class we run together a repeated theme when working with refugee people from around the globe is an exploration of our common love of nature: rivers, trees, gardens, birdlife, orchards, mountains and the forests of home. Many people have had to leave their beloved landscapes behind because of devastation of their environment, a theme central to this novel.

The real story of Dr Ryad Alsous, a Syrian refugee who is on a mission to save Britain's bees, was the catalyst for Nabil's bee-keeping ancestors.